CRISIS COUNSELING

"Now. Tell me what's wrong."

Georgina pulled herself into a ball, knees to her chest, and rocked back and forth, sobbing. "Diane's dead."

"Your therapist? My God! Are you sure?"

Georgina nodded her head, her lips a thin, tight line. "Look."

Georgina pointed. I stood and passed through a pair of French doors. A cold wind blew in off the lake. I stood shivering on a balcony, surrounded by tall trees. Ivy snaked along a brick wall that separated the Sturges property from the park. Inside its boundaries lay piles of dead leaves, patches of snow, a small cedar tree, rocks, a blue shoe. Another blue shoe, attached to the leg of a woman wearing a blue suit. A woman whose body now lay broken over the face of a boulder, one leg bent cruelly under the other, her left arm flung out over her head, her eyes blank and wide. From the size of the dark stain that had spread over the surface of the boulder and from the unnatural angle of the woman's head, I knew she was very, very dead.

Also by Marcia Talley
Sing It to Her Bones

For my friends at the Charlotte Hobbs Memorial Library!

UNBREATHED MEMORIES

A Hannah Ives Mystery

Marcia Talley

Marcia Talley

A Dell Book

Published by
Dell Publishing
a division of
Random House, Inc.
1540 Broadway
New York, New York 10036

Dell® is a registered trademark of Random House, Inc.

ISBN: 0-7394-1201-9

Manufactured in the United States of America
Published simultaneously in Canada

In Memoriam
Lois Elizabeth Tuckerman Dutton
1917–1980

Mother

Acknowledgments

I owe special thanks to many people who generously helped in the writing of this book. All mistakes are mine alone and should not be attributed to any of the wonderful folks mentioned below.

To my husband, Barry, for his unqualified love and support.

To my daughters, Laura Geyer and Sarah Glass, for making me laugh whenever I'm in danger of taking myself too seriously.

To Carolyn, Pauline, Katherine, and especially to Gretchen, for their candor and courage.

To my editor, advocate, and friend, Jackie Cantor, and to the amazing Abby Zidle, who can do anything.

To my creative and indefatigable agent, Jimmy Vines.

To my writers' groups—Sujata Massey, John Mann, Janice McLane, and Karen Diegmueller in Baltimore, and Christiane Carlson-Thies, Janet Benrey, Trish Marshall, Mary Ellen Hughes, Sherriel Mattingly, and Ray Flynt in Annapolis—I couldn't have done it without you!

To Malice Domestic, Ltd., for the grant that opened the door, and to the members of Chesapeake Chapter of Sisters in Crime, for all they do to support newly published authors.

To Thomas Tracey, M.D., Shirley Aronson, and Donna Yates, for medical advice and background information.

To Barbara Parker, feng shui consultant and Web maven extraordinaire (*http://hometown.aol.com/ mardtal/homepage.htm*).

To Linda Sprenkle, location scout, intrepid guide, and dear friend.

To Vicki Cone, former Assistant Librarian at St. John's College, for an insider's tour of the renovated library and its special collections.

To Rear Admiral Robert McNitt and his wife, Pat, who invited me to dinner at Ginger Cove, little suspecting where it would lead.

To Ed and Donna Hudgins, who helped invent All Hallows Church, which might have been more Episcopally-correct, had it not been for all the wine.

To Kate Charles and Deborah Crombie, partners in crime and best of friends—Long live "Plot Fest"!— and to Ken and Angela Pritchard at Pickford House, Beckington, Somerset, for the British hospitality that made it possible.

And to Carol Chase, best of best friends, for her cyber-hugs and sympathetic ear, for St. Hilda's and Edington and everything else.

Hard-handed men, that work in Athens here,
Which never labour'd in their minds till now;
And now have toil'd their unbreathed memories
With this same play, against your nuptial.

William Shakespeare
A Midsummer Night's Dream
Act 5, Scene 1

UNBREATHED
MEMORIES

BELIEVE IT OR NOT, THERE ARE ADVANTAGES TO HAV-
ing had cancer. When the bloodmobile folks come to
town, for one, they're not the least bit interested in si-
phoning blood from you, even if you've got some rare
blood type known only to God and six people on a remote island off the coast of South Carolina. Two, I get
my mammograms at half price. Third, I've discovered
one can get away with being a bit eccentric. If you decide to take up skydiving or transcendental meditation,
for example, or suddenly become a vegetarian addicted
to broccoli sprouts, people may think you're a little
nuts, but they don't give you a hard time about it. They
just nod their heads, peek at each other sideways, and
whisper knowingly, *cancer.*

That's probably why my sister Ruth thought I'd be interested in those New Age gizmos she sells in her shop
on Main Street in downtown Annapolis when they've
never particularly interested me before. She had just
telephoned to say she'd be coming over with "a little
something" to show me. I shuddered. The last time she'd

brought me "a little something"—bamboo curtains meant to slow down fast-moving *chi* between the family room and the kitchen—it had ended up costing me seventy-four dollars just to get them hung.

While I waited for Ruth, I sat at my kitchen table going through the mail. The kitchen was particularly pleasant that day, unusually warm and bright, with sunshine flooding the room, reflecting off the thin layer of snow covering the ground outside. Spread out before me were all the Christmas cards I had missed while I was out in Colorado attending the birth of my first grandchild—a little girl named Chloe, after one of my son-in-law Dante's clients. A particularly wealthy and grateful woman, she had brought him a lot of new bodies to massage. To me, "Chloe" was the title of a raucous old Spike Jones tune with gongs and bells, but my daughter Emily liked the name because it sounded like a warm, spring breeze. I looked it up—"Chloe" is a Greek word meaning "young, green shoot." Not very zephyr-like, but I wasn't going to mention it.

I shuffled through the greeting cards, looking first for ones from absent friends. With enthusiasm I slit the envelopes open with a kitchen knife so I could catch up with lives via hastily scribbled notes or elaborate, mass-produced Christmas letters in which happy family groups smiled out at me smudgily from poor-quality photocopies.

Beneath an oversized seasonal communication from State Farm Insurance, I uncovered a manila envelope from a plastic surgeon in Severna Park I had consulted about reconstructive surgery just before leaving for Colorado Springs. Reconstruction. I liked that word. It evoked visions of something new and wonderful rising from the ruins. I daydreamed about it while putting the teakettle on to boil, wondering what my chest would look like after surgery when they removed the bandages for the first time. The plastic surgeon had shown me samples of her work; photographs of other women, naked from the waist up, with black rectangles covering their eyes. I imagined my own picture—a dark oblong wearing light brown curls, a crooked smile, and just below my shoulder and to the right, a pert little hill jutting out of a ravaged plain.

I measured some jasmine tea into a silver tea ball and dropped it into the pot to steep. While I waited, I opened the envelope from the doctor. It contained a letter encouraging me to call her office "at my convenience" to confirm the surgery, and a two-page, legal-looking consent form. Reading this stuff required a strong stomach and an equally robust cup of tea, so I poured myself a mug, covered the pot with a cat-shaped tea cozy, and had just settled down to plow my way through the small print when the telephone rang.

"Hi, Hannah, whatcha doing?"

"Looking over some stuff from Dr. Bergstrom. I'm trying to decide about reconstructive surgery."

"I'd sure have it if I were you."

Easy for her to say. My sister Georgina was a C-plus-plus to my insignificant A-minus.

"Listen to this." I dragged a chair over to the telephone and settled into it. " 'These are my wishes if I am ever in a persistent vegetative state . . .' Yuck! I'm nervous enough about going through more surgery without being reminded of all *that*!" I tossed the document toward the kitchen table, where it ricocheted off a potted geranium, floated to the tiles, and slid under the refrigerator. It had been a little over a year since my mastectomy, and the memory of the surgery and my long recovery was still fresh in my mind. "I'm thinking about not going through with it, now that they mention the risk."

Georgina sounded bubbly. It must have been one of her up days. I could hear high-pitched squabbling in the background, the twins from the sound of it, Sean and Dylan, who were seven. "It will be fine, Hannah. You'll be fine. Better than fine."

I rested my head against the wall with the receiver to my ear and didn't say anything. My sisters didn't talk to me very much about *It* these days. I suspect they had convinced themselves that if you didn't talk about *It, It* wouldn't exist.

Keeping the receiver clamped to my ear and uncoiling the cord as far as it would go, I walked to the refrigerator, stooped, and retrieved the document, shaking off a couple of greasy dust bunnies that clung to the edges. "I think I'll add a line to this form, Georgina. If I should end up in a persistent vegetative state, I'm saying I want them to start hydration and artificial nutrition and then I want you to remind Paul to call his lawyer and sue the pants off them."

Georgina chuckled. "I'll try to remember that."

"You better, or I'll come back to haunt you." I laid the document on the table near the Christmas cards and took another swig of tea. "How's it with you?"

"Busy. Trying to keep the kids out of Scott's hair while he's working."

"Why doesn't Scott get an office outside the house? I don't know how you stand it! As much as Paul and I enjoy each other's company, we'd soon be at each other's throats if I had him hanging around the house all day."

"Scott's working on it. He's got his eye on a place off York Road in Towson, and if he can land this big Mahoney account, he'll have it made." Scott was a CPA, and I couldn't imagine how he managed to work, let alone land any big accounts, with three children under-foot. Sean had evidently popped Dylan, or vice versa, because there was a piercing wail and Georgina's voice became muffled. "Sean! Cut it out! Now! Trucks are for playing, not for hitting. And turn down that TV!" Poor Georgina. I sometimes baby-sat for my nephews, identical down to the sandy hairs on their mischievous little heads, and it was exhausting. No wonder Georgina stayed so thin. And now there was baby Julie to trip over, born when Georgina was in her late thirties, just turned four and prancing about everywhere.

Over the background of the TV, playing cartoons at a decibel level high enough to rupture all eardrums within a half-mile radius, Georgina persisted, "Help me remember something."

"How do you stand the noise?" I asked, but she didn't give any indication that she heard me.

"Where did we live when I was two?"

I didn't have to rack my brain to come up with an answer to that. I could still remember the sunny days, the faultless blue of the Mediterranean sky, and the smoky outline of Mount Vesuvius in the distance across the sea. "Dad was stationed in Sicily then."

"Who took care of us?"

"What do you mean, who took care of us? Mother did. And Marita, the maid. Why do you ask?"

"It's something I need to know for my therapy."

Georgina had been seeing a therapist who was helping her deal with a protracted postpartum depression. In my opinion, all she needed to cure what ailed her was to get her husband out of the house and hire a baby-sitter once or twice a week, and I told her so.

"It's not just the pressure at home, Hannah. Lionel was absolutely beastly at church this Sunday."

The Senior Warden at All Hallows Church in Baltimore where Georgina played the organ was a piece of work. After listening to Georgina's complaints, I decided that he was the psychotic who needed therapy, not Georgina. I thought about the organ concert where I had last seen the odious Lionel—Mr. Streeting to his friends—pacing self-importantly in his slimy, silver-gray polyester suit, peering over the tops of oversized tortoise-shell eyeglasses and making two-finger come-hither gestures as he seated the audience. How Georgina could stand even to look at the man—his black hair, laced with gray, parted too neatly on the side, and so thick with hair cream you could see the tooth marks of his comb—was beyond me. Streeting controlled every aspect of All Hallows, from the choir director to the Junior Warden, from the Altar Guild to the church secretary, even the rector, with an uncompromising hand. Look up "prick" in the dictionary and there's his picture, right between "pricey" and "prickle."

Georgina's antipathy knew no bounds as she launched into her latest diatribe. "The hymns are always too loud for him, never too soft. I'm to play faster or slower, depending upon the phase of the goddamn moon. During the prelude today I caught sight of him in my mirror, flapping his arms like a wounded bird. I thought someone had died, for Christ's sake! Then the light on the console started flashing off and on and I knew he wanted me to quit playing but I only had sixteen bars to go so I ignored the SOB." She paused for breath. "And then, do you know what he did?"

"I hate to think."

"He oozed up to me after the service, tapped his watch, and said, 'We simply *must* start the services on time. Your prelude was two minutes over, Mrs. Cardinale.' Honestly!"

"Why don't you quit?" I asked.

"I thought about applying for the organist position at Union Memorial downtown, but I've been Episcopal since forever, and All Hallows is so close to home."

It seemed to cheer Georgina up to bitch about Lionel, so we spent some hilarious minutes trashing the jerk. I laughed out loud when Georgina told me how she'd sneak down to the fellowship hall for a Diet Coke during the sermon.

"How do you know when it's time to come back?"

Georgina snickered. "When Lionel records the sermons, he turns the sound up full blast. Father Wylands doesn't know it, but they're probably debating his views on the Prodigal Son up on Mars."

I heard the front door open. "Hannah!" My older sister was calling.

"Gotta go, babe. Ruth's just arrived."

By the time I said good-bye and made it to the entrance hall, Ruth was disappearing into my living room, leaving the front door gaping wide and all the heat pouring out onto Prince George Street. She was carrying an objet d'art about two feet tall, made of copper. I shut the door securely and followed her, wondering why I ever thought it would be a good idea to give my sister a house key. "What on earth is that?"

"It's a fountain. Water represents prosperity, harmony, and peace." Ruth set the fountain down on the floor, then surveyed the room, turning slowly in a complete circle. She looks a little like me, except her hair is long and gray, caught up at each side above her ears with silver butterfly clips. Neither one of us can figure out how we're related to Georgina, who has green eyes, hair the color of buttered sweet potatoes, and is drop-dead gorgeous, either a throwback to a great-grandmother on our mother's side or simply delivered by the stork to the wrong house.

Ruth zeroed in on a vase, now filled with irises, that I had kept for years on an antique table between two windows. "Here." She lifted the vase off the table and handed it to me. I stood there like a dummy, holding the arrangement, my mouth open, but no protest came out. I knew it would be a lost cause. I hated myself for allowing Ruth to steamroll me like that, but I told myself that if I really hated the darn fountain, I could put the irises back after she left.

Ruth keeps insisting that my health problems and past troubles with my marriage were related to poor feng shui. She's made it her life's work, or at least this year's project, to bring my house into harmony. While Ruth went to the kitchen on some mysterious errand, I looked around for a new home for the silk flowers, finally stowing them under the dining room table to deal with later. Ruth returned in minutes with a saucepan of water, which she dumped into the base of the fountain. She yanked the cord attached to a pottery lamp out of the wall, plugged the fountain into the same receptacle, then stepped back to admire her handiwork. "There. Isn't it pretty?"

I had to admit that it was. A graceful sculpture of bamboo stalks and leaves, down which water cascaded in a pleasantly gurgling spiral.

"Now for the mirror." She extracted a tissue-wrapped object from her purse, an octagonal disk about the size of a saucer.

"Your shop must be doing well if you can take time off to come here at the drop of a hat to give me all this stuff." I waved my arm, beginning with the mirror still in her hand and including in its sweep the fountain, a red-tasseled bamboo flute hanging over the front door, some wind chimes she had brought over last November, and a crystal hanging between the front door and the stairs, all selected by Ruth to cure various deficiencies in my home environment.

Ruth surveyed the room critically, looking for the best place to hang the mirror. "Of course I can afford it." She homed in on a watercolor, a particular favorite of mine, a painting of Emily cradling Sunshine, a calico cat long gone to that happy catnip garden in the sky.

"Now wait a minute!" I was suddenly tired of being a doormat. "I *love* that picture there! Leave it right where it is. Please!"

Ruth, her eyebrows thick and brushed straight up, scowled at me over her shoulder. "It's the best place for the *ba gua*, my dear. We need to deflect the negative energy coming in through that window from the street."

"Well, I don't care. You can hang your *ba* whatzit up if you want, but it'll have to deflect negative energy somewhere else."

Ruth wandered into the dining room, finally selecting an alternate location over the stove in the kitchen. "Here. Come hold this up so I can see how it looks."

I took the little mirror from her hands and positioned it at eye level against the floral wallpaper.

"Why waste time on me?" I asked. "Why not help Mom and Dad get settled in their new place?"

"I tried." Ruth squinted at me, her head cocked to one side. "Up a bit," she instructed.

I inched the mirror up the wall.

"Mom told me to stop fussing and come back in a couple of weeks when the movers were gone and things were less hectic. Sort of kicked me out, if you want to know the truth."

"Imagine my surprise," I said.

"As it turns out, I won't be around in two weeks. I'm going on a buying trip to Bali."

"Bali! That sounds like a classic boondoggle."

"Bali's the feng shui capital of the world."

"Seriously?" I was still standing at the stove holding her stupid mirror against the wall.

"Seriously." She pulled up a chair and sat down. "First I'm taking a wood carving course, then I'm checking into a health resort in Ubud. I need to get rid of all the poisons in my system." She moaned with pleasure. "Saunas, herbal wraps, meditation, vegetarian meals, mountain hikes—"

"And don't forget the souvenir T-shirt." I jerked my head toward the wall, just in case she had forgotten about the mirror. "How long will you be gone?"

"About a month. Sunnye is taking care of the store."

"What about Eric?" Eric Gannon was Ruth's ex-husband. He still owned a half interest in the shop and used that as an excuse to pop in from time to time and fiddle with the displays, just to annoy her.

"Mon-sewer zee artiste won't even notice I'm gone. Last time I saw him he was walking down Main Street arm in arm with that Sylvia creature who used to work at Banana Republic." She heaved an exaggerated sigh. "Thank God we didn't have any children." Ruth wiggled her fingers. "A little more to the right."

I complied, although my arm was beginning to ache. You'd think she was building the space shuttle or something. When the telephone rang, seconds later, I made an eager move to answer it.

Ruth raised her hand, palm out. "You stay there, I'll

get it." She snatched the receiver off the wall. "Ives residence." She turned and looked at me, head tilted, considering the present placement of the mirror. "Oh, hi. How're you doing?"

She waved her hand, indicating that I should move the mirror a few centimeters to the left. I was praying she'd find a cosmically acceptable position soon.

"Sure. She's right here. I'll get her." She extended the receiver in my direction. "It's Georgina." Ruth wore that puzzled look where her eyebrows nearly met. "Apparently she doesn't want to talk to me." She held the receiver by the cord with two fingers, as if it were dirty and she'd forgotten the Lysol.

I set the mirror down on a chair, walked to the phone, and took the receiver from where it hung from Ruth's outstretched fingers. "What's up, Georgina?"

"Sorry to trouble you again, Hannah, but I thought of a couple more questions I wanted to ask about when I was a kid."

"Why don't you ask Mother? Or Ruth? Ruth was nine when you were born. She might remember more than I do. I was only seven."

"I can't talk to Mother and I don't want to ask Ruth. She's so . . . judgmental." Georgina was practically whispering, as if she thought Ruth might overhear.

"If it's for therapy, I'm sure we'd *all* be willing to help."

"Don't give me a hard time, please, Hannah. I'd rather talk to you, is all, if that's OK."

I sighed. Might as well get it over with. "Sure. Shoot."

It seemed forever before Georgina actually spoke. Strange, for someone so anxious to talk. "Why was I hospitalized in kindergarten?"

That was easy. "You had your tonsils taken out." I remembered how jealous we'd been when Georgina'd been allowed all the ice cream she could eat.

"Are you sure?"

"Of course I'm sure."

"How long was I in the hospital?"

"Oh, I don't know. Maybe two days."

"I seem to remember it being longer than two days."

"Georgina, you were only five. Two days away from your family would seem like forever to a five-year-old."

"I guess so." Georgina paused. She didn't sound convinced.

I made a brave effort to change the subject. "Speaking of children, how are the boys liking Hillside?"

Georgina ignored me. Her next question caught me completely by surprise. "Tell me. How did Mary Rose die?"

Mary Rose was our infant sister who died when I was barely three, long before Georgina was born. I felt guilty that the only memory I had of Mary Rose, other than photographs, was from the tantrum I threw when the new baby moved into my room and I had to share a bedroom with Ruth. But I will never forget my mother grieving over the empty crib. "It was SIDS," I told her, not believing that she didn't already know this.

"Are you sure?"

"Of course I'm sure! If you don't believe me, ask Mother."

"I told you, I just can't talk to Mother about this stuff. She wouldn't understand."

I turned my back to the stove where Ruth had her head under the exhaust hood and was using the heel of her shoe to pound a nail into the center of a white rose on the wallpaper. "I'm not sure I understand either,

Georgina." I paused, waiting for her to reply. When she didn't say anything I said, "Look, I've got to go help Ruth. She's running amok in my house, feng shui-ing all over the place. Call me back later if you still want to talk."

"I thought that you, at least, would understand," she said in a small, sad voice; then she hung up abruptly, leaving me with a dial tone buzzing in my ear. I shrugged and returned the receiver to its cradle, feeling like I'd just bought a one-way ticket into the Twilight Zone.

Ruth stepped back to the kitchen table and surveyed her handiwork. "Good!" she said. Then after a few thoughtful seconds asked, "What'd Georgina want?"

"She was asking me some damn fool questions about when we were little."

"Questions? Like what?" Ruth mumbled around a nail that wobbled between her lips.

"Like when she had her tonsils out and why Mary Rose died."

"How odd."

"She says it's to help with her therapy."

One eyebrow arched. "Therapy? What the hell's she in therapy for?"

"She's been depressed. Although what having one's tonsils out has to do with depression, I have no idea."

"I'm glad she's getting help, Hannah, but why on earth didn't somebody tell me about the therapy? *You*, for instance."

I poured us each a fresh cup of jasmine tea and motioned for her to join me at the table. "I didn't think it was important." But in less than forty-eight hours, with my hands wrapped around a similar mug of tea, I would learn how very wrong I could be.

OTHER THAN TO MAKE AN APPOINTMENT WITH DR. Bergstrom, for the next few days I didn't worry much about my reconstructive surgery. Or about Georgina and her imaginary problems. Instead, I spent my mornings engrossed in a project an old friend at St. John's College had steered my way. I had been temping at a local law firm, filling in for a secretary on maternity leave. I confessed to my friend over lunch at El Toro Bravo that I was glad the woman was coming back. I was pretty damned tired of doing nothing more constructive than answering the telephone and filing updates as thin as Bible pages into fat black legal loose-leaf binders.

"Have you heard of L. K. Bromley?" my friend asked.

Of course. Everybody had heard of L. K. Bromley, the famous mystery writer, who in her time was crowned "America's Agatha Christie," writing more than seventy mystery novels in a career that spanned fifty years. But few people knew that L. K. Bromley was also Nadine Smith Gray, that tweedy, straight-backed, white-haired Annapolitan who lived in a wee brick house on the corner of College and North Streets and walked her dachshunds every day on the back campus. She looked more like a Navy widow or someone's sweet old grandmother. So when she moved to the Ginger Cove retirement community at the ripe old age of eighty-two and left her entire library—or, rather, L. K. Bromley's library—to the college, along with the money to process and maintain it, everyone was surprised. No one at the college could figure out why Ms. Bromley had singled out St. John's for that honor. Maybe it was in gratitude for all the lectures she attended there, someone speculated, or the classic film series, or the privilege of letting her dogs poop on the well-manicured lawn. Ms. Bromley, as mysterious and tight-lipped as her protagonists, wasn't saying.

A delighted St. John's needed someone with experience to organize and catalog the collection. I had just spent an enjoyable and productive two days perched on a low stool in a bright workroom on the southeast side of the recently renovated college library. There I sorted through Ms. Bromley's novels, putting plastic covers on to preserve the dust jackets and deciding what to do with the large number of books that she used as references. There were guidebooks, maps, train schedules, trial transcripts, and books on forensic evidence, just the thing if you live a quiet suburban life and need to know what a bullet can do to a person's head at close range. I pored over *Coroner's Quarterly* with the same morbid fascination that I used to give to my grandfather's medical texts, delighted in the old maps of Savannah, Georgia, and Reno, Nevada, and marveled that in the 1950s you could catch a train from Annapolis to Baltimore every hour. In recent years the tracks had been torn up, and you were lucky if you could find a bus going there once or twice a day.

The librarian had suggested that I complete the Bromley collection by rounding up copies of the author's short stories. They had been serialized in publications such as the *Saturday Evening Post* and *Collier's*, so I was expecting to spend a great deal of time with *Reader's Guide to Periodical Literature*, visiting other libraries that kept complete runs of popular magazines, and shelling out dimes by the ton for photocopying. I was fascinated by the work, and after only a day had decided that even if the creeps who had laid me off last year from Whitworth & Sullivan wanted me back, even if they crawled down Route 50 after me, begging on their hands and knees, I'd never agree to work in Washington, D.C., again.

The part-time job also gave me the flexibility I needed to help my parents with their recent move to Annapolis from Washington State. Dad had graduated from the academy in 1950 and had been stationed there again when Ruth and I were in high school. He liked the town so much he always swore he'd retire there, so after leaving the Navy in 1980 and spending nineteen years as a consultant to the aerospace industry, he and Mother made plans to move east. Mom seemed relieved. My recent illness had affected her more than she let on, and we both had the telephone bills to prove it.

Now the calls were local, but I preferred the face-to-face contact I had missed when we were separated by a continent. Recent afternoons found me heading for my parents' new home in the Providence community, out Greenbury Point Road, just past the Naval Station. It was a comfortable, ranch-style house on a quiet street, one block from the water. As a housewarming gift Paul's sister, Connie, had painted a mailbox featuring entwined anchors, a mermaid, and other nautical flora and fauna. I noticed it had been installed at the head of the drive. "Capt. George D. Alexander, USN, Ret." gleamed from both sides in bold, gold letters.

Mother was removing glasses from a packing barrel and layering them into the dishwasher when I arrived shortly after lunch. She swiped with the back of her hand at a damp tendril of graying hair that hung down onto her forehead, then nodded in the direction of the laundry room. "Hang your coat up in there, darling, then come give me a hand."

I smiled at my mom, a petite woman not more than five feet tall, wearing black jeans, a faded red cardigan, and a favorite pair of fleece-lined slippers from L.L. Bean. Rolls of shelf liner, a ruler, and a pair of scissors lay out on the kitchen table. "Be a dear and finish up with that cabinet over there, so that it'll be ready when these glasses come out."

I dutifully measured the shelves, then used the scissors to cut the paper to fit, following the preprinted grid on the back of the sticky paper while Mom continued unpacking. At one point she held up a Peter Rabbit bowl that had been mine as a child. There was a chip in the rim where I had once banged it too hard with my spoon. "Remember this, Hannah?"

"I sure do." I remembered my favorite bowl well, but had no clear recollection of the temper tantrum that had resulted in the damage. Mom must have told me about it. I had been two and a half; no one could remember back that far. Now Georgina was trying to dredge up memories from when she was that age. I didn't believe it was possible.

I was trying to think of a way to bring up the subject of

Georgina's therapy with my mother, but wasn't sure how much she knew. "Mom, have you talked to Georgina lately?"

She looked at me sideways over her shoulder. "Not for several days. Why?"

"She's been calling and asking idiotic questions about her childhood. I told her what I knew about it, but can't understand why she doesn't ask you."

"She's probably afraid her father will give her an earful after the phone call he had with her last week. I overheard him saying that if she didn't get herself to a *real* doctor, he didn't want to talk about it any more."

So they knew about the therapy sessions. I put down the scissors. "I thought she *was* seeing a doctor."

"Dr. Sturges is a therapist, but she's not an M.D."

"I thought therapists *were* M.D.s."

"Not always. Some are psychologists or social workers."

"But surely she's competent."

"Your father doesn't think so."

"That woman is a quack." My father entered the kitchen from the dining room carrying a wrought-iron pot rack and a hammer. He brushed my cheek with his lips, handed me the hammer, then climbed onto a stool and positioned the rack on the wall over the stove. He turned, towering over me, a handsome, broad-shouldered man, his close-cropped sandy hair only slightly gray at the temples. "She's filled your sister full of the damnedest nonsense I've ever heard." He extended his hand, and I put the hammer in it. He used it to bang away at a nail, swore when the nail bent double, and wrenched it out of the wall with the claw end of the hammer, sending it ricocheting off the wall and skittering across the tiles. He inserted another nail in the hole he had started and began pounding again. "God!—damned!—quack!"

I looked at my mother, her brown eyes serious and unblinking. "Why don't you use a drill and some proper screws, George?" When my father didn't answer, she shrugged. "I'd invite you to stay for tea," she said to me, "but we haven't found the teapot yet." She gestured vaguely in the direction of still more boxes piled up in the corner of the kitchen, spilling out into the adjoining family room. "There's coffee."

"No thanks, Mom." I gave her a hug. "I've got to get going anyway. I promised Paul I'd make chicken curry tonight, now that I'm a woman of leisure. More or less."

I squeezed my father's leg where he stood on the stool. "Bye, Dad."

He patted my head. "See you later, pumpkin." As I shrugged back into my coat I heard him say, "Lois, I'll take some of that coffee, if you don't mind. On second thought, make that a martini."

In the fifteen minutes it took to cross the Severn River, drive home, and find a parking spot in front of our house on Prince George Street, I worried about Georgina. What on earth was going on in that screwball head of hers? At the turn onto the Severn River bridge, I was cut off by a silver Toyota speeding down the hill through a red light. I honked at the driver, a young man with a cell phone grafted to his ear. I had owned a Toyota once, until I drove it into a pond at my sister-in-law's. I'd recently replaced it with a 1996 Chrysler Le Baron convertible in a pale purple color the used car salesman had described, with an expansive sweep of his hand, as wild orchid. Paul called it the Grannymobile, my midlife-crisis car. Could well be. In any case, I figured it was a heck of a lot cheaper than Georgina's shrink.

At home, I retrieved the mail from the floor where it

had fallen through the mail slot. Nothing but bills, and the U.S. Postal Service had torn the cover of my *New Yorker* magazine again. I tossed the lot onto the hall table, hung up my coat, draped the strap of my purse over a doorknob, and headed for the kitchen. I pulled some chicken breasts out of the freezer and put them in the microwave to defrost, and had just settled down with a steaming cup of Earl Grey when the telephone rang. I wiped my hands on a towel, sighed, and resigned myself to giving the brush-off to another telephone salesman. Nobody else ever called me at three o'clock in the afternoon.

"Hello."

I heard a strange, disembodied whispering, like summer wind through the trees.

"Hello?" I said again.

The same plaintive sound sighed down the line, but this time it separated into two recognizable syllables. "Han-nah!"

"What? Who is this?" My heart began to pound.

"Hannah, it's me, Georgina." Her voice was so husky I hardly recognized it.

"Georgina! You sound terrible. What on earth's the matter?"

"Hannah, you've got to come and get me!"

"My God, what's happened?"

"I'll explain later," she whispered. "Just come!"

"OK, but I can't do anything until you calm down and tell me where you are."

"At my therapist's."

"Are you OK?"

"Yes." Georgina drew a ragged breath. "No! Oh, please hurry!"

"I'm thirty miles from Baltimore. Even if I drive like a

bat out of hell it'll take me forty-five minutes to get there. Will you be OK until then?"

Whatever Georgina meant to say was lost in a noisy snuffle. She began to wail.

"Breathe, Georgina! Breathe." I could hear her gasping, so I tried to distract her. "Where's your car?"

"Scott . . . dropped . . . me . . . off."

"Look, he can get there faster than I can. I'm going to call him right now."

"No, Hannah, don't! He's home with the kids. He'd have to bring them along. They can't . . ." Georgina paused as if listening for something, then said, "I think somebody's coming. Please hurry!"

I knew that Diane Sturges lived on Lake Roland, a city park since 1861, yet one of Baltimore's best-kept secrets. Georgina had pointed out the back of the elegant, ultramodern Sturges home last fall when we had been hiking with the children along the footpath that ran through the woods and along the lakeshore. We had parked down by the bridge like everyone else and had walked up the dirt and gravel path, holding hands and singing. I wasn't sure I knew how to get to the house directly.

Georgina's breathing had steadied, but she began moaning. I found myself shouting, hoping to get her attention. "How do I get there, Georgina? Roland to Lake and turn right on Coldbrook?"

"Pleeeease!"

I could see that I was on my own. I checked my watch. Three-fifteen. If I was lucky, I could beat rush-hour traffic and make it to Baltimore well before dark. After dark, I doubted I'd be able to find a white elephant in the deeply wooded, exclusive neighborhood, even if it were wearing a neon tutu. I threw the packet of chicken into the fridge, scribbled a note to Paul suggesting he nuke a Stouffer's frozen macaroni and cheese, and headed for my car.

As I sped up Interstate 97, I wondered what on earth had happened. Did Georgina have a difficult therapy session? If so, what? What could be so awful that she couldn't share it with her husband? Was their marriage on the rocks? Or maybe she had worked herself up into such a state that she didn't want her children to see her that way. I had pressed Georgina pretty hard for answers, but she only cried harder and pleaded with me to hurry.

I took the ramp to the beltway at thirty miles over the posted limit, exited at the BW Parkway, and broke all speed records getting to the stadium, where I peeled off on Martin Luther King and headed straight through the city to the JFX. At the Northern Parkway exit I darted across three lanes of traffic to make a left turn on Falls Road, then headed east on Lake Avenue. I had reached the Boys Latin School when I realized I must have overshot the turning to Coldbrook Lane, so I U-turned in the school's drive and headed back down the hill. Coldbrook appeared almost immediately on my right. I turned and drove slowly along the narrow, forested lane, hoping I would recognize the Sturges house from the front, but none of these expensive homes had been built anywhere near the street.

At the end of the lane, I came to a dead end at a wooden gate. I steered to one side, parked my car on the soft earth near a pile of leaves, and climbed out. The Sturges house had to be near here somewhere. I remembered seeing this gate during our hike.

To my left, a driveway angled up steeply and disappeared around a corner. A box containing salted sand and a small shovel stood near the mailbox, but there was no name painted on the mailbox, just a number. Still, it seemed a likely candidate. I looked around, feeling guilty, then opened the mailbox and thrust my hand in. I pulled out a packet of magazines and long envelopes held together by a rubber band. The letter on top was addressed to Diane V. Sturges, Ph.D., and another envelope announced that she was a member of the Mystery Guild book club. Her husband, Bradley, had investments with Salomon, Smith, Barney and read *Sports Illustrated* and *Forbes*. I stuffed the mail back in the box, then, leaving my car parked on the street where it wouldn't get blocked in, I hurried up the drive.

At the top of the hill, the driveway widened enough to accommodate two cars and circled around under an elaborate, pillared portico attached to a substantial, modern, yellow brick dwelling. A spur led to a three-car garage, also made of brick. One garage door stood open. No cars were in sight.

I stepped up to the front door and stood there for a few minutes, my finger hesitating over the bell. What if I rang it and somebody answered? What would I say? *Excuse me, but may I use your phone, I seem to be lost?* I could always claim to be collecting money for charity. Or be a Jehovah's Witness. I mashed the doorbell button with my thumb. *Silly.* I would simply ask for my sister.

When no one came to the door after several minutes, I peered through a window. Everything inside was dark. Where was Georgina?

To the right of the entranceway a flagstone path led around the house, passing through a well-tended garden that, in summer, would be brilliant with color but now contained mostly boxwood, rhododendron, and ivy.

I picked my way carefully along the path, hugging the foundation of the house, then stopped. A sign, "Office," hung on a white-painted door. The door stood ajar.

I pushed it open with my palm. "Georgina?" There was no answer. I stepped into a small, prettily wallpapered entrance hall simply furnished with a small table, an umbrella stand, and a brass coatrack with Georgina's green winter coat and paisley scarf hanging on it. Ahead of me a short flight of stairs, lushly carpeted, led up to a landing. I took three steps. "Georgina?"

I gasped when Georgina appeared unexpectedly at the head of the stairs, looking like a madwoman. Her hair tumbled loose about her shoulders, and her mascara had melted into black streaks that ran down her cheeks. "Thank God you're here!" She stumbled toward me and hugged me so fiercely that I thought my ribs would break and we'd go tumbling backward down the stairs together.

I took hold of my sister's arms and eased her into a sitting position on the landing, keeping one arm around her shoulder. "Now. Tell me what's wrong."

Georgina pulled herself into a ball, knees to her chest, and rocked back and forth, sobbing. "Diane's dead."

"Your therapist? My God! Are you sure?"

Georgina nodded her head, her lips a thin, tight line. "Look."

Georgina pointed. I stood and passed through a pair of French doors into a simply but elegantly furnished office, dominated by a large walnut desk. Someone, probably a decorator, had arranged small Oriental rugs casually about on the oatmeal-colored wall-to-wall carpeting, A perfectly normal-looking black leather sofa stood against the left wall, a matching overstuffed armchair angled next to it. I strolled around the desk. A green blotter. A pen. An appointment book. A framed photograph of a handsome man in his mid-sixties. Dr. Sturges's husband? Her father? Who could say. Nothing appeared to be out of the ordinary.

"What are you talking about, Georgina?" I yelled. "There's nobody here!" I was afraid my sister had really lost her marbles.

"The balcony."

Beyond the desk, a set of sliding glass doors led out to the balcony that I had admired last summer. Through the glass I could see an iron bench, a small glass-topped table, and, next to it, a large urn containing an evergreen of some sort. Traces of snow remained piled here and there in the corners where the rays of the winter sun couldn't reach. Again, nothing appeared out of order. Yet something must be wrong to have frightened Georgina and upset her so badly. I slid open the door and stepped out onto the deck.

A cold wind blew in off the lake, roaring across my ears and whipping my scarf back over my shoulder. I stood shivering at the end of the balcony, surrounded by tall trees. Through their bare, dancing branches I could see the waters of the lake just below. Off to the left, a lone bicyclist stood on his pedals, then shifted to a lower gear as he huffed and puffed his way up the bike trail. The trail curved toward me, then away again toward the lake, over a small bridge.

Ivy snaked along a brick wall that separated the Sturges property from the park. Inside its boundaries lay piles of dried leaves, patches of snow, a small cedar tree, rocks, a blue shoe. Another blue shoe, attached to the leg of a woman wearing a blue suit. A woman whose body now lay broken over the face of a boulder, one leg bent cruelly under the other, her left arm flung out over her head, her eyes blank and wide. From the size of the dark stain that had spread over the surface of the boulder, and from the unnatural angle of the woman's head in relation to her shoulders, I knew she was very, very dead.

I grasped the railing and swallowed hard, fighting the urge to throw up. Without touching the doors, I hurried back to Georgina. "What happened? Did you see her fall?"

"She was like that when I got here." Georgina gasped, one hand to her mouth. "I came for my appointment like always and I looked all around . . . Oh, God." She sniffed noisily and wiped her nose with the back of her hand. "Diane wasn't in her office, and then I felt a draft and noticed that the doors were open. Oh, God! Oh, God!" She rocked faster and faster. "I wish I'd never gone out there!"

I took Georgina by the arms and shook her. "Why didn't you call the police?"

"I was too scared. I called you."

"We have to call the police!"

"But my fingerprints are all over the place! Oh, Hannah, just get me out of here! I'm her last patient on Fridays. Nobody needs to know I was here. We can call the police from the pay phone down by the pizza place."

She started to cry again, great racking sobs just like when we were kids and I was stuck baby-sitting her. I was a sucker for it then and even worse at resisting it now. "Georgina, we have to call nine-one-one. If there's even the slightest chance she could be alive . . ." I stepped back in the direction of the office. I hadn't seen a phone on the desk, but there had to be one in there somewhere.

"No!" Georgina's scream caught me off guard. When

I turned around a split second later, she had bolted down the stairs, grabbed her coat and scarf, and disappeared.

I raced after her—out the door, up the path, down the driveway, and into the street, where I caught up with her at my car, pounding on the locked door with her fist. "Stop it, Georgina!" As serious as the situation was, the first thought that came to mind was that she would ruin my paint. I unlocked the driver's-side door and popped the locks. "Get in."

Georgina silently obeyed, settling into the passenger seat, hugging her bunched-up coat like a security blanket. I knew I should go back to the house and call the police, but I was afraid to leave my sister alone. No telling what she'd do in her present condition. I considered the forest, deep and thick, surrounding us on three sides and, only yards away, the lake, dark and cold, its shoreline rimmed with ice. Against my better judgment I gave her a disapproving, big-sister glare and said, "OK, we'll call from the pizza place. I don't suppose it matters where we call the police from, as long as we call them."

Five minutes later, I was standing in a phone booth at the Lakefalls Pizzeria dialing nine-one-one. "There's been an accident. A bad fall," I told the operator. "Two twenty-one Coldbrook." When she asked for my name, I panicked and hung up. *Why did I do that?* I leaned against the wall and counted slowly to ten. In the light from the restaurant, I could see Georgina, where she sat huddled in the front seat of my car. I went inside the pizzeria and bought her a Coke.

"Here, drink this."

"I'm not thirsty."

"You should drink something. Here." I grabbed her left arm and pulled it toward me. Her hand came out of her pocket, clutching several sheets of paper. "What the hell's that?"

Georgina thrust the paper back into the pocket of her sweater, like a child. "Nothing."

"Yes it is. Let me see." I set the Coke down on the floor of the car and held out my hand, palm up.

"No."

"Georgina!"

Slowly Georgina pulled the crumpled wad from her pocket and held it out to me, eyes downcast. "It's pages from her appointment book. I took it because my name's in it."

"For the love of God, Georgina! You're her patient! Your name's *supposed* to be in there!" I snatched the pages from her fingers. "First you make me guilty of leaving the scene of an accident—maybe even a crime!—and now you're tampering with the evidence!" Sirens began wailing, approaching in our direction down Falls Road. I stuffed the pages from Dr. Sturges's appointment book into the depths of my bag. "And it's too late to put them back now, the police are already on their way." I threw my head back against my headrest and closed my eyes. "Oh, God, what a mess! I'll deliver these to the police myself, but in the meantime, I'm taking you home. You're going to have a nice, hot bath and tell Scott all about it. You're going to pull yourself together. Then, first thing in the morning, you're going to talk to the police."

But it didn't quite work out that way. I should have known better after watching *Homicide* all those years on NBC. The Baltimore police would turn up on Georgina's doorstep the following morning, even before Sean and Dylan made it out of bed to turn on the television.

NOTHING THAT HAPPENED AFTER I BROUGHT GEOR-
gina home from Dr. Sturges's prepared me for an early-
morning visit from Baltimore's Finest, least of all the
wine. It would help me to relax, I reasoned; but after too
many glasses to count, I decided I'd just sleep forever,
even on the lumpy mattress that spat cookie crumbs all
over me when I wrestled the ancient hide-a-bed open in
Georgina's TV room. Whatever was in Scott's Box-o'-
Chablis knocked me out cold from eleven-thirty until
five, at which time my eyes flew open and my throbbing
head told me it wished I'd had the brains to take some
Alka-Seltzer before putting it to bed. As I lay flat on my
back with the pale light of a gray dawn creeping around
the corners of the window shade, I relived the previous
evening.

Georgina had been a total wreck. The minute we hit
the house she collapsed into a chair like a puppet with
cut strings, leaving me to explain to Scott what had happened. He listened, nodding, with red-rimmed eyes as
cold and pale as arctic ice, then folded his catatonic

wife into his arms and led her away in the direction of the bedroom. I think Scott really wanted me to go home. To tell the truth, I felt like a fifth wheel, but after everything that had happened, I just couldn't face the long drive home after dark.

Sean watched his mother's retreating back, his face impassive. "Daddy's giving Mommy her pills now." Dylan, sitting cross-legged on the floor with a picture book on penguins spread out before him, nodded sagely.

"Mommy's got a headache," offered Julie. "Just like Abigail." She held out her stuffed toy for inspection, a plush pink rabbit whose fur had been loved off in many places.

I stroked Abigail's threadbare ears. "Does Abigail need an aspirin?"

Julie shook her head. "Uh-uh. Abby took her Prozac."

Under other circumstances, I might have laughed. But, sadly, last night appeared to have been business as usual in the Cardinale household, and that was no laughing matter.

So I ended up staring at the ceiling for hours, comforted by the familiar noises a house makes at night—the compressor cycling on and off in the refrigerator, the ice maker dumping its cubes, the furnace in the basement rumbling to life. I waited, dozing, for the sound of running water or a flushing toilet to let me know that someone else was stirring, an indication it might be OK to get up. But the first sound I heard was not the flushing of a toilet, but the thump of heavy footsteps on the porch, followed by two short rings of the doorbell.

I checked the display on the VCR: 6:45. Who could be calling at this hour?

I threw off the quilt and swung my legs over the side of the bed, then stopped. *You can't answer the door like this, you idiot.* In lieu of a nightgown I was wearing one of Scott's extra-large T-shirts with an insurance company logo emblazoned in yellow and black across my chest. My only accessory was a pair of fuzzy orange socks. The doorbell rang again, more impatiently, it seemed. I stumbled into the living room, calling for Scott. Somewhere a door banged. In the entrance hall I grabbed a raincoat off a hook, then peered through the long, rectangular window to the right of the door. Two people stood on the porch, a man and a woman, similarly dressed in winter overcoats. They both wore gloves. The woman was slapping her upper arms for warmth while the man held our *Baltimore Sun*, wrapped in a yellow plastic bag, in his hand. I doubted he was the paperboy.

"Just a minute!" I called through the door. "I'm not dressed." I slipped into the raincoat and pulled it securely around me before opening the door.

"Yes?"

The woman stepped forward. "Mrs. Cardinale? I'm Sergeant Williams, and this is my partner, Detective Duvall, Baltimore City police." She flipped open a leather wallet containing her badge and held it about ten inches from my nose. "We'd like to talk to you about Dr. Sturges."

My heart fluttered, then began pounding wildly. "Dr. Sturges?" I stammered.

"Yes, ma'am," said Officer Duvall. "May we come in?"

I took a deep breath, recovered my manners from wherever they'd fled to, then swung the door wide. "Sure, but I think it's my sister, Georgina, you'll be wanting to talk to, not me. She's still asleep." I led them toward the living room, which was seldom used. "You'll have to excuse my appearance." I shrugged within my overcoat, my hands buried in its pockets. "I decided to spend the night with my sister quite suddenly, and I left home without a change of clothes."

Sergeant Williams turned her sharp black eyes on me. "Suddenly?"

Oops! I'd have to watch my choice of words. I was trying to think of a nonincriminating reply when Scott's voice boomed from behind me. I nearly jumped out of my socks.

"Hannah was baby-sitting for my wife and me. We were out quite late."

I swallowed a gasp and stared, amazed, at my brother-in-law, who had shambled into the room, shirtless, still zipping up his jeans.

Scott ignored me. "How can we help you, Officers?"

"May we sit down?" Sergeant Williams gestured toward the chintz-covered sofa.

"Sure, sure. Be my guest." Scott waved his hand vaguely. "Hannah, why don't you go see about the children?"

I had no intention of leaving the room. Scott had already told one lie, and if he was going to tell any more whoppers, I wanted to know about it. I looked hopefully at Sergeant Williams. "Don't you need me here?"

"No, not right now. Go ahead and see to the children, but we'll want to talk to you before we leave." *Not the right answer.*

When I left the room rather reluctantly, Scott slid the pocket door shut between us. I thought about doing as I had been told, but as my mother will tell you, I've never been very good at that. So I stood outside the door instead, my ear practically glued to the paneling.

"We understand your wife's a patient of Dr. Sturges's." Officer Duvall spoke with a rich Jamaican accent.

"She is. So what's the problem?"

"Diane Sturges was killed sometime yesterday afternoon."

"Killed? Oh my God! How?" I could just imagine Scott, the consummate salesman, shaping his face into a mask of surprise and dismay.

"In a fall off her balcony." Officer Duvall cleared his throat. "That's why we'd like to talk to your wife. We understand she had an appointment with the doctor yesterday afternoon."

"Surely the fall was an accident."

Officer Duvall started to say something, but Sergeant Williams cut him off. "The case is still under investigation."

"My wife would hardly have had anything to do with Diane's death. Diane was the thread that kept Georgina tethered to reality." Scott's voice was edged with concern.

"There's no need to get upset, Mr. Cardinale. We're talking to all her patients." Sergeant Williams's voice oozed Southern comfort.

"You don't understand, Officer. This news is going to come as a great shock to my wife. She's not at all well. I'm afraid this may send her right over the edge."

"May we speak to your wife, sir?" Sergeant Williams addressed my brother-in-law as if he were a second-grader.

"Like Hannah said, she's still asleep."

"Then I'm afraid you'll have to wake her up."

"I'd rather not."

"Most people would rather not deal with the police, Mr. Cardinale, but my partner and I are here. Your wife's here. So the way I see it, she can cooperate with us now, or talk to the grand jury later. Her choice."

"How did you find out my wife was a patient of Dr. Sturges's, anyway? I thought a doctor's files were supposed to be confidential."

"Dr. Sturges kept her appointments on a computer," Officer Duvall explained. "We have all her patients' names and telephone numbers."

"Duvall!" Sergeant Williams's voice had a sharp, elbow-in-the-ribs edge to it. Duvall will get his knuckles rapped good for letting that bit of information slip out, I thought.

Scott grunted and the chair springs creaked a warning as he stood up. I scurried toward the kitchen, where he found me seconds later noisily tapping used coffee grounds into the trash from a gold-mesh filter. "The kids are fine," I told him, having absolutely no idea whether they were or not. They could have been building campfires in the middle of their bedrooms and I wouldn't have known.

Scott smiled wearily when he saw what I was doing. "Make that a big pot, Hannah. I think we're going to need it."

I filled the coffeemaker with enough water for twelve cups, my hands shaking. *Why had Scott lied to the police about yesterday? More importantly, what was I going to do about it?* I opened several cupboards before I remembered that Georgina kept the mugs in the cabinet over the microwave. I picked out five at random and set them on a hand-painted tray. As I opened the refrigerator looking for the milk, I realized that if the police had the doctor's computerized files, there was no need for me to volunteer the calendar pages that Georgina had stolen. I could save her that embarrassment, at least. I found the milk easily—two gallon jugs stood on the bottom shelf—and only spilled half a cup on the counter when I tried to transfer a small amount of the liquid into a pitcher. From a glass canister on the counter, I filled the sugar bowl and set it on the tray with several spoons and a handful of paper napkins. *Should I tell the police what I know? Should I tell them now?* I decided to wait and see what Georgina had to say.

I was serving coffee to the two officers when Scott arrived a few minutes later with Georgina in tow. Literally. He held her hand and dragged her into the living room behind him. She wore a long, plush bathrobe, loosely belted, and her slippers were on the wrong feet. Her glorious hair was caught behind her head in a careless ponytail with a fat red rubber band. She looked sleepy and confused, as if she had awakened in a strange hotel room in a foreign city where everyone was speaking Hungarian. Scott led her to the chair he had recently vacated and held on to her hand until she was comfortably seated. Then he perched beside her on the arm of the chair. "Georgina, these people are from the police. They want to talk to you about Dr. Sturges."

Georgina looked from Sergeant Williams to Officer Duvall with wide, frightened eyes. Her lips formed a tight line and she shook her head back and forth like a reluctant child.

"I've explained to my wife that her doctor is dead," Scott said. "I'm afraid she's in shock."

Georgina stared at her hands, which were folded tightly together in her lap.

"Tell them what you told me, honey." Scott's voice was soft, almost a whisper. His big hand reached out to envelop hers.

Georgina glanced from my face to her husband's and back again, as if she were watching a tennis match.

"Come on, baby."

Georgina bowed her head and gazed up at her husband through lowered lashes. When she spoke, it was to Sergeant Williams. "I went for my regular appointment at three. It was at three, wasn't it, honey?"

"Yes, at three. I drove you there myself."

"I opened the door, went up the stairs, and sat down on the couch like always. But she never came." Big tears coursed down my sister's pale cheeks. "Diane never came."

"Did you notice anything unusual while you were waiting for the doctor, Mrs. Cardinale?" Officer Duvall leaned forward, his elbows resting on his knees.

Georgina shook her head.

"Anybody coming or going?"

"No."

"What did you do when the doctor didn't show up?"

"Walked."

"Walked? Walked where?"

Georgina raised her head. "Home, like I always do." She glared at me as if daring me to contradict her. I was beginning to suspect she wasn't as out of it as she seemed.

I opened my mouth to reply, then thought better of it.

"Walking relaxes her," Scott volunteered. "Sometimes if it's been a difficult session, she'll call me for a pickup, but this time, she walked."

Now Scott was lying, too. I couldn't figure out what was going on. Why was Georgina afraid to mention that she had discovered the doctor's body? True, we had run off without calling 911, but that wasn't a crime. Not that I knew of, anyway. Besides, we *had* made that call. Eventually.

I was leaning back against the mantelpiece digesting all this when it suddenly came to me. *My God! Scott must think Georgina did it!*

Georgina began to sob, shoulders shaking. I reached out to smooth her hair while Scott sat silently, holding her hand in both of his. "I think my wife needs to go back to bed now, Officers. She's on medication."

Officer Duvall set his coffee mug down on the tray and stood up. "Fine. But we will want to talk to her again later."

Scott led a dazed Georgina away, leaving me alone with the officers and in a fine pickle. I knew I had to say *something*, but was paralyzed with indecision. I had been at the scene, after all, and I hadn't been wearing rubber gloves. It would be hard to explain away my fingerprints if I didn't tell them what I knew about Georgina.

I began to gather up the dirty mugs.

"Here, let me help you with that." Sergeant Williams slipped her notebook into the pocket of her blazer and picked up the tray.

"Uh, thanks."

Sergeant Williams followed me to the kitchen. As we passed the TV room, I could hear the blare of early-morning cartoons. I peeked in. Sean and Dylan lay on my unmade bed, chins cupped in their hands, watching Spider-Man. Julie sat cross-legged on the floor, drinking juice from a sippy pack, Abigail Rabbit resting between her knees.

"The children should be getting ready for school," I said.

"It's Saturday," Sergeant Williams reminded me.

I slapped my forehead with my palm. "So it is! All this has got me completely discombobulated."

In the kitchen Sergeant Williams set the tray down next to the sink, then leaned against the counter. "I've been watching you," she said, "and I have the feeling there's something you're wanting to tell me."

I was dizzy with relief. "That obvious, huh?"

She nodded. "I could see the war going on all over your face."

I paced back and forth between the stove and the refrigerator. "I don't know quite how to put this . . ."

Sergeant Williams simply stared at me, breathing evenly. I watched the gold necklace she wore move slightly with each throb of the pulse at her throat. I'd read about this technique. Keep your mouth shut and the suspect will keep talking just to fill the void.

It worked. My brain churned through the silence, worrying about my sister, who appeared determined to paint herself into a corner with lies she'd never be able to explain away once the truth became known. I was little Miss Goody Two-shoes, about to spill the beans. *Tough love, Hannah. You'll have to do it.*

"I'm afraid my sister didn't tell you the full truth just now." My stomach lurched. I paused to take a deep breath, stalling for time. I wanted to put what we had done in the best possible light. "Georgina called me from Dr. Sturges's in hysterics," I babbled. "When I got there, we saw Dr. Sturges lying on the rocks. I was going to dial nine-one-one, but Georgina panicked and ran away. I found her by my car. After I managed to calm her down, we called nine-one-one from a nearby pizza place."

"What time was this?" *As if she didn't know*.

"About five o'clock."

Sergeant Williams made a notation in her notebook. "If your sister's appointment was at three, that means she was alone in the doctor's office for two hours."

"It took me almost an hour to get there."

"An *hour*?"

"I live in Annapolis."

Sergeant Williams raised a suspicious eyebrow. "Why didn't she call her husband?"

I shrugged. "He was watching the children."

Sergeant Williams slipped her ballpoint pen into her purse. "Thank you for telling me, ma'am. I know how difficult it must be for you."

"I honestly can't figure out why Georgina didn't tell you about this in the first place. She didn't commit any crime."

Sergeant Williams's face gave nothing away, so what she said next took me completely by surprise. "You're not going to like this, but we'll need to take your sister down to the station for questioning."

Tears pricked the corners of my eyes. "Oh, God! *Please* don't tell her you learned anything from me! She'll never forgive me." I felt like Judas Iscariot.

"I realize your sister's not well. We'll make it as easy on her as possible. We'll need to take her fingerprints anyway, for purposes of elimination."

"But Georgina's fingerprints will be all over the place! She visits Dr. Sturges two times a week."

"Then they won't turn up where they shouldn't," she said reasonably. "Now, would you call your brother-in-law for me, please, Mrs. . . . ?"

I filled in the blank. "Ives. Hannah Ives." When she

asked, I gave her my address and telephone number. I felt like a worm. A low-down, sludge-crawling, big-mouthed, mud-eating worm.

I found Scott in the bedroom holding a glass of water for Georgina, who sat on the edge of the bed in her nightgown, knocking back pills. In another thirty minutes she'd be a zombie. *Good luck getting anything out of her then, Sergeant Williams!* I told Scott the police needed to speak to him again. I didn't say about what. Then I skulked away to hide out in the TV room with the children.

"Hi, Aunt Hannah." Sean looked up as I entered, but Dylan's eyes remained glued to the TV set where an armada of cartoon tanks was flattening an invading army of robot mice. The sound track was deafening.

"What'cha watching, kids?" I shouted.

"Some stupid boy show." Julie had laid Abby aside and was using blunt-nosed scissors to cut pictures out of an old *National Geographic* magazine. At least I hoped it was an old one.

"Can I help you, Julie?"

"Grown-ups don't like to cut out."

"This grown-up does."

She grinned and handed me the scissors. I was in the middle of trimming neatly around the whiskers of a satin-eyed baby harp seal when my brother-in-law's voice exploded behind me.

"You are *not* going to take my wife with you!"

The children, lost in their own worlds, appeared oblivious.

"I'll be right back, kids." I backed out of the den, pulling the folding doors shut behind me.

Georgina and Scott stood in the hallway just outside the kitchen. Still in her nightgown, Georgina shrank against the wall while Scott stood protectively between his nearly comatose wife and Sergeant Williams.

"I'm afraid we are, sir. You may come with her, if you want."

"If I want? Of course I want! And I'm going to call my lawyer, too."

"That is your prerogative."

Scott faced Georgina, took her by the shoulders, and spoke to her softly. I didn't hear what he said. My sister nodded mutely. With Scott's arm around her, they shuffled into the bedroom, emerging five minutes later with Georgina dressed in a loose-fitting pair of tan slacks, a red cable-knit sweater, and clean, white tennis shoes. His hand rested lightly on her back as he guided her down the hall.

Suddenly Scott seemed to notice me. At first he looked puzzled and I panicked, thinking it might have occured to him who was responsible for Sergeant Williams changing her mind about questioning Georgina at the police station. But the puzzlement quickly evaporated, to be replaced with wide-eyed distress.

"The children!" Scott's face was flushed; he wiped his forehead with his hand. Tears pooled in his eyes. "What about the children?

I rushed to his side. "Scott! Don't worry. I'll take care of the kids." I hugged him hard and he clung to me, breathing heavily and raggedly into my hair. He kissed my forehead. Then he kissed Georgina and watched, grief-stricken, as she was escorted down the front walk to the officers' car. He followed in his burgundy SUV, reversing out of the drive in a spray of gravel and squealing tires.

I watched from the front porch, the door standing half open behind me, until both vehicles disappeared over the hill at Church Lane. When I turned, Dylan and Sean stood framed in the doorway. "They're taking Mommy to jail!" Dylan wailed. His brother's lower lip trembled and he, too, burst into tears.

"That's nothing," Julie proclaimed, elbowing her way between the boys. She laid her cheek against the sparse fur of her toy rabbit. "Abby's been to jail *hundreds* of times."

"JULIE! WHERE'S YOUR HAIRBRUSH?" I WAS HELP-
ing the children pack a few of their belongings and had
given them each a plastic grocery bag from Giant to put
them in.

"I want my suitcase," declared Dylan.

"Me, too. The red one." Sean slouched in the doorway of the bedroom he shared with his brother, pouting.

"I have no idea where your suitcases are, kids. Besides, we're just going to be gone for a little while.
Maybe only one night."

Sean folded his arms across his chest. "I don't want
to go."

"Me, neither," Dylan agreed.

"You are silly boys," announced Julie. "Granddaddy
has a pool table." That seemed to make all the differ-
ence. Julie, I decided, had a future in politics.

I left the boys arguing over which of their Star Wars
action figures to pack in their bags while I wandered into
my sister's bedroom. I told myself I was searching for a
hairbrush for Julie, but to be honest, I was snooping. As

I expected, the room was a mess. The clothes Georgina had worn the day before were heaped in a corner next to the dirty clothes hamper, as if someone with very poor aim had tossed them there. A dresser drawer stood open; another drawer had been hastily closed over some item of clothing, probably the corner of a T-shirt. Compulsively, I picked up the scattered clothing and laid it on the bed, then looked around the room for the missing hairbrush. I was about to give up when something caught my attention, propped up on my sister's side of the bed between the box springs and the leg of her bedside table—a framed photograph of Georgina at the age of three. I recognized the pose. It was from a snapshot of us girls Dad took for our Christmas postcard the last year we lived in Sicily. But Georgina had cropped Ruth and me out of the picture altogether and blown herself up to a fuzzy eight-by-ten. I tried not to feel annoyed.

I studied the picture and was struck by how much Julie now resembled her mother at that age. I stroked the smooth mahogany of the frame with my fingers. The kids had certainly been handling the picture, poor little tykes. I hadn't seen picture glass so smudgy with fingerprints since my photograph of Paul McCartney, the love of my life in junior high school.

I placed Georgina's picture between a lamp and an alarm clock on her bedside table, then made a valiant stab at tidying up the rest of the room, but the clutter of soaps, cleansers, cosmetics, and vials of prescription drugs from three or four different doctors defeated me and I moved on to the less personal and more familiar territory of the family room and kitchen. While the kids took their sweet time packing, I folded up the hide-a-bed, reduced the scattered magazines to a single pile on the coffee table, moved the children's breakfast dishes from the sink to the dishwasher, and gave the kitchen table and countertops a badly needed swipe with a damp rag. Around eleven, I got the house locked, the kids loaded into the car, and my Le Baron headed east around I-695 toward Annapolis. On car trips when we were small, my sisters and I used to dream up irreverent lyrics to "Over the River and Through the Woods to Grandmother's House We Go," until Daddy, laughing, would threaten to pull over and leave us by the side of the road. Kids haven't changed all that much. While I drove, Sean and Dylan lounged on one side of the backseat and butchered "Grandma Got Run Over by a Reindeer," while Julie, belted in behind me with Abby, pretended to ignore her brothers and wondered aloud why we couldn't put the top on my convertible down.

"It's winter," I told her. "There's snow on the ground."

"The sun's out," she said, reasonably.

"It's too cold."

"You could put the heater on."

I took my eyes off the beltway traffic for a second and looked at her in the rearview mirror. "I could, but our heads would freeze off."

Julie giggled. "If we didn't have heads, we couldn't eat. Is Gramma going to have cookies?"

Julie must have been thinking of my mother's famous soft, melt-in-your-mouth ginger cookies. I figured that Mom hadn't even had time to unpack the cookie sheets, let alone bake anything on them. "I don't know, Julie. But we could stop at the grocery store and get some pizza."

"Yay, pizza!" Dylan lived for pizza.

"Pepperoni!" chimed in Sean. "No mushrooms."

"Abby likes mushrooms," said Julie. "Don't you, Abby?"

I felt as if I'd stepped into a time capsule and been whisked back forty years. As I drove south on I-97 listening to the happy patter and good-natured squabbling of the children, I recalled wondrous cross-country trips as the U.S. Navy moved us from one duty station to another. Sometimes Daddy would hitch up a trailer to our big Chrysler and drag it behind. We'd camp in national parks along the way—Yellowstone, the Grand Tetons, Yosemite. I smashed my finger in a door at the Tetons and bled all over my new plaid shirt. Mother washed it out in a tub of cold water, using an old-fashioned corrugated washboard. Funny the things you remember.

Sometimes we'd pull off the road where a flashing neon sign announced "Vacancy" and "Free TV," and, if we were really lucky, "Heated Pool." We loved staying in inexpensive motels where my sisters and I would get a room of our own. With our parents locked safely behind the connecting door, we'd watch TV late into the night, falling asleep while the black-and-white images still flickered on the cheap knotty-pine paneling.

"The Doorknob to Hell," a small voice intoned from the backseat. We were heading east on Rowe Boulevard, just approaching the Naval Academy stadium where a water tower shaped like a golf ball on a tee towered over the parking lot.

I glanced into the rearview mirror and tried to catch Dylan's eye. "Who told you that, Dylan?"

"Nobody. Looks like a doorknob is all."

"Yeah," Sean agreed. "There was this giant . . ." and the twins launched into an improbable story involving dinosaurs, devils, and underground caverns, interrupting each other to heap one extravagant detail upon another until Julie clamped both hands over her ears and even I screamed for mercy. But in the left-turn lane at

Taylor Avenue, waiting for the light, I looked back over my shoulder toward the stadium. The kid was right. Darn thing did look like a giant doorknob.

Ignoring our pleas, Sean reached the climax of his story and began making *woo woo* noises and waggling his fingers at his sister.

"Make him stop, Aunt Hannah! He's scaring Abby!"

The light turned green just then, of course, so I couldn't deal with Sean until we had pulled into the parking lot at Graul's Market.

I unbuckled my seat belt and swiveled around. "If you can't behave yourself, Sean Patrick, I'll have to leave you in the car while the rest of us go shopping."

I wouldn't have, of course, but Sean didn't know that. He hung his head until his dimpled chin touched his chest, tucked his hands snugly between his knees, then looked up at me through white-blond lashes. "Can I pick out the pizza?"

"You can *each* pick out a pizza." Auntie Hannah wasn't usually so generous. I just wasn't in the mood for any hassles. Exhausted with worry and racked by guilt, I could focus only on getting to my parents', anxious to find out if my passion for truth had ruined my sister's life.

A few minutes later, I paraded into the supermarket, three perfectly behaved children in tow. It was too good to last. Dylan wanted to take the shopping cart and tear through the aisles like Mario Andretti, but I nipped his racing career in the bud by putting him in charge of my purse, a large bookbaglike satchel that contained everything I own. He hung it around his neck like a feedbag. At the checkout, he reached in and solemnly extracted a twenty-dollar bill from my coin purse and handed it to the cashier. Sean, meanwhile, correctly pegging me as a softie, had selected two candy bars and tried to slip them into the shopping cart when he thought I wasn't looking. Julie, ignoring us all, danced Abby up and down the tabloid magazine racks. Abby laid a noisy kiss on Leonardo DiCaprio, then moved on to smooch with Bill Clinton. Cheeky little rabbit. I had forgotten how it was, shopping with kids.

Back in the car, the children were strangely subdued, and I wondered if they were worrying about their mother or had simply run out of gas. By the time we reached the spot where the road forks left to Providence and right to the Naval Academy golf course, Sean and Dylan had fallen asleep with chocolate on their lips and the bag of groceries sandwiched between them.

I pulled into the drive behind my father's black Lincoln and set the brake with relief. Paul's blue Volvo was parked on the street in front of the house next door. "We're here, sports fans!" I reached back to unbuckle Julie, stepped out onto the driveway, then pushed my seat forward so the kids could get out. As Sean started to run off, I grabbed him by the hood of his jacket. "Not so fast, big fella. Carry the bag for me, will you?"

He wrapped thin arms around the bag in a bear hug and plodded up the walk. "Help, Aunt Hannah! I can't see!"

I flipped down the automatic door lock and smiled after my nephew, as he staggered with slow, exaggerated Frankenstein steps up the walk, acting for all the world as if the bag weighed fifty tons. How could someone as screwed up as my sister Georgina have managed to raise such sweet kids? *Oh, Lord!* What if she *had* killed her therapist? What if she went to jail? I couldn't imagine Scott handling the kids. Especially Julie. Inside that clever head of hers wheels were turning, measuring, weighing, taking everything in. And that defiant little chin, just like our Emily. At least Emily had turned out all right—eventually—although there had been times when she was in high school when I would gladly have strangled her. I shuddered, remembering Dr. Sturges's distorted face. *Not nice, Hannah. You shouldn't joke about stuff like that.*

I stepped through the door the kids had left open. Amid stacks of packing boxes still piled in the entrance hall, Paul greeted me with a hug and a soft kiss, his lips lingering on mine just long enough that I began to forget where I was and what brought me here. "Hold that thought," I whispered against his ear. "Right now I have to cook up a few pizzas for lunch. Want some?"

"Pepperoni, no mushrooms?" Paul asked, hopefully.

"Pepperoni, no mushrooms."

Paul touched my lips with his index finger. "I love it when you sweet-talk me like that." A long, satisfying minute later, he followed me into the kitchen where Sean had abandoned the grocery sack, leaning crookedly against the refrigerator door.

Paul tore open the pizza boxes while I fiddled with the high-tech dials and buttons on Mother's new stove, trying to get the oven to turn on. "Where are Mom and Dad?" I asked.

"In the living room. Watching TV. They were waiting for the news, at least that's what they were doing until the recent invasion of adoring rug rats."

I rummaged through the cabinets, looking for something to bake the pizzas on. "What a mess! How are they taking this?"

"Neither one's saying much. Could be shock, I suppose. Your dad's wearing a hole in the carpet with his pacing while your mother's keeping a stiff upper lip. She's confident it will all turn out to be a colossal mistake."

I found the cookie sheets—Mother had unpacked them, after all—and Paul slid the rock-hard pizzas onto them. While we waited for them to bake, I quietly brought Paul up to speed on the events of the past twenty-four hours and my role in them. I was relieved when he hugged me and told me that he thought I had done the right thing by telling the officers the truth.

After pizza and Coca-Cola, consumed around the big coffee table in the living room, talking of everything else but, the children entertained us with a corrupted version of Monopoly. Even though they made up their own rules, which the boys kept changing to benefit themselves, it was Julie, I noticed with satisfaction, who ended up own- ing all the railroads, with hotels on both Boardwalk and Park Place. Paul eventually settled the kids in the base- ment recreation room with a bag of videos he had rented from Blockbuster, while the grown-ups waited upstairs for news from Scott. Mother sat in an upholstered Queen Anne armchair and kept trying to smile and make small talk—"I think the garden is going to be lovely once I get my roses in"—while Daddy busied himself between mugs of coffee by taking books out of boxes and arranging them in order by size on the bookshelves. How much coffee could my father drink before his blue eyes turned brown, I wondered.

Sitting next to Paul on the sofa, I threw out conversa- tional tidbits—jokes I had read on the Internet—that glowed, then quickly died, like sparks from a campfire.

My mother laid aside the magazine she had been flip- ping through without actually reading anything in it. "Why doesn't Scott call? He's got to know that we're worried sick."

"I guess he's got a lot on his mind right now, Mom."

"But you'd think he'd at least check in to make sure the children are OK."

"He knows the children are OK. They're here with us."

Mother sighed. "I suppose so." She chewed on her thumbnail, a habit she had recently acquired when she finally gave up a two-pack-a-day cigarette habit.

I didn't think I could stand one more minute of not knowing. I had to do something. Anything. Surprised I hadn't thought of this before, I excused myself, went into the kitchen, and picked up the phone. My sister-in-law's boyfriend, Dennis Rutherford, was a Chesapeake County police officer. Although Chesapeake was several counties to the south of Annapolis, I was convinced Dennis would have an inside track with his colleagues up in Baltimore. But Dennis wasn't home. Disappointed, I left a detailed message, then rejoined the family broodfest.

When the phone finally rang, it wasn't Dennis, just somebody selling a lawn care service. Mother screamed into the receiver, "We don't want any!" slammed it back into the cradle, and burst into tears. Dad stood by the fireplace with a book in each hand, staring helplessly at his sobbing wife.

It was Paul who saved the day. "C'mon, Lois. I'm taking you shopping."

Mother and I always enjoyed a little retail therapy now and then, but this was a new role for Paul.

Mother pulled a fresh tissue from the box on her lap, dabbed at her eyes, and looked up doubtfully. "Where to?"

Paul shrugged, palms up. "Home Depot?" The giant do-it-yourself store would carry many of the items on Mother's list, things she needed for the house, such as towel bars, curtain rods, and lightbulbs. I was amazed at what the previous owners had taken away with them.

My parents had been operating for almost a week without toilet-paper holders. First things first. No wonder Mother had sent Ruth and her dandy little mirrors and wind chimes packing.

After Paul had helped Mother into her coat and the door had slammed shut behind them, Daddy flipped on the TV, and we caught the five o'clock news. The anchorman on Channel Two, with hair so sculptured his hairdresser deserved a line in the scrolling credits, didn't tell us anything we didn't already know. Dr. Sturges had fallen or been pushed over the balcony during an apparent struggle. Robbery had been ruled out. The police were still waiting for the medical examiner's report. My father must have been listening to the broadcast, although his eyes weren't on the TV. Suddenly, the pile of books he was holding teetered, then collapsed into a heap on the floor. "Dammit to hell!" he muttered, just loud enough for me to hear. Without picking anything up, he left the room, smack dab in the middle of the report. "I don't want to hear it."

I watched, puzzled, as he threaded his way through a maze of packing boxes on his way to the kitchen. What had upset him? Something the reporter had said? Or maybe he was just sick to death of unpacking books and wired from too much caffeine. Whatever, I was relieved when he returned a few minutes later looking normal and holding a cold bottle of beer. Coffee and beer. Uppers and downers for the masses. Daddy perched on the arm of the sofa and took a long drink, then turned his attention to the TV. But now the reporter had moved on to describe a fire that was burning out of control in a warehouse near Fells Point. Daddy grunted.

"They didn't mention anything about Georgina, Daddy."

He set his beer down on top of the *Capital*. I watched as the moisture from the bottle slowly soaked into the newspaper. "That little girl doesn't have her head screwed on straight, but there's no way in hell she could have killed anybody. What can the police be thinking?"

They're thinking they don't like to be lied to. I didn't tell Daddy about that. I couldn't predict how he'd take the news that I ratted on Georgina. If he found out about it later, it wouldn't be from me.

Leaving the TV playing on low volume, I helped Dad unpack books, fighting the old librarian's urge to put them in alphabetical order by author and title. Size is good. So is color. I rearranged a shelf so all the blue bindings were together, then ended the row with a two-volume set of yellow-bound essays. The complete works of Patrick O'Brian, my father's favorite novelist, went on the next shelf down. I left him to check on the children from time to time, finding them happily eating popcorn and watching *The Lion King* for the umpteenth time.

When the doorbell rang, I was thumbing through an ancient paperback copy of *Thunderball*. I rushed to the door, thinking it might be Dennis, but the officer with her index finger on the button wasn't Dennis. She was Sergeant Williams, with her partner, Detective Duvall. It didn't compute. *What the hell were they doing here in Annapolis?*

Suddenly I panicked. "Where's my sister? Has something happened to Georgina?"

Officer Williams didn't answer. "May we come in, Mrs. Ives?"

I stood in the doorway like a stone fool, one hand grasping the doorknob, the other balled into a tight fist.

My heart was pounding. *Something must be wrong with Georgina!* I took a ragged breath. "Not until you tell me why you're here."

Officer Williams shifted her weight from one foot to the other, then ran her short, stubby fingers through her light brown hair. "There's no need to worry. Your sister's fine, under the circumstances. We sent her home with her husband over an hour ago."

An hour ago? I couldn't believe Scott hadn't called. What a selfish clod!

I continued to block the door. "Then why are you here?"

"We'd like to talk to your father."

Daddy appeared suddenly at my shoulder. "What about?" The deep, confident voice that had caused many a young sailor to quake in his deck shoes had no perceivable effect on this lady. She didn't even blink.

"Is there someplace we can go where we won't be interrupted?"

That was odd. It wouldn't have surprised me if they'd come to talk to *me* after everything I'd blabbed to Officer Williams. But Daddy? What could they want with him? I glanced quickly at my father, hoping for a clue. He looked bewildered and didn't answer right away, so I blurted out, "We can go to the kitchen, I suppose." I tugged on his arm.

My father led the officers down the hall with me following close behind. Once in the kitchen, Daddy leaned against the dishwasher and waved the officers toward the table. "Have a seat."

Officer Duvall turned to me and drawled, "We'd like to speak to your father alone."

"Daddy?"

He frowned, deepening the natural crease that separated his eyebrows. "I'd rather she stayed."

Officer Duvall shrugged. "If that's what you want."

"I've nothing to hide."

Officer Duvall settled his ample behind into a chair that groaned alarmingly under his weight. I wondered if the chair had been screwed back together securely after being disassembled for the move. He pulled a small notebook from his inside breast pocket, turned to a blank page, and smoothed it open on the tabletop. Officer Williams remained standing by her chair and regarded my father coolly. "Your daughter believes you had something to do with Dr. Sturges's death."

If it had been me, I would have shouted it, but Daddy's voice remained calm and steady. "That's perfectly ridiculous!"

"Mrs. Cardinale claims that Dr. Sturges invited you to come to her office last week in order to assist with her therapy." Officer Williams sat down, laced her fingers together, and laid her hands on the table in front of her.

Daddy looked thoughtful and began chewing on the knuckle of his index finger. A sure sign of nerves. Something was getting to him.

"She says you became angry during the session. She says you lost your temper."

Officer Williams hadn't taken her eyes from Daddy's face and, with the long practice of a commanding officer, he had traded her gaze for gaze. But now he looked away. "I wasn't there."

"Are you telling me that your daughter is lying?"

His head snapped around. "Of course she's lying."

"You saw her this morning," I reminded the officers. "Georgina was a mess."

"True. But in this case, we have a corroborating witness. The housekeeper claims she heard raised voices."

My father shrugged. "Sturges is a shrink. I imagine voices get raised in that office all the time."

"But, sir, your name appears in her appointment calendar."

I felt like I'd been punched in the stomach. "Daddy?"

I caught his eye, but he looked away. His shoulders sagged. Clearly the interview wasn't going the way he had expected. "Get me a cup of coffee, would you, honey?"

I emptied the dregs from the coffeepot, thick as syrup, into his cup. My heart raced. When I returned to the table, he was sitting down at it. Anyone coming in just then would think we were about to play a hand of bridge.

Daddy took a sip from the cup I gave him, grimaced, and said, "OK. I'll admit that I attended that damn-fool therapy session. But that was the only time I was *ever* in that loony woman's office."

Duvall made a notation in his notebook. "Just that once?"

"Yes."

Officer Williams leaned forward. "Tell me, what was it that made you lose your temper?"

"I'd rather not say."

The two officers exchanged glances. "I think it'd be fair to tell you, sir," Officer Williams continued, "that your daughter told us all about it."

My father's face grew pale beneath a sheen of sweat. "If my daughter were completely sane, she wouldn't be seeing a therapist, now would she?"

"I'll ask you again, sir. What was the argument about?"

Daddy closed his eyes and rubbed his temples. When he opened his eyes again, I saw that they were pooling with tears. "That damn therapist was supposed to be helping my daughter get well. Instead, she was filling her head with nonsense." He took a deep breath. "It's all a pack of lies."

"Lies? What kind of lies?"

Daddy looked at me, desperation in his eyes. "Don't tell your mother," he pleaded.

I grabbed his arm and shook it. "Don't tell her what?"

Daddy took another deep breath and exhaled slowly. The silence roared in my ears. When Daddy finally spoke, I thought at first that I'd misunderstood what he'd said. "That woman has Georgina convinced that I sexually abused her."

"What!" My head swam.

A tear ran down his cheek and dripped, unchecked, onto the front of his shirt. "How can she say such a thing?"

I sat there, too dumbfounded to speak.

"Exactly the question I was going to ask, Captain Alexander. Why would your daughter say such a thing?"

"She's delusional, Officer." He swiped at his cheek with the back of his hand. "I'll admit I went there for the therapy session. I thought maybe it would help. But then, they bushwhacked me. Georgina looked me straight in the eye and accused me of all sorts of atrocities!" He jabbed a finger in the air. "And that damn woman sitting behind her desk, egging Georgina on . . ." A shudder ran through his body. "I tell you, I just cracked. Lost my temper and yelled at the two of them until my throat was sore. Goddamn therapist!" He searched my face for understanding. "I got out of there, pumpkin. Jesus! It was like Jonestown without the Kool-Aid! I got out of that hellhole and never went back."

I turned from him then, sick with confusion. It seemed a hundred miles to the sink, but I managed to get there and lean over it, the metal hard and cold beneath my hands. Outside the window, a bird hopped gaily from limb to limb of the sycamore tree. I felt like popping it one. Why should he be allowed to be so happy when our world was falling apart?

"Granddaddy? Are you sick?" I spun around. *Julie!* My niece stood at her grandfather's knee, Abby dangling by one bedraggled ear from her chubby fist. *How much had she heard?*

My father raised his head from where it rested on his arms and smiled at his granddaughter. "No, honey, your granddaddy's just a little bit tired." He laid a gentle hand on top of her head, then stroked her cheek with his thumb.

Julie studied him seriously, a worried look on her face. She was the image of her mother at the age of four; her copper ponytails hung like fat sausages, just grazing her shoulders. "Abby wants a drink."

I took Julie's hand and steered her gently away from the table. "Let's take care of Abby," I said. While the officers made small talk behind me, I rummaged quickly in the refrigerator, coming up with a carton of orange juice and a Pyrex dish of yellow cheese cubes covered with plastic wrap. I hustled Julie out of the room. When I had her settled again on the family room couch I watched with affection as she offered her cheese first to Abby, then when Abby didn't appear to care for cheese, thank you, nibbled on it herself.

Abby wasn't the only one who had completely lost her appetite. I didn't think I'd ever be able to eat again. *How could Daddy? How could anybody?* I swallowed hard. "Impossible," I said aloud. "Absolutely impossible."

I DECIDED TO HIDE OUT DOWNSTAIRS WITH THE children until the police had finished their business. I couldn't bear to watch my father shrivel with humiliation before my eyes. He was my hero—the man who had bought me a cowgirl suit with cap pistols on my sixth birthday; who had wiped away my tears when the boy of my dreams jilted me for a bleach-blond cheerleader; who had walked me down the aisle, tall and proud, the day I married Paul.

When I heard the front door slam and felt my spine relax into the sofa cushions, I realized how tense I had been. But my brain still churned. What would I do if Daddy continued to insist that I not tell Mother about Georgina's wild claims? Yet Mom had looked drained, the deep lines in her brow already reflecting the wearying burden of the mess Georgina had gotten herself into. How could I heap on this new disaster?

When their grandfather appeared at the foot of the basement stairs, Sean and Dylan each grabbed a hand and dragged him toward the pool table. Dad spent the time jockeying a little footstool around so they could reach the table to play eight-ball. In his grandchildren's company, I watched the worried frown evaporate. Daddy wore the benign countenance of an innocent man with an unshakable belief in the infallibility of the system. As he racked up the balls for the boys, I wanted to slap him hard on both cheeks and shout, *Wake up! Life is not like the movies. Truth doesn't always reign triumphant.*

I left the children sending the cue ball ricocheting dangerously around the table and dashed upstairs to clean up the kitchen, reasoning that Mom would surely notice how the coffee cups had multiplied in her absence. I was inverting a souvenir mug from New Orleans over a peg in the dishwasher, feeling like my father's accomplice, when the front door slammed again. I hardly had time to turn around before Mother was standing in the kitchen doorway, her eyes wild with panic. Paul towered like a protective giant behind her. Even in the darkened hallway I saw that his arms were laden with bulky plastic bags from Bed Bath & Beyond.

"What were the police doing here? Have they arrested Georgina?" My mother's voice trembled.

Paul set the bags down in the doorway and laid a comforting hand on my mother's shoulder. "We saw the police car pull out of the drive," he explained.

"Georgina's fine, Mom. They've even sent her home."

"Then what . . . ?"

I took in my mother's unusual pallor and decided a half truth would do. "The police are talking to everyone who saw Dr. Sturges in the last few weeks. Apparently Daddy went with Georgina to one of her therapy sessions."

Mother shrugged out of her down jacket, handed it

to Paul, and collapsed into a kitchen chair. "Of course. I knew that." Relief flooded her face with color. "So, what did they want to know?" A strand of pale peach hair had fallen forward over her cheek, and she tucked it back behind her ear.

"You'll have to ask Daddy about that."

"Where is your father?"

I nodded toward the basement door. "Playing pool with the kids."

"I suspect Georgina—" She paused and swallowed. "—or Scott will come to collect them before long."

"But if they don't, the children can spend the night with us." Paul had returned from the utility room and I hugged him from behind, my arms encircling his narrow waist. "As grandparents ourselves now, we need a refresher course in kid control."

"Absolutely not!" My mother's voice carried even over the sound of the dishwasher kicking in. "They'll stay here with us. Look at this place!" She made a broad sweep with her arm. "If we didn't plan to have everyone over, we wouldn't have bought a house with so much space."

As bad an idea as I thought this was, I found it hard to reverse the parent/child roles. I could never outrank my mother. Still thinking that she might be overwhelmed by the rambunctiousness of her grandchildren, I quickly added, "Do you need me to stay?"

Paul swiveled his head in my direction, a pout beginning to materialize on his lower lip. It morphed into a smile as Mother said, "No, we'll be fine. Georgina needs a rest."

If she only knew the half of it. I prayed Daddy would tell her everything tonight.

I touched her arm. "Are you sure?"

"Don't be silly."

"The boys are pretty lively."

"It's a *pleasure* to have them. We lived so far away for so long. I've missed watching them grow up." She stood and pulled her sweater close around her. "I'll just go look for the sheets."

Paul stood in the doorway like a guardian angel, watching until my mother was out of sight. "She's gone upstairs," he said.

He took a step in my direction, then stopped short when I snapped, "Where's the damn phone?" After holding it in with my mother, my father, and the kids, my nerves just fell apart.

Paul pointed to a beige telephone mounted on the beige wall between the utility room and the refrigerator, a puzzled look clouding his face. Of course he didn't know anything about Georgina's accusations. I punched the auto dial button marked "G&S." "Let me check with Scott. See what he wants us to do," I told Paul.

"Need me?" He raised a hopeful eyebrow.

I wanted to tell him all about it then, but shook my head and blew him a conciliatory kiss instead. "Later, love."

"I'll just take these down to the basement, then." Paul gathered up the bags containing Mother's purchases. "Hold that thought," he said, and disappeared down the stairway.

After four exasperating rings, I got the answering machine and Georgina's naturally breathy voice telling me untruthfully that nobody was home. "Scott. I know you're there. Pick up." The silence stretched into an endless minute while I breathed quietly into the recording. "Pick up, dammit!" The line merely hissed and crackled.

I hung up, counted to ten, and dialed again. This time Scott answered on the first ring. "Sorry, Hannah. I was putting Georgina to bed."

Almost unconsciously, I checked my watch. Six-thirty. Scott was putting his wife to bed like a child. "So, what happened with the police?"

"Oh, God! They questioned her for hours. But she hung in there! Your baby sister hung right in there, Hannah. A regular trouper."

Yeah, sure. I could see it now. Flashing those jade-green eyes, seeking Scott's approval for every lying word. I wondered how well Georgina's demure damsel-in-distress act had played with the businesslike Sergeant Williams.

Beating around the bush was never an option with my brother-in-law, so I got right to the point. "So, Scott, tell me this: What did Georgina say that made the police think they needed to talk to Daddy?"

"How—?"

Good. I'd caught him off guard. "They showed up in Annapolis over an hour ago."

Scott cleared his throat and mumbled something I didn't understand.

"Scott? Are you there?"

"Sorry." He sighed heavily. "Seems your father went to a therapy session with Georgina. He had a disagreement with the doctor."

I was hoping Scott would be more forthcoming about Georgina's interview than the police had been, so I wasn't about to make it easy for him. "A disagreement? What about, for Christ's sake?"

"Her treatment, I suppose. Or maybe her medication."

Liar, I thought. Aloud I asked, "What kind of treatment?"

I knew I'd touched a nerve when he snarled, "You know I can't talk about that!"

"You mean it's something you can talk about with the police—who the last time I noticed were complete strangers—rather than with your family?"

"That's not what I mean and you know it."

"Then I ask you again, Scott. What kind of treatment?"

He paused before answering. "Diane was urging Georgina to confront her demons head-on."

"Demons?"

"If Georgina is going to be pulled from the abyss, she has to face what happened to her."

I hadn't made it as far as the abyss. I was still stumbling over the demons. And then I made the awful leap. The words tumbled out of my mouth before I could stop them. "Daddy? A demon?"

"So. You know about it." His voice was calm, matter-of-fact.

"You think Daddy's a demon?"

"I didn't say that, Hannah. You did."

I lost all patience with my brother-in-law. "That's the biggest crock of shit I've ever heard! How can you believe such crap?" I fumbled for the right words. "Daddy never touched us inappropriately. Never!"

"Well, Diane was certainly right about that!" Scott sounded disgustingly pleased with himself.

"Right about what?"

"She warned Georgina to expect denials."

"Well, of course I'm denying it! Nothing like that ever happened."

"Hannah, you realize that by refusing to face this issue head-on, you're no better than a coconspirator?"

I gasped. "We're all coconspirators, then. Ruth, Mother, Paul, probably even the paperboy and the Avon lady." I fell back against the wall, breathless, as if I'd just taken a quick punch to the stomach. Scott was hopeless. If he wanted to label us coconspirators, I had a label for him, too. Enabler.

I took a deep, steadying breath. "I want to talk to Georgina."

"She can't come to the phone right now."

I'll bet. Another handful of colorful pills had sent her off to la-la land. I wondered what Scott would do if those prescriptions ever ran out. "Will you have her call me when she wakes up?"

Scott neatly sidestepped my question. "I'll tell her you called."

I knew that nothing I said that day was going to change his mind about Daddy, so I tried another tack. "Have you completely forgotten that we have your children?"

"Of course not!"

"What about the children, Scott?"

I could feel a request being formulated in the silence. "Do you think they could spend the night? Georgina's in no fit state to take care of them right now."

"How about their father, then?" I asked. "Somebody put you on psychotropic drugs lately?"

"Give me a break, Hannah! I'm looking after your sister and I have a business to run. The business, need I remind you, that pays for all her medical treatment."

I stared at a jumble of dirty spoons in the kitchen sink and didn't say anything.

"I'll be down to pick the children up in the morning," he said at last.

Scott was slippery. I pushed for specifics. "When, exactly?"

"Uh, around eight; time for Sunday school. Georgina needs to be playing by nine anyway."

I doubted Georgina would be ready to play the radio or anything else in the morning, let alone a pipe organ. "See that you are. Mom and Dad aren't as young as they used to be."

"What? Aren't the children with you and Paul?" Scott was shouting so loudly I had to pull the receiver away from my ear. What was his problem?

"No. We're at Mother's. They're spending the night here."

"No way! Not after what Georgina told me. No way they'll stay in the same house with your father."

My stomach tightened and I tried to swallow, but couldn't. He really believed it, then. It wasn't just a husband's blind, unquestioning support of a disturbed wife. He believed every one of Georgina's lies. I took two deep breaths and found my voice. "If that's the way you feel, then I suggest you get in your goddamn car and come pick them up yourself."

Scott must have had rocks for brains. "Are you sure they can't stay with you?"

"As you so succinctly put it, Scott, no way. No effing way." I hung up before he could reply and pressed my forehead against the cool enamel of the kitchen doorframe, wondering when this nightmare would be over.

When I turned around, I was surprised to see Mother standing in the doorway between the kitchen and the dining room, juggling a large box marked "Sheets / Twin."

Oh, God! How much had she overheard? I hurried to relieve her of the box and set it down on the kitchen table. "You won't need these tonight, Mom. Scott decided to come get the kids after all."

The light left her eyes. "I'm sorry about that."

"Me, too, Mom. Me, too."

While we waited for Scott, Mother and I arranged towels and sheets in the upstairs linen closet and Paul called for Chinese carryout. After the delivery boy left, it didn't take long to turn the kitchen table into a disaster area of red and white cartons, paper plates, overturned sauce cups, crumpled-up napkins, and the odd chopstick. At eight o'clock Scott pulled his SUV into the drive and honked. After a strained conversation with Scott in which I determined that Georgina would probably sleep through till morning, we sent the kids scurrying off with kisses and hugs and tummies full of shrimp fried rice. I had managed some hot-and-sour soup, but that was all I had the stomach for. When Mother gave me That Look, I claimed I was still too full of the pizza I had wolfed down at lunch.

By the time Mother and I returned to the kitchen after escorting the children down the drive, Paul was ready to go, holding my coat folded over his arm. With my back to him, I struggled into it while he waved the coat around behind me like a matador, trying to anticipate where I'd put my arms. "Where's Daddy? I want to tell him good-bye."

Mom kissed my cheek, handed me my cashmere scarf, then shoved me gently in the direction of the front door. "He's gone up to his room." I recognized that wounded expression. Daddy'd probably taken a bottle of scotch up with him. "Look after her, Paul." Her eyes darted to the food, half-eaten, on my plate. "She needs to keep up her strength or she'll be too weak for the surgery."

His lips brushed her cheek. "Don't worry, Lois, I will." Paul's arm snaked around my waist. "And Lois?"

"Yes."

"You're a damn fine shopper."

Mother looked from Paul to me, a half smile brightening her face. "Be forewarned," she said, shaking an index finger. "It's in the genes."

Once we pulled the front door shut behind us, I stood on the porch, sick with dismay. I wanted Paul to bundle me into his arms and get me out of there. I wanted to snuggle against him as he drove me home, and the hell with mandatory seat-belt laws. I wanted a hot bath. A warm bed. But both his car and mine were parked out front.

I must have moaned, because Paul squeezed my shoulder. "I'll drive," he said, instantly in tune with my mood. "We'll come back in the morning to pick up your car."

I stared up into his eyes. "You are a prince, Mr. Ives."

He kissed my forehead. "Just an overachieving frog, my dear."

I thought I could wait until we got home to tell him about Daddy, but once in the car with the key already in the ignition, I reached out to touch Paul's hand before he could start the engine. "Honey, I need to tell you something."

He faced me then, his cheeks a sallow yellow in the light from the street lamp overhead. I struggled for the words. I didn't want to cry, but a combination of worry and anger made my eyes overflow. I felt a tear slide down my cheek. I brushed it away with my fingers.

Paul took my chin in his hand and turned my face gently toward his. "Hannah, something's been eating you all evening. What is it?"

I sputtered, gasped, then broke down, sobbing against his chest with my cheek resting against the soft flannel of his shirt, smelling freshly of Tide. I told Paul about Daddy's interview with the police and about Scott's crazy conspiracy theory.

"God, Hannah. Just when I thought things couldn't possibly get any worse." We sat there while I blubbered, Paul stroking my hair.

After a few minutes I straightened, wiped my face with an old napkin Paul had scrounged out of the glove compartment, and said, "Take me home."

Paul started the engine and drove home cautiously, making attentive noises as I ranted. As we waited for the traffic light at the intersection of College and King George, he put a comforting hand on my knee and squeezed gently. In the darkened car, his handsome profile reflected red in the light from the turn signal of the car just ahead of us, blinking to turn left.

Ten minutes later, back at the house, I stood in the entrance hall like a zombie with my coat still on.

Paul unwound the scarf from my neck and unbuttoned my top button. "I'll see what I can do, Hannah. I'll talk to Iris Templeton at the Navy clinic. She's been in the therapy business for ages; I'm sure she's had to deal with this kind of stuff before."

"And I'll talk to Ruth. If there was ever anything funny going on, surely she'd have known about it." While Paul pawed through the closet looking for a hanger for my coat, I sat on the carpeted steps that led upstairs. "I just can't get my mind around this! Tell me I'm going to wake up and find out that I've been dreaming."

Much later that night I found my escape. Paul and I made slow, gentle love and I fell asleep in the crook of his arm, dreaming of sunny days and soft breezes and the warm waters of a Caribbean lagoon sliding over my naked body, which, in the way of dreams, was once again perfectly whole.

chapter
6

RUTH HAD A CASUAL POLICY ABOUT OPENING UP ON Sundays—if you asked her, she'd say "noonish." I had been cooling my heels outside Mother Earth for ten minutes before she appeared at the intersection of Main and Conduit carrying a bag of bagels from Chick 'n' Ruth's deli. I caught sight of her strolling down the street, munching on half a bagel, window-shopping as if she were a tourist with all the time in the world. Under her mohair shawl she wore a natural linen outfit in dark lavender which I thought would be more suitable for May than for January. The slacks flopped loosely around her ankles, casually rumpled, as if she'd been sleeping in them. Knowing Ruth, though, she'd probably paid extra for the wrinkles.

Customers weren't exactly lining up at the door as if waiting to buy tickets to the next *Star Wars* movie—I was the only one, in fact—so I hoped we'd have time to talk before the tourists and day-trippers finished with their Sunday brunch specials and started wandering in.

Ruth finally noticed me. "Hannah! What a delight!"

She stuck the bagel bag under her arm, sorted through a collection of keys on a large ring, unlocked the door, and stood aside while I walked ahead of her into the shop. Once inside, she jiggled the bag enticingly under my nose, but I turned it down. I didn't have any appetite, and Ruth didn't, either, after I told her a few minutes later what Georgina had said about Daddy.

Ruth nearly choked on her bagel. "Bullshit!" she exploded. A speck of cream cheese clung to her lip. She threw the bagel down on the display case so hard that it bounced, landing cream-cheese-side down on the glass.

Even though I shared her anger, I was surprised to find myself playing devil's advocate. "What if—"

"Don't go there, Hannah. Our sister's delusional."

"But—"

"Didn't happen. Never happened."

"Can you be certain?"

"OK. Supposing, just supposing it were true. Don't you think it odd that Daddy would abuse Georgina but not either one of us? And we didn't notice a thing." She sat down with a grunt in the wrought-iron chair behind the counter. "Sexual abuse! I can't even think it. Makes me ill."

"Me, too." I pushed aside an elaborate kinetic clock made out of brass and sat down on the edge of a display table near the front of the shop. "Georgina keeps asking about Sicily, as if the key to this whole mess lies in Italy somewhere. Tell me about Sicily, Ruth."

Ruth thought for a few moments. "I was nine when we lived in Sicily; you were seven. Georgina was just a baby, toddling around after the maid, thumb in her mouth." She stared out the window toward the street, her face grim, then looked back at me. "You know, Mom and Dad were hardly ever home. They were out doing the social, hands-across-the-sea sort of thing—receptions, cock-tail parties—sometimes two in one night. Mom kept all the invitations in a scrapbook. Probably still has it somewhere."

The chimes over the door jingled and a customer came in. Ruth suddenly noticed the wayward bagel, scraped it off the counter, and tossed it into the trash. I wiped the glass clean with a napkin while Ruth helped the woman pick out some natural bath salts especially designed to relieve stress. I could have used a few pounds of that just then.

"And besides," Ruth continued as the chimes sounded as the door closed on the woman's blue-jean-encased behind, "Daddy was often too drunk after parties to do anything more than fall into bed."

I looked up in surprise. "I don't remember that!"

"You were probably too young to notice."

I considered what Ruth had told me. "Could he have done something during an alcoholic blackout?"

"Get real, Hannah. Georgina shared a room with the maid. A two-hundred-pound man crawling into bed with a toddler would hardly go unnoticed."

My stomach lurched at the picture. I'd read about sickos like that in the newspapers. And my father was no sicko, I was certain of that. This had to be some ghastly misunderstanding. "What are we going to do about Georgina?"

Ruth turned a switch that started the water gur-gling over the stones in a miniature rock garden. She shrugged. "I just don't know."

"Won't Georgina have to *prove* Daddy abused her? And there'll be no proof of that, will there, because it simply didn't happen!"

I fell back against the counter. "I can't decide which

is worse—Daddy being arrested for murder or Daddy being branded a child abuser." I pressed my hand against my chest, as if to contain my heart, which was beating wildly. "Oh, my God! Or both!"

"Frankly, Hannah, I suspect the police aren't particularly concerned about the sexual abuse angle."

"Why not? Isn't it against the law?"

"Sure, but I seem to remember reading that sexual abuse has to be reported within a certain amount of time. The statute of limitations may have run out a long time ago." She chewed thoughtfully on her thumbnail. "Besides, if something happened in Sicily, the jurisdiction would be military, not civilian. I doubt that police in the States could touch him; and Daddy's long out of the Navy."

"Whether it's true or not, it gives Daddy a powerful motive to have murdered Georgina's therapist," I suggested.

"If it were me, I'd have been so angry that I'd want to kill Georgina."

"I think he blames the shrink, not Georgina. You should have seen his face, Ruth. He was crushed by what Georgina said. Absolutely numb."

"Don't the police suspect Georgina, then?"

"I have no idea what she told them, but they must realize how much she depended on Dr. Sturges just to get through the day. I think they consider her a witness, not a serious suspect."

While I perched uncomfortably on the edge of the table, Ruth began to move nervously around the shop, realigning bottles of herbal shampoo, folding and refolding batik wall hangings, standing incense sticks up in ceramic Japanese bowls of powdered lime. She held a match to one of the sticks and soon the pleasant odor of sandalwood filled the shop. "By the time I get back from

Bali, the police will probably have arrested that therapist's ex-husband or her spurned lover, or a vagrant maybe. Trust me. The whole thing will have blown over."

I remembered how much I had wished the whole mess with Paul and that student had simply blown over, but it had never been satisfactorily resolved, and the doubt I had carried about with me like a heavy stone had nearly wrecked my marriage. Fortunately, Paul and I had moved beyond that a long time ago. Jennifer Goodall, the cause of so much unhappiness, was serving on some aircraft carrier in the middle of the Persian Gulf. She was the Navy's problem now.

Ruth stood in the center of the store, her hands on her hips, glaring. At first I thought she was angry with me, but then I noticed she was staring at something behind me. "Oh damn. Just what I need. Here comes old S.H."

"Who?"

"Old shithead. Brains in his crotch."

"Eric?"

Ruth smirked. Eric was Ruth's ex-husband, Eric Gannon, who still owned a half interest in Mother Earth. They had been married nine years when he began alleviating the painful onset of an early midlife crisis by taking a string of newer models out on test drives. The day Ruth realized he was of no more use to her than her Water Pik shower massage, she pitched him and his prize collection of 33$^{1/3}$ records out on the street, but, being Ruth, kept the turntable he needed to play them. Eric had dyed his graying hair dark brown since I'd seen him last, but his face was young, unlined, and, despite it being January, incredibly tanned. Ruth, who had friends who kept her informed of Eric's every move, would probably tell me that the bimbo du jour was some sweet young thing he met at the tanning studio out on West Street.

"What's he doing here?" I whispered.

"Drops in from time to time to rearrange the displays and generally annoy me."

Eric breezed through the door, caught sight of me, and aimed a dazzling smile in my direction. "Hi, Han. How the hell are you?"

"Doing good," I lied. Eric always called me "Han," even though he knew I hated it. "Been worried about you, Han. Heard you're facing additional surgery."

I stared at him stupidly, wondering who'd blabbed. "I haven't decided about that yet."

"Well, good luck with it." He ran the back of his hand along a set of brass wind chimes, setting them to dancing and singing.

Ruth emerged from behind the counter, grabbed me by the arm, and dragged me toward the street. "Watch the store for a bit, will you?" she called over her shoulder.

Eric shrugged and shook his head. "Can't, I'm afraid. I'm meeting someone."

"Get off it, Eric. As long as you continue to own part of Mother Earth, you can sit your buns down behind the counter every once in a while."

"But—"

"Don't you 'but' me. I'll be back in an hour. Hannah and I need to talk."

Ruth left Eric stammering useless protests and steered me down Main Street to the city dock. We bought decaf cappuccino at Starbucks and carried it to a bench overlooking the water. "So what are we going to do now?" I asked. I watched a red cigarette boat noisily exuding smoke, hops, and testosterone belch its way up the narrow channel called Ego Alley, U-turn, and mosey back out to the bay. Thank God it was winter or we'd have been treated to the sight of the operator's bare torso, with gold chains tangled in his chest hair. I wrapped my hands around my paper cup to warm them. "Is it possible to be cured of something that never happened?" I wondered aloud.

"You mean learn to live with something you believe happened when it actually didn't?" She removed the plastic lid and sipped her coffee. "I don't know."

We sat in silence for a few minutes, watching the tourists stroll back and forth on the crosswalk between the city dock and the market house.

Suddenly I had a brainstorm. "Wait a minute! That's the key! It's not up to Georgina to prove it did happen. We have to prove to her that it didn't." I set my coffee down on the brick planter next to me and turned toward my sister. "Think about it, Ruth! If such a thing happened, wouldn't there have been signs? Physical signs?"

"Possibly."

"I wonder where Georgina's medical records are?" I asked.

"Lord only knows, we've moved so many times. If Mother doesn't have them, they must be at some Navy hospital somewhere. Where are yours? Or mine, for that matter?"

"Mine have been overtaken by events," I said, thinking about the fat folder in Dr. Wilkins's office with sheet after sheet detailing my cancer surgery, chemotherapy, and extensive follow-up treatment. Being able to lay my hands on a record of a tetanus shot I had back in 1959 seemed the least of my worries. "Help me put it together, Ruth."

Ruth leaned back on her hands and stared into the

pale winter sky. "Georgina had her tonsils out when she was five . . ."

"But they wouldn't necessarily have been looking . . ." I turned my head away. ". . . down there."

"I vaguely remember a severe bladder infection . . ." Ruth's voice trailed off and the silence was filled with the chatter of a group of boisterous tourists.

I couldn't see any way around it. "Somebody needs to ask Mother, then."

"Oh, sure!"

"Maybe I could inquire about my early records. Say I need the information for my reconstructive surgery." The minute I said it, I realized what a stupid idea that was. Mother was no fool. In my eagerness to avoid talking to Mom about Georgina's accusation, I was grasping at straws. I sat quietly and we stared at a seagull pecking energetically at a dirty pretzel.

I retrieved my coffee and took a grateful sip. "At this late date, I have a feeling it's a case of 'he said, she said.' "

"Hannah, I told you. Stop worrying. By the time I get back from Bali, this will all have blown over."

This was the second time in less than an hour she'd mentioned her damn trip. How could she be going about business as usual when our world was coming apart around us? I turned to face her. "I can't believe that you're still talking about that trip!"

Ruth's eyebrows lifted in surprise. "I've been planning this trip for over a year. Paid for it in advance. It's a package deal, Hannah. Nonrefundable."

"One might consider the situation at home somewhat in the nature of an emergency."

"One certainly might, but it's not going to do me or anybody else any good if I stay home moaning and groaning."

"I need you, Ruth."

"And I need this retreat! It's something I'm doing for myself, Hannah. You, of all people, should understand the importance of that." She slipped the plastic lid inside her empty cup and squashed the cup flat. "I need to be extra careful now that you've screwed up the odds."

"Odds? What odds?" I didn't have a clue what she was talking about.

"Having a sister or mother with breast cancer increases my risk of getting it by twenty-five percent."

I leapt to my feet and glared down at Ruth, who frowned and shook her head slowly from side to side. "I always warned you that working in Washington—"

"It's not *my* fault I got cancer! I can't believe you're laying this on me! Not here. Not now."

I must have been shouting, because she grabbed my hand and pulled me down onto the bench beside her. "Shhh. I'm just trying to explain why I won't give up my trip. It's for my health, as much as for my business."

At that point I felt like wishing her good-bye and good riddance, but as satisfying as it would have been to punch her in the nose, I really wanted Ruth to stay and I told her so. Begged her even. Said I'd run an ad myself offering to sell her reservations.

"I only regret I won't be back in time to help out when you have your reconstruction." She slipped her arm around my shoulder and drew me close.

I shrugged her arm away. "*If* I have it." I didn't even try to hide the anger in my voice. "Georgina's certifiable, Daddy's flirting with hard liquor again, one or both of them may have killed that damn therapist." I grabbed my sister's arm and squeezed. "Have you seen Mother? She looks like something the cat dragged in! The family's falling apart, Ruth, and you're leaving me all alone to pick up the pieces."

"Everything will be fine, Hannah. You'll see."

But I didn't think so. What I thought was that Ruth or no Ruth, I would do whatever it took to uncover the truth. If only I knew where to begin.

MONDAY DAWNED CLEAR AND COLD. I STARTED THE coffee and put water for the oatmeal on to boil before dashing outside in my pajamas to pick up the newspapers. I walked back to the kitchen, preoccupied, scanning the headlines. Nothing new about the Sturges case in the Baltimore paper. I wondered if no news was good news, and told Paul that I would be holding my breath until someone I wasn't even slightly related to was arrested for the crime.

Twenty minutes later, Paul left for the academy. I thought he'd be staying home on Martin Luther King Day, but he claimed he had work to catch up on. I was still sitting at the table over a cup of cooling coffee. I had no game plan; but I had promised Paul I'd think twice before going off half-cocked. So far I had thought no further than planning to put in a few hours at the library, then check in with my parents.

At nine, dressed in jeans, a white turtleneck shirt, and a warm tweed jacket, I left the house and headed up Prince George Street toward College Avenue. At the replica of the Liberty Bell I turned left and cut across campus on the grass. There was probably some rule against walking on the grass, but nobody was around to stop me.

The St. John's College Library loomed large before me, a square brick building trimmed in white that had once been the Maryland Hall of Records. Now extensively remodeled, the dark, claustrophobic lobby of the old state archives had been transformed by an atrium that suffused the building with light. A grand staircase bisected the atrium, where counters of variegated granite contrasted attractively with warm cherrywood shelves. Interior windows offered glimpses of the main reading room and portions of the book collections just on the other side of the wall. I felt marginally cheered and decided it wouldn't be such a hardship to work at St. John's full-time.

I nodded to the circulation assistant on duty, then passed through the glass-enclosed office of the assistant librarian, through a workroom, and into a room they had assigned me in the southeast corner of the building. There the Bromley books lay stacked on carts and strewn about on a round gateleg table. From overhead, light fixtures like ice cube trays cast a stark, white light over my project. I draped my coat over a chair and decided to see what I could find out about childhood sexual abuse. I tapped the terms into the library's online catalog, but got no meaningful results, unless you count an obscure book about a case of child abuse in the eighteenth century, a handful of books about Sigmund Freud and something by Piaget. Not surprising for a college whose curriculum is based on concentrated study of the classics, like Aristotle, Copernicus, and Descartes, in their original texts.

I launched Netscape instead, typed the terms into Lycos.com, and sat back in my chair, stunned by the enormity of it all. I needed some way to narrow down this mountain of information. I needed an expert, is what, someone to sort through all the gobbledegook, but I didn't know any experts and I didn't feel like waiting around for Paul to locate Iris Templeton.

I was resting my chin on my hands, staring at a bronze bust of Dante Alighieri on a tall cabinet and thinking how little he resembled my son-in-law, Dante, when a student aide poked her head through the door. "Coffee's fresh."

I looked up, startled. "Thanks, Laurie. I'll get some in a minute."

"Done!" She held out a mug of steaming coffee.

"You read minds?" I set the mug on a folded paper towel so as not to spoil the finish on the antique table.

She chuckled. "Daily." She took several seconds to look around the cluttered workroom. "So, tell me what you're doing."

I turned away from the computer, blanking the screen almost guiltily, and pointed to the books.

"Well, first I sorted them by publication date, but the British, German, and Japanese editions of any particular title all came out in different years, so that got messy. Finally, I decided to put them in alphabetical order by English title, but that wasn't easy either." I picked up two books, one in each hand—*Tangled Web* and *A Talent to Deceive*. "Look. Here are two editions of the same novel." I waved the British edition in the air. "You wonder what could have been wrong with a title like *Tangled Web* that would compel Bromley's American publisher to change it."

"You got me." Laurie pivoted on her heel and headed toward the door. "Well, back to work. I live to shelve!"

I looked closely at the book in my hand. *Tangled Web,*

I noticed, had first been published in 1949. On the cover a raven-haired beauty appeared caught in a giant spiderweb, her hand splayed palm out before her face, her mouth a bright red "O." *Oh, lady. I know just how you feel.* I turned the book over. Pictured on the back, in a casual pose with a Jack Russell terrier, was Ms. Bromley. She had been a handsome woman in '49. I wondered if she still wore her hair in that postwar bob, brushed back from her forehead and curled softly around her ears.

The next book on the cart had hit the best-seller list thirty years later—*Triple Jeopardy*. It was the sailboats pictured on the cover that first intrigued me. I turned to the jacket flap, curious if the boats had anything to do with the plot or were just some illustrator's fantasy:

> When Tony met Amy on a package tour of Mexico, he thought he'd found the girl of his dreams. How could he know, when she became his bride three months later, that he'd married Lisa and Veronica, too. Soon Tony's quiet world was turned into a nightmare of doubt and suspicion when her memories of a troubled childhood, long suppressed, threatened not only his marriage but his life.

There was more about an illegal adoption and a missing will, but it barely registered. I skimmed quickly through the pages. Amy believed she had been sexually abused by her uncle. It wasn't until after the poor man committed suicide that Amy and the reader learned it wasn't true. I sat and digested that bit of cheerful news. I wondered if the novel had been based on a true story. Ms. Bromley was famous for her meticulous research. She'd often spend months gathering background material before she began writing. If this Amy character was anything like Georgina, maybe Ms. Bromley could offer me some real-life background information or point me in the right direction. I decided a visit to Ginger Cove was in order.

When I telephoned, saying I wanted to talk to her about her books, Ms. Bromley surprised me by inviting me to join her for lunch. Thanking my lucky stars that I didn't have to punch time clocks anymore, I hurried out Riva Road, turned left at the big Greek church, and wound down the narrow road that led to the waterfront retirement community.

Ms. Bromley's apartment was on the second floor of building eight. When I knocked, she opened the door so quickly I thought she might have been standing just behind it, waiting. She was of average height and wore a simple dark blue skirt and a pink turtleneck. A colorful silk scarf was held together at her breast by a silver slide. Her hair was a little shorter than in her book jacket photo, slightly curlier, and almost entirely gray.

"Ms. Bromley?" I extended my hand.

She grasped it firmly. "Delighted to meet you, my dear." Behind her I glimpsed a small, comfortably furnished living room. Just beyond was a dining nook, where dozens of flowering plants hung on hooks or were arranged on racks under an enormous bay window. A cheerful kitchen was on my left. I was puzzled that the counters were spotless, with no sign whatsoever of lunch being prepared.

Ms. Bromley opened a closet and pulled a gray wool cardigan from its hanger. "Let's talk over lunch. I'm starved." She followed me into the hall, pulled the door behind her, and jiggled the knob to make sure it locked.

"Don't know why I didn't move here years ago," she confided as we strolled down the hall. "A certain number of meals in the residents' dining hall come with the price of admission," she told me, a smile spreading across her face. "I can cook or not. Mostly it's not."

We continued down the carpeted corridor to an elevator, which carried us, with excruciating slowness, to the ground floor. When it finally disgorged us, I sprinted ahead to hold the door, more out of politeness than any need to assist Ms. Bromley, who was the spriest eighty-two-year-old I had ever seen.

She breezed past. "When it rains, I can get to the dining room through the corridors of the building." She waved a hand. "They're all connected. But it's so beautiful out today." She stopped and turned her face full into the sun, eyes shut. "Ahhhh! I can't wait for spring." She resumed her purposeful pace over the sidewalk that crossed the croquet field, and I scurried to keep up. "I discovered people are either summer people or winter people. Which are you, Mrs. Ives?"

"Call me Hannah, please." I paused for a moment, considering her question. "Summer," I said. "Definitely summer. In fact, if anyone ever tells you that I've retired to Maine, you will know that aliens have come and taken over my body."

Ms. Bromley's shoulders shook with laughter and her face wore a lopsided smile. At the community building, she tugged on an outer glass door. I held it open and watched as she entered, walked across a small vestibule, and inserted her house key into a slot. When the inner door opened, I followed her along a corridor hung with artwork, some of it, she said with pride, created by the residents.

She paused and stood before an accomplished water-color of a cat curled up on a chair. I thought I recognized the window. "Yours?"

She nodded.

"Impressive."

She ran a fingertip along the aluminum frame as if checking it for dust. "Art is my pleasure now. What do you do in your spare time, Hannah?"

"Read mostly, or sail, but not at this time of year. My husband's sister has a boat."

When we reached the dining room, I had to mask my surprise. Each of the waitstaff, clad in black trousers, white shirts, and bow ties, greeted my hostess by name. The tables were set with quality china on white table-cloths; red napkins, elaborately folded, sprang from each water glass like astonished birds. Because there were no leaves on the trees, a pleasant view of the South River lay beyond the window. There were restaurants in Annapolis not nearly as attractive as this.

A petite blonde, her hair held back at the crown by half a dozen miniature butterfly clips, showed us to a table set for two by the window. Her name tag said "Trish."

I settled comfortably into a chair while Trish held Ms. Bromley's chair and scooted it closer to the table. Once the elderly woman was comfortably seated, Trish laced her neatly manicured fingers together and held them against her chest. "The specials today are spaghetti Bolognese and shrimp scampi. I'd recommend the scampi," she announced with a grin. "And if you clean your plates, ladies, there's our famous apple pie."

"The scampi will be fine for me. Hannah?"

"The same."

"And some tea, too, Trish."

"Okeydokey!" Trish flounced away and returned almost immediately, carrying a teapot and a saucer of lemon slices. She set the teapot on the table with a flourish, knocking over the bud vase in the process. A puddle of water spread across the tablecloth. "Oops! Sorry. I'm a butterfingers today." She handed me the lemons, then dabbed at the water with a napkin she'd snitched from an adjoining table.

Ms. Bromley seemed unruffled. "Never mind, Trish." She pulled the napkin from the waitress's hand and waved her away. "We'll take care of it." She folded the napkin in half and laid it carefully over the stain.

When Trish was safely back in the kitchen, Ms. Bromley poured a cup of tea for each of us. "So you're the young woman they've saddled with all my children." She dropped a thin slice of lemon into her cup and watched it float to the surface.

I chuckled. "And I'm honored." I slipped a sugar cube into my tea and mashed down on it with the tip of my spoon, persuading it as gently as possible to dissolve.

"You said on the telephone that you had some questions to ask me."

"Yes, ma'am."

"Goodness! I feel old enough without you ma'aming me. Call me Nadine, please. Or Naddy."

I could no more call this famous woman I had just met "Naddy" than I could call my grandmother Laureen. I decided I'd avoid the issue altogether, if I could manage it. "I'm making good progress on your collection, getting all the titles together. Are all your books included?"

"Every blessed one. Including a few in Portuguese." She noticed that the level of the tea in my cup was a tad low, lifted the pot, and raised an eyebrow.

I nodded, and she topped it off.

"And your short stories?" I asked.

"They're all on the list I gave St. John's. But I'm afraid I didn't always keep copies of the short stories."

"I've located sources for most of them and arranged to get photocopies through interlibrary loan." I sipped my tea. "The newspaper and magazine interviews are more difficult, but I stumbled across an article in *Parade* magazine that was fascinating."

"I remember that one. A near disaster. Carrie—that was my dog—nipped the reporter on the ankle and drew blood. We had to report the naughty girl to dog control." She leaned back in her chair, her face alive with the memory.

Remembering my husband's unfortunate experience with the press the previous spring when reporters had lurked about on the street outside our house, ambushing him whenever he appeared, I said, "Give the pooch a medal."

Ms. Bromley crinkled her nose thoughtfully. "I wrote a radio play once for NPR, but it was never produced."

"I don't remember running across any of your plays."

"And you won't, my dear. There was only the one, and it should stay well and truly buried."

The waitress brought our food at that moment and the conversation turned to children (mine) and pets (hers) and grandchildren (hers and mine). I confess I even dragged out my wallet-size photos of Chloe, aged one month and already cute as a button. When our plates were taken away and Trish went off to fetch the world-famous pie, I figured I had beaten around the bush long enough. "I was interested in one of your books in particular."

Ms. Bromley looked up from her tea. "Oh, yes?"

"*Triple Jeopardy?*"

Ms. Bromley cast her eyes upward as if what she was

about to say was written on the ceiling. "Ah, yes." She
laid her elbows on the table, made a tent with her fingers, and rested her chin on her thumbs. The eyes studying my face were green, flecked with brown. "That was
an interesting one. I spent some time with a woman in
Charleston whose therapist claimed to have identified
twenty-three distinct personalities. She wasn't so much a
woman as a club!" She straightened her back and leaned
forward, confidentially. "Can't imagine what I'd do with
all those people cluttering up the place. I have a hard
enough time managing the one personality I've got."

Trish set a thick slice of pie crusted with cinnamon in
front of each of us. Ms. Bromley took a bite from the
pointy end and chewed it thoughtfully. "I wrote that
back in the days when multiple personalities were all
the rage. You probably remember *Sybil*?"

I nodded.

"But before that, there was *The Three Faces of Eve*."

"Joanne Woodward," I said.

"Exactly." She took another bite of pie. "That theory's
been largely debunked, though."

I was surprised to hear that. If you believe what you
see on Lifetime TV, one woman out of three is harbor-
ing multiple personalities. "It's not the multiple personalities I'm curious about, actually. It's the idea that
memories of things that never happened—like sexual
abuse—can be recovered."

I watched her face carefully when I said that. I didn't
want her to think that *I* had been sexually abused.

"The two are related," Ms. Bromley said matter-of-
factly. She dabbed her lips with her napkin, then rearranged it in her lap. "Some therapists theorize that
abused children develop these alternate personalities as
a coping mechanism to help them deal with the abuse.

The only way to integrate these individuals, they feel, is to help them remember the traumatic experiences that triggered the split." She leaned back in her chair and studied me thoughtfully. "I suppose there may be genuine instances of memories being deeply buried, then remembered sometime later, but unless we are to believe that there's been a recent epidemic of child sexual abuse, most experts now discredit this theory, too."

I felt my spirits soar. "They do?"

She nodded. "Experiments have shown how easy it is to create false memories in even the most levelheaded of people. I think you'll find a lot of background material on this in my files."

She laid down her fork. "And there have been recent cases . . ." She looked thoughtful. ". . . a big article in *The New Yorker*, even. They've coined a term for it— false memory syndrome."

What a relief! If Georgina's symptoms had a name, maybe there was a cure.

Ms. Bromley folded her hands on the table in front of her. She spoke so softly that I had to lean forward to hear her. "Hannah?"

"Yes?"

"This isn't one of those I-have-a-friend-who conversations, is it?"

When I didn't answer right away, concern clouded her face. "Were you . . . ?" She paused, as if unwilling to put words into my mouth.

I considered how much to tell this woman I'd just met. Maybe I had read so many of her books that I just felt that I knew her. Maybe she reminded me of my grandmother. For whatever reason, I instinctively knew she would be discreet, so I decided to trust her.

"No, not me. I was curious about your character

Amy, Ms. Bromley, because she reminded me of my sister Georgina." I pushed my pie aside and leaned toward her over the table, my voice a whisper. "She has just accused our father of sexually abusing her while we were living in Sicily."

Ms. Bromley reached out and laid her hand, warm and soft, on mine. "I'm so sorry, my dear." I felt so relieved! She really understood.

"And it's obvious to everyone in our family—except for Georgina and her husband—that these so-called memories are totally false!"

"Have you tried talking to your sister?"

"Several times. At first I didn't know what she was getting at. She kept asking me all these weird questions. By the time I figured it out, her therapist had been murdered, and now we're all in a fine pickle."

"Murdered?" Her teacup grazed the edge of its saucer. "Is this the therapist up in Baltimore that I heard about on the news?"

I nodded.

"You poor thing!" She shook her head. "I've written about murder all my life. I've stabbed 'em, shot 'em, poisoned 'em . . . even threw a victim out of an airplane once, but it was all the fruits of an active imagination. Never hit me close to home, thank goodness." She reached over and patted my hand, which was nervously converting what was left of my roll into tiny crumbs.

"The police suspect my sister, I'm afraid, although they also questioned my father."

"How perfectly dreadful!"

"It's actually my sister who pointed the finger at Dad. It's tearing the family apart, Ms. Bromley! My brother-in-law won't even allow his children to visit their grandparents anymore!"

"That's a great pity. I can't imagine . . ." She sat quietly for a moment, as if lost in thought. "There are good therapists and bad therapists out there, Hannah. But if you're convinced your sister's gotten herself into the hands of one of the bad or careless ones, it will take some kind of proof." She stared out at the bare trees for a moment. "For instance, I read about an unmarried woman who claimed she had been systematically abused by her father, even aborted his child. It wasn't until a medical exam showed she was still a virgin at twenty-eight that she recanted."

"I'm afraid Georgina's not a virgin."

"But there may have been some exculpatory evidence earlier; do you have access to her medical files? Her school records? Abused children are often absent from school."

"My older sister and I thought of that. I'm going to ask Mother about them this afternoon, although my parents have just moved, so God only knows where they're packed or if they're even still around. I hate to upset my mother."

"Take some advice from an old woman. Your mother probably already knows. You'll need to work on this as a family, my dear. And when you do, you'll find support groups out there. One in particular. The FMS foundation."

"FMS?" I thought of the financial management system I used in my former life at Whitworth & Sullivan.

Ms. Bromley paused while Trish cleared away the empty teapot and our dirty dessert plates. When the waitress was out of earshot, she continued. "The initials stand for false memory syndrome. You can link up with other people who have gone through the same experience." She leaned comfortably back in her chair. "I have to warn you, though. This FMS group is very controversial in psychiatric circles. Some see it as just another way of saying 'I don't believe you' to rape victims."

"But I know Georgina hasn't been raped." I watched a squirrel scamper up a tree outside the window and thought about my options. Up until now, there weren't any. This was the first positive lead I'd had. "How do I contact them?"

"Your best bet would be through the Internet. Search Yahoo or Lycos."

I was impressed that this woman, who had come of age during the Depression, would know so much about the Internet. Although I tried not to think in stereotypes, my astonishment must have shown on my face, because she added, "Another one of my hobbies."

She laid her crumpled napkin on the table and sighed. "Everyone's a victim these days. It's the most popular sport in America. If I'm failing in school, it's some teacher's fault for not preparing me properly. If I wreck my car, it's the manufacturer's fault. If I'm depressed, it must be due to some dark secret in my past." She scooted her chair backward and stood.

I reached for my purse. "Whether Georgina was abused by my father or not, we still have the problem of what to do about Diane Sturges's murder."

"Sherlock Holmes said it best: 'When you have eliminated the impossible, whatever remains, however improbable, must be the truth.'"

"I see. Roughly translated, since my sister and my father are innocent, then someone else must have killed the therapist."

"Exactly."

I pulled out my wallet to pay for our lunch, but Ms. Bromley waved it away. "No, no, Hannah. Your money's no good here. Besides, you're *my* guest. It's the least I can do after all the work you're doing on my moldy archives."

"Well, if you're sure, then thank you." I stuffed my wallet back into my purse and began rummaging in the bottom for my car keys. One day I would simplify my life and learn to carry one of those itsy-bitsy wallet-size purses on a string, but for the time being, I'd have to sift through the old lipsticks, loose change, paper clips, and pencils jumbled about on the bottom of my tote. My fingers eventually closed around a key chain–shaped object underneath a plump packet of folded paper. "What on earth?" And then I remembered. I still had the pages from Diane Sturges's appointment book, right where I had stashed them the night I drove Georgina home.

"Thank you!" I said again, fingering the crisp folds of paper and remembering the list of names they contained. "And now I think I have a very good idea about where to start looking."

I WAS SURPRISED WHEN NO ONE ANSWERED THE door at my parents', because my father's Lincoln was sitting, big as life, in the driveway. I jiggled the doorknob, but the front door was locked. Making a mental note to ask my mother for a key, I wandered around back, along an uneven path of slate paving stones that wobbled under my weight. The path led through a side gate into a pocket garden where brownish grasses and scraggly gray weeds flourished. I bent over to pull up a clump of crabgrass and smiled, thinking, *Watch out, weeds!* By spring this plot would respond to my mother's green thumb, and bloom with color.

Although I was thinking about her, I was surprised when I turned the corner to discover my mother, bundled in her purple parka, sitting at the picnic table. Her elbows rested on the sun-bleached redwood boards next to a can of Diet Coke, and she was smoking a cigarette.

"Jeez, Mom, I thought you gave that up."

Mother exhaled a steady stream of smoke, which was snatched away by the wind. "I did."

"Then why . . . ?"

"Ask your father."

I sat down on the opposite bench, facing her. In spite of the cold, Mom wore no gloves or hat, and the wind lifted her peach-pale hair and tossed it about carelessly. "Where is he?" I asked. "Nobody answered the door."

"Gone for a walk along the beach, I suppose. It's been a rough morning." A column of smoke drifted into her eyes, and she kneaded them with her fingers.

"So Daddy told you about Georgina?"

She nodded and took a drag on her cigarette. "If that therapist weren't already dead, I'd kill her myself."

"You'd be at the head of a very long line."

"When did you find out about it, Hannah?" She fixed her eyes on mine with such intensity that I looked away to hide my embarrassment.

I didn't want to tell Mother exactly when I knew; I didn't want her to discover that I'd heard about Georgina's accusations against my father long before she did. "Scott told me," I said. "That's why I'm here."

Mother flipped the filter of her cigarette with her thumbnail and watched the ash particles spiral to the ground. "You're not the first. The police were here most of the morning."

I gasped. "Again? What did they want this time?"

"They had a search warrant." She pointed the end of her cigarette, glowing hotly in the wind, toward the house. "Made a mess."

"What were they looking for?"

She shrugged and dropped the remains of her cigarette through the slot in the top of the Diet Coke, where it sizzled out.

"Did they find anything?"

"As far as I know, they went away empty-handed."

That was something, anyway. I squirmed uncomfortably on the bench. The wind was leaking between the seams of my tweed jacket, and I shivered. "Hey, Mom, it's cold out here. Let's go inside."

"In a minute." She reached for a pack of Salems that lay on the table in front of her. I wanted to snatch it out of her hand and send it flying over the neighbor's fence. Mother had given up smoking three years ago. It broke my heart to see her resuming what had once been a two-pack-a-day habit.

She tapped another cigarette out of the pack and, by cupping her hands around it, got it lit on the third match. "I wish you wouldn't smoke," I told her.

She studied me with tired eyes. "I wish I wouldn't, either, but it seemed like the thing to do at the time." She took another drag, held it in her lungs for a long time, then exhaled slowly. "I suppose you want to know what I think."

I laid a hand on her arm. "Mom, I don't believe a word of what Georgina says."

She slipped the cellophane from the pack of cigarettes, toyed with it briefly, then crumpled it into a ball. "That's a relief. Because it isn't true, you know." She tucked the Salems into a pocket of her parka and zipped it shut. With the cigarettes out of sight, she seemed to notice me for the first time. "My God, you're not dressed for this kind of weather, Hannah. Go on inside. I'll just be a minute."

"No, I'll wait." I sat and watched in silence as my mother smoked her cigarette down to the filter, then ground it into the grass with the toe of her tennis shoe. I noticed that her ankles were badly swollen and worried that she had been spending far too much time on her feet lately. I stood when she did, and when she came around to my side of the table, we linked arms and walked through the back door together.

I didn't know what I would see when I entered the house—drawers and closets yawning open, clothes and papers strewn about willy-nilly—but it wasn't what I expected. The kitchen seemed untouched, but in the rest of the house, boxes which had been neatly stacked in corners or against the walls had had their packing tape ripped off and had been moved and carelessly stacked in the opposite side of the room. Thankfully my parents had just moved in, so there hadn't been much in the closets and drawers for the cops to paw through. Mother followed me to the office off the front hall, still wearing her parka.

"It's not as bad as I thought," I commented. I took in the open boxes around me and the piles of papers on my father's desk. "Was Daddy here when they came?"

Mother nodded. She backed into an overstuffed chair next to the window and sat down, her hands pressed between her knees. "One officer sat with us in the kitchen while two others rummaged through our things." She rested her head on the back of the chair and closed her eyes. "I can't believe this is happening to us."

I lowered myself into my father's desk chair and stared at the computer monitor, busily crawling with a hungry caterpillar screensaver. "They looked there, too."

I turned to face my mother. "Where?"

"Your father's computer. One of the officer's diddled around with it for an hour or so, then copied some files onto a Zip disk and took it away with him."

"What kind of files?" I asked, although I could guess. Kiddie porn. That's what they were looking for on my father's computer. I felt ill.

When mother simply shrugged, I added, "Well, there

couldn't have been much to find; the computer just came out of the box. Unless some software manufacturer with more money than God is up to some funny business."

My fingers clamped down on the arms of the chair, as if by tightening my grip I could keep the world from spinning out of control. First the police. Then my sister's deteriorating mental condition. My mother's smoking. Daddy's drinking. Not to mention my own precarious health. What next? Even a merry-go-round designed by Satan has to grind to a halt sometime. Or so I hoped.

Mother eased herself out of her chair and onto her knees, then rummaged listlessly through a box of videotapes and computer manuals that I was certain had been packed much more neatly before the police had gotten their grubby mitts on them. She held up a videotape for my inspection. "Emily's Graduation, Bryn Mawr" was printed neatly on the label in black Magic Marker. I smiled, remembering how proud we had been of our daughter on that day. Mother and Dad had flown in from Seattle. Paul and I had driven up with Connie.

Connie. Long before Dennis. Now I wondered why Dennis had never returned my call.

I fished around in my purse for my address book, then picked up the phone.

Mother heard me punching buttons and looked up. "Who are you calling?"

"Dennis Rutherford."

She pressed a hand flat against her chest. "Can't we keep this in the family? I just don't know what your father will do if word of this leaks out."

"For heaven's sake, Mother! Dennis *is* practically family. I'm thinking he might be able to find out what's really going on with the police up in Baltimore."

She continued to stare at me without moving.

Dennis's phone rang four times before the answering machine kicked in. I left another message, then called Connie.

Connie didn't have much use for modern contraptions like VCRs and answering machines, so I let it ring and ring. I was just about to hang up when she picked up, sounding out of breath. "Hello?"

"Connie, it's me. Hannah."

"Oh, hi! Just a sec. I've got an armload of old newspapers I need to do something with." The phone tapped against a table and I heard a door slam. In a minute, Connie was back on the line. "Whew! If I just took them out to the barn every day instead of once every twenty-five years, it wouldn't be so much of a hassle."

I got right to the point. "Connie, do you know where Dennis is?"

"That's a slap in the face. Haven't talked to you in ages and practically the first words out of your mouth are 'Where's Dennis?' "

"We've got a crisis on our hands. I really need his help."

"Crisis? My God, is everybody all right?"

"Sort of." Realizing that my mother was still in the room, I said, "I'll explain later."

Connie sprang into action. "Dennis has been out of town at a conference. Look, I'm going to hang up now and call his beeper. He should get right back to you."

She was true to her word. The next time the phone rang it was Dennis. I nearly fainted with relief when I heard his voice—deep, sympathetic, and extraordinarily reassuring. While he didn't offer to kiss everything and make it all better, he did promise to do what he could.

Although I'm not very good at staying put, I agreed to hang out at Mother's until I heard from him.

After that, I persuaded Mother to make us some tea while I rallied the troops. I telephoned Ruth and Paul. Paul joined us in mid-afternoon and Ruth when she closed the shop, a tad early, at four o'clock. Dad had returned from his walk shortly before then, looking more dead than alive. When we tried to cheer him up, he made it clear to everyone we should keep our distance. There wasn't much for us to do except concentrate on unpacking the boxes—putting dishes in the cupboards, books on the shelves, and towels in the bathrooms. Ruth and Paul hung pictures while I took out my aggressions on the packing boxes, ripping off the masking tape and squashing them flat before lugging them down to the basement. As we worked, we limited our discussions to where best to put what lamp, what to do about the glassware that wouldn't fit in the dining room cabinet, and whether to tie back the drapes or leave them hanging straight. No one mentioned Georgina or the police. It was as if an eight-hundred-pound gorilla had plopped himself down on the living room rug and everyone simply stepped around him, too polite to notice.

Around six, I opened a few cans and heated up some tomato soup, then assembled a platter of ham sandwiches. As I worked I kept praying for the phone to ring, but when the ring finally came, it wasn't the phone but the doorbell. At the first *bur-ring* Mother jumped like a startled deer, then closed herself in the downstairs bathroom.

"Mother!" I stood outside, my ear pressed to the door she had just slammed in my face.

"I don't care who it is, Hannah. I don't want to see anybody."

While I tried to persuade Mother to pull herself together and come out and join her family, Paul answered the door. "It's Connie! And Dennis," he shouted. Ruth and I nearly collided in the hallway, we were so anxious to see them.

In the several months since I had last visited Connie, she had allowed her reddish hair to grow out. I had always liked it short and curly, but had to admit that the way this new do waved smoothly under and just skimmed her shoulders was damned attractive. Dennis probably thought so, too. He stood directly behind her, his sandy hair hidden under a knit cap.

My father had never met Connie's boyfriend, so we made introductions all around, although the pleasure-to-meet-yous rang rather hollow under the circumstances. After hanging up their hats and coats, Connie and Dennis gravitated toward the kitchen, where we arranged ourselves around the table. Paul dragged a seventh chair in from the dining room for Mother, who had finally decided to end her self-imposed exile.

Dennis rested his elbows on the table and laced his narrow fingers together. "First off, I need to explain that cops share information on a 'need to know' basis, even with other cops." Disappointment must have been written large across my face, because Dennis reached over and patted my arm. "But I've got this buddy up in Homicide who owes me one after I nabbed a guy he was looking for last year. So I gave him a call."

My father snorted. "I'm afraid to ask."

"Well, sir, it seems your daughter's story kept changing every five minutes, so the officers got a warrant and searched the Cardinale home."

"Georgina's house? When?" My father was shouting.

"Early this morning."

"But that doesn't explain why they came here," my mother complained.

"It's what they found at Georgina's that led them here."

Ruth set the coffeepot down on the table with a thunk. "So, what did they find?"

"Georgina has been keeping a diary." I heard Ruth's sudden intake of breath.

Dennis glanced in Ruth's direction, then continued. "The handwriting is sometimes hard to read and she rambles a good bit, but tucked between the pages they found a letter." His green eyes settled squarely on my father. "A letter from you, Captain."

Daddy scooted his chair back, stood, and began pacing between the table and the refrigerator. "I know what you mean."

"George?" Mother's eyes were wide.

"After that session with the therapist, Georgina wouldn't talk to me, Lois! I called her on the telephone, but when she recognized my voice, she hung up. When I called back, Scott picked up and said Georgina didn't care to speak to me."

"So you wrote her a letter." Ruth set a plate of Oreos down in the middle of the table along with a handful of spoons.

"I wrote her a letter." Daddy sat down and Ruth nudged a mug of coffee in his direction, which he ignored. "In the letter I refuted her accusations one by one and ordered her to get away from that therapist. I insisted that she find a doctor who could help her. A *real* doctor. An M.D."

Connie looked from Daddy to Dennis, her nose

wrinkled in confusion. "I don't understand. What's so incriminating about that?"

"Tell her, Captain."

My father lowered his eyes and studied his thumbnails. "I may have made a few threats."

For some reason, Dennis turned to me. "Your father wrote Georgina that if she didn't consult a real doctor soon, he would disown her."

"That's it?" I was incredulous.

"And something about making the therapist see reason."

"Oh, Lord!" My mother began to massage her temples, a sure sign that a migraine was on the way.

"So, what were they looking for here?" I asked.

"Turner didn't say. But I know they came away empty-handed."

I realized Ruth had been holding her breath when she puffed air out through her lips. "Whew!"

But Dennis wasn't finished. "Now, *this* is what concerns me. They found your fingerprints, Captain, on the glass door leading to the balcony from the therapist's office."

Daddy's eyebrows shot up. "I'm not denying the possibility of that. I must have left them there during that god-awful session with Georgina."

"That could well be, except the Sturgeses' housekeeper claims that she carefully cleaned the glass, inside and out, on the day before the murder."

Daddy frowned. "Maybe that housekeeper's not as thorough as she thinks."

"Turner says that Georgina told him you never went near the balcony that day."

"She's very much mistaken, then." Daddy shook his head. "That office was stifling. I needed some air."

Dennis waved a hand. "The word of the housekeeper in itself is not going to cut much ice with the detectives, so if that's all they've got . . ." He pinched the bridge of his nose between his thumb and forefinger. "But I wouldn't risk it. To tell you the truth, sir, I think you need a lawyer."

"Wait a minute!" I croaked. "We know when Dr. Sturges died. The police were asking everyone what they were doing between the hours of noon and three on Friday." I swiveled to face my father. "You told them what you were doing then, didn't you, Daddy? If you were here in Annapolis, you can't have been murdering people up in Baltimore!"

Daddy shrugged. "I was at Home Depot buying stuff for the house."

"So you have credit card receipts!"

"I paid cash."

"But you still would have receipts," I reasoned.

"Hannah, I can't find them. I'm sure they went out with the trash on Saturday."

Mother, who had begun sobbing quietly, got up and left the room. I heard the door to the bathroom firmly close and the unmistakable sound of running water.

Connie spoke for the first time in a long while. "Dennis, even if he doesn't have a rock-solid alibi, surely the police don't really believe that Captain Alexander killed that woman! He's a solid citizen. A war hero. When I think about all he went through in Vietnam . . ."

Using his fingers like a comb, Dennis smoothed his pale hair back from his forehead. "Under the circumstances, I wouldn't be surprised if he's still considered a suspect."

Daddy pounded the flat of his hand on the table so hard that the spoons jounced and clattered. "I'll clear it up right now! I wrote that letter to Georgina and I meant every word I said. I wanted to kill that damn therapist. I could have strangled her with my bare hands for what she's done to my little girl. *Wanted* to, notice, but didn't. After that session I drove home, wrote the letter, and cooled off. End of story."

Daddy's face turned scarlet; crooked, purple veins pulsed in his forehead. I had never seen him so angry.

Dennis must have decided Daddy wouldn't bite, because he stood up and faced him, practically nose to nose. "Captain Alexander, we've just met, so I'm going on gut feeling here, but I believe you. Now, we'll just have to hope you come up with a more solid alibi, or that somebody else pops up on Homicide's radar screen, because right now, sir, you are what's behind door number one."

"Dennis, isn't there anything you can do?" Connie spoke softly, her voice pleading.

Dennis shook his head. "Out of my jurisdiction. And Turner has already stuck his neck out for me on this."

"Somebody's got to do something!" Ruth moaned.

Since she was flying to Bali come hell or high water on Thursday, I figured it wouldn't be Ruth doing the something that needed doing. I surveyed the glum faces clustered around me. Maybe Dennis's hands were tied, but not mine. First thing in the morning, if Georgina still refused to talk to me about Diane Sturges, I'd start trying to track down the owners of some of the other names in the doctor's appointment book.

chapter

9

GEORGINA WASN'T TAKING ANY CALLS. SCOTT, TEE-
tering on the edge of rudeness, made this abundantly
plain when I telephoned the following day. So, with Paul
drowning in beginning-of-semester tasks and Ruth resolutely Bali-bound, I prevailed upon Connie to help me
locate the patients on Diane Sturges's list. Connie had
to prepare a shipment of her painted gourd figures for
an art gallery in New York, but she had hired Dennis's
twenty-something daughter, Maggie, to help out. Usually Connie strong-armed me to manage the packing,
so I was relieved to learn that she had made other arrangements. It was also encouraging to hear that Maggie
was feeling up to it. It had been over a year since her
mother's death, but Maggie was still grieving and not yet
comfortable with the undeniable romance between her
father and Paul's sister. Perhaps this was the first sign of
a thaw. Connie promised to get Maggie started and see
how it went.

After breakfast, I kissed Paul good-bye and stood on
the front stoop watching him walk up Prince George

Street until he turned the corner on Maryland Avenue on his way to class. I poured myself a second cup of coffee and carried it down to our basement office. I retrieved the pages Georgina had taken from Dr. Sturges's appointment book from the filing cabinet where I had hidden them and spread them out, in chronological order, on the worktable. It was the first time I had given them more than a cursory glance.

The pages covered approximately three weeks in Diane Sturges's busy practice. Sunday and Monday appeared to be her days off, but between ten and five on all other days she had appointments scheduled back to back, six per day and sometimes seven, with no break for lunch. Fridays she knocked off early. Georgina's appointment at three was Dr. Sturges's last scheduled session on that day.

I flipped backward and confirmed that Georgina also visited the doctor on Tuesdays at eleven. On the Tuesday immediately before the murder, Georgina's name was duly listed and there was an additional notation— G. Alexander. Tuesday. Poor Daddy. He hardly had time to unpack his suitcase before Georgina managed to drag him into her private hell.

Most of the patients, like Georgina, visited the doctor twice a week. A handful made single visits and two lucky individuals bared their souls to the doctor each Tuesday, Wednesday, and Friday. I wondered what Sturges charged them. One hundred? Two hundred a session? I did some mental arithmetic. With thirty sessions per week, that was a healthy chunk of change.

I decided that anybody needing therapy three times a week was probably too screwed up to be of much help and moved on to consider the others. B. Smith. *Hah!* No way I could find a Smith in the phone book. Gini.

Could have been anyone—a patient or an appointment with her manicurist. J. Riggins. Maybe. A. Jacobs. Good bet. F. Wandowsky. Even better. Once I had a list of possible candidates, I drove to the public library on West Street, parked, and headed straight for the shelves of telephone directories. Believe it or not, there were four people named A. Jacobs in the Baltimore metropolitan area, but there was only one F. Wandowsky. I jotted down that telephone number and those of a few other likely individuals, knowing it was just the tip of the iceberg. Most telephones were still listed in the husband's name, so there could have been any number of A. Jacobs married to those John, Henry, and Thomas Jacobs listed in the directory. Back home, I tried another resource. I logged on to the Internet and clicked over to the white pages on the Lycos search engine. J. Riggins might be the J. S. Riggins living on North Charles Street. The A. Jacobs was definitely Andrea, I decided, because her address on Cold Spring Lane was just off Roland.

Exhilarated, I picked up the phone, then dropped it back in its cradle. What the hell was I going to say? Doctors' records are supposed to be confidential. I puzzled over that while I went for another cup of coffee, hoping the extra caffeine would jump-start my brain.

Wait a minute! If the police had already contacted all of the doctor's patients as they claimed, I could pretend to be Officer Williams, simply following up on something. But then I thought better of it. The last thing my mother needed was for another of her daughters to get arrested, this time for impersonating a police officer. If I impersonated anybody, it couldn't be Officer Williams. I'd be a departmental secretary or something.

I tapped in the first number.

"Ms. Wandowsky?"

"Ain't no Ms. Wandowsky here."

"Ms. F. Wandowsky?"

"Name's Frank. Whatcha selling?" The voice screamed tattooed arms, beer belly, and a round-the-clock five-o'-clock shadow.

"Sorry, sir. I'm afraid I have the wrong number."

I hung up, then thought, *You dope!* Just because F. Wandowsky was a man didn't mean he wasn't a patient of Dr. Sturges's. But the man didn't sound very forthcoming—probably resented my interruption of his daytime television viewing—so I went to the next name on my list. Andrea Jacobs wasn't able to come to the phone just now, but if I would leave my name and number, and day and time that I called, she would get right back to me. I hung up before the beep.

J. S. Riggins answered in a voice heavy with sleep. It wasn't so much a "hello" as a "hmmph."

"Ms. Riggins?"

"Yes? What time is it?" She sounded as if she had a mouth full of peanut butter crackers.

"I'm sorry if I woke you, Ms. Riggins. This is Betty Smith calling from the Baltimore City Police Department. I'm working with Officer Williams, following up with Dr. Sturges's patients on something from the other day."

"I already told you people all I know. Can I go back to sleep now? Christ! I work nights."

Bingo! My heart did a flip-flop in my chest. "This will only take a minute," I said.

I took her grunt for a yes.

"Who referred you to the doctor, Ms. Riggins?"

"Nobody did. I saw a notice on the bulletin board at Fresh Fields about a self-help group that meets on

Wednesday nights at a local church. I'd been having trouble losing weight, so I thought I'd give All Hallows a try."

"All Hallows?" I squeaked. That was Georgina's church! I coughed, hoping to cover up my squeak. I didn't imagine that squeaking was a sought-after trait in selecting an employee for the Baltimore City Police Department. I doubted that Officer Williams's voice ever got squeaky.

"Diane Sturges was in the group?"

"Hell, no. She was facilitating it."

"So, how did you get to be her private patient?"

"Diane was helping me see that in order to be cured of what was troubling me, I'd have to come to grips with some things that happened in my past. She convinced me that one-on-one therapy would be beneficial."

Where had I heard that before? She and Georgina were certainly singing out of the same hymnbook. "So," I persisted. "Some of her patients knew each other?"

"Of course we knew each other. After working in that group, we knew each other inside and out."

"How many of her private patients were also in the All Hallows group?"

"Four or five, maybe. I can't say for sure. They came and went."

"Do you mind telling me who they were?"

When she didn't answer right away, I thought for a minute she might have dozed off.

"Ms. Riggins?"

"Look, you've got all the names in front of you. Ask them yourself!"

I had almost forgotten I was supposed to be working for the police, so I scrambled to salvage the situation. "Just one more question, Ms. Riggins, then I'll let you get back to sleep. Based on what you know about these other women, do you think any of them had a reason to kill Dr. Sturges?"

Ms. Riggins sputtered into the receiver. "Hardly. She was getting us through some pretty tough stuff." She paused for a moment. "One of the husbands might have done it, I suppose. A father, maybe. Or a Catholic priest or two."

I chuckled and was instantly sorry.

"You may well laugh, Ms., uh, Smith, was it? But I'm perfectly serious about the priests."

I was dying to ask if she knew my sister. Since the group met at the church where Georgina played the organ, it couldn't possibly be a coincidence. But I had already come dangerously close to blowing my cover, so I didn't want to risk it. "Thanks for your time, Ms. Riggins. I'm sorry to have troubled you."

She grunted and hung up without saying good-bye, and I never did learn what the *J* stood for.

I sipped my coffee, now cold, sat back, and considered the other names I had jotted down. I was about to dial someone named C. Cameron when I noticed that the caller ID box attached to the phone was flashing red and the digital display said "Message Waiting." I punched the review button and learned I had two calls—one from Connie and another from an unknown number that had come in at 10:02. I dialed the answering machine and checked my messages. Regretfully, Connie wasn't coming. She didn't feel comfortable leaving Dennis's daughter alone, especially when their relationship was so fragile. *Well, nuts!* The unknown number was my plastic surgeon's receptionist, reminding me that I had a consultation for my breast reconstruction the following day. In all the confusion, I had completely forgotten about the appointment. They were expecting me to appear with all the necessary papers signed, and I was still being wishy-washy about it. What frightened me the most was the anaesthesia. At night, lying in bed listening to the click-click-click of the portable alarm clock, I'd worked myself up into a cold panic. They give you something to shut down your lungs, I'd read somewhere, then they hook you to a machine that breathes for you. I wasn't sure I had that much trust in machines.

Our office has a single window, a narrow rectangle, high up and splattered with mud through which the rays of the late-morning sun were just able to penetrate. Dust motes danced in a shaft of light that caught a photograph on top of the filing cabinet in its spotlight. I picked up the photo and blew a layer of dust from the glass. The picture had been taken five years before and showed Connie and me lounging on the bow of *Sea Song*, holding beers and toothily grinning. Connie wore a red striped bathing suit and I was squeezed into a chrome yellow bikini that Paul used to say made him break out in a sweat. Lord, I had good legs then! Nice boobs, too, swelling out over the top of the bikini. Paul had insisted that the decision about reconstruction was up to me, but how could he *not* prefer a less lopsided wife? If I had been teetering on the status quo side, seeing that picture again tipped the balance.

Before I completed the forms the doctor expected me to bring, I finished my detective work by writing all the names from Dr. Sturges's appointment book down on a yellow tablet, in columns. Beside A. Jacobs I wrote Andrea, then penciled in a big question mark. Next to J. S. Riggins I drew a check mark and wrote in the wide column to the far right: Husbands? Fathers? Priests? As I did this, I wondered if I was wasting my time, but as

the list took shape, I felt good about it. At least I was doing something.

I smiled to myself. The police must be at their wits' end.
Every one of these people could be telling stories that
would make the hair of even Baltimore's Finest who had
probably heard everything stand on end. Based on what
Ms. Riggins had told me, they could have dozens of sus-
pects by now, all of them hiding secrets ugly enough to kill
for. I slipped the tablet into my purse and zipped it up securely. But no matter how you cut it, it was my father's fingerprints that had turned up on Dr. Sturges's plate-glass
window, not some suburban housewife's funny uncle.

I was agonizing over this when the telephone rang.
Even before I checked the caller ID, I knew who it was.
This wasn't the first time something like this had hap-
pened; it must have been telepathy.

"Hannah?"

"Hi, Daddy." His voice sounded as if it were coming
to me from inside a barrel at the bottom of the bay.
"Where are you?"

"I took the telephone into the closet. I didn't want
your mother to hear."

Tears stung my eyes. "Oh, Daddy."

"Your mother's not coping very well. She sat up in
bed all night, hardly sleeping, propped up on pillows.
She didn't even get out of bed this morning."

"That's not good."

"She says she believes I'm innocent, but then she
gets this look in her eyes like the woman I know and
love has gone away somewhere. I feel like I'm losing her,
Hannah."

"She's started smoking again, too," I said, feeling like
a snitch.

"I know. What worries me is that she doesn't even bother to hide it."

"I don't know what to say, Daddy."

"Help me, Hannah! If it were up to me, I'd be out beating the bushes to find the real killer. As it is, I can't leave your mother in her present condition." He paused to take a deep, steadying breath. "I don't know what she'll do if I'm actually arrested for killing that woman."

Even though I had no clue about it one way or the other, I tried to reassure him. "I don't think that arrest is likely, Daddy. The evidence against you is very slim."

"I've been doing a lot of thinking about this whole situation. Once I got over being angry with Georgina, I started worrying about her. She needs professional help more than ever now."

"Don't I know it!"

He paused, breathing audibly, then blurted, "You don't suppose her life's in danger?"

This was a new thought to me, but I didn't consider it likely. "Georgina's her own worst enemy."

Daddy paused to ponder what I had said. "But if I didn't do it and neither did Georgina, the real killer could be connected with one of her other patients. I can't be the first father who wanted to silence that charlatan." He ran possible scenarios by me, each wilder than the next, his words tumbling through the receiver and into my ear at one hundred miles per hour. How about a spurned lover, he suggested, or a jealous husband? Maybe she had a sister or brother who killed her for her share of an inheritance? Maybe Diane Sturges had to be silenced before she passed on some incriminating information that a patient had shared with her? I let him wind down, then said, "OK, Daddy, I promise to do what I can. I've got an appointment with the plastic surgeon early tomorrow afternoon, but after that, I'll stop by Georgina's and see if I can't get her to talk to me. It's possible she knows some of the other patients."

His voice brightened. "Thanks, honey. You know she won't have a thing to do with me."

"I know. But that will change. I know it will." I tried to put a smile into my voice. "Now, you do something for me. Drag Mom out of bed, get her dressed, and take her out for a nice lunch somewhere."

"I'll try."

"Just *do* it, Daddy."

When I hung up a few minutes later, I decided if Georgina still refused to speak to me tomorrow, I'd camp out on her doorstep until she did.

I HATE TO ADMIT THAT I'M OLD ENOUGH TO REMEM-
ber the good old-fashioned G.P. who sometimes made
house calls. Nowadays, every doctor has a specialty. I
swear I've got a doctor for every part of my body—my gy-
necologist, my surgeon, my oncologist, the ENT guy who
once dug a plug of wax out of my ear. Most of the doctors
I see in Annapolis have relocated from downtown to offices on Bestgate Road or out by the new hospital facility
being built near Annapolis Mall. Consequently there
had to be some sort of rule that the best plastic surgeon
in the county had established her office in a 1970s-
style office building on Route 2 halfway to Glen Burnie,
a soulless, wall-to-wall corridor of strip malls, fast-food
joints, and car dealerships.

I'd spent a restless night thinking about what I would
say when I saw the doctor, but got up in the middle of
the night and padded down to the basement to take another look at myself in the yellow bikini. Whatever it
took, it was worth the price.

At Dr. Bergstrom's the nurse ushered me into a small

office with comfortable chairs and a large TV set on a mahogany credenza. I was glad I didn't have to undress. Dr. Bergstrom had done all the examining and clinical photography on a previous visit; today I was supposed to have made up my mind about options. At first she had recommended a saline implant that would be pumped up with water every week, gradually expanding the tightened skin across my chest until it had stretched far enough to remove and slip a permanent implant underneath. I wasn't particularly comfortable with the idea of carrying a foreign object around in my body. With my luck, I'd no sooner get it installed than the FDA would outlaw whatever it was they were using in place of silicone these days. I asked to see the introductory video again; about halfway through I decided on a free TRAM flap procedure. They'd take a mound of tissue and skin from my abdomen and transplant it to my chest. Sounded like good news/good news to me. Lose a chunk of stomach flab and gain a breast. Afterward, they'd do a bit of touch-up and tattoo a nipple on. My son-in-law, Dante, would get a kick out of that. I had never made any secret of my dislike for the elaborate tattoos that snaked up and down his arms.

The videotape ended and began to rewind automatically. I stared at the blue screen for a while, trying to relax. Eventually Dr. Bergstrom breezed into the room, her pink lab coat flying. She flipped on an overhead light and perched on the corner of the credenza.

"Well, Hannah. Made up your mind, or do you still have questions?"

"No, I've decided to go for the TRAM flap thing."

She sprang to her feet. "Wonderful! I know you won't regret it for a minute." She beamed. "Except for the few days immediately after surgery, when you'll be a little sore."

I favored her with a half smile. "You'll prescribe something for that, I trust."

"Of course." She laid one hand on the doorknob and handed me my folder. "Take this to the receptionist and she'll make all the final arrangements."

I took the folder from her outstretched hand, but didn't move to leave. "Doctor?"

"Yes?"

"I've made up my mind to do this, I really have, and I know that we blocked out the date on your calendar, but because of some pressing family matters . . . well, what would be the possibility of postponing it for a couple of months?"

"Cold feet, Hannah?" Her smile was sympathetic. "We *could* put it off, of course, but I have to attend a medical conference in Helsinki in three weeks. My calendar is full. If we don't do it now, it will be months before I can reschedule."

"When would be the earliest?"

"You'll have to check with Cindy, but not until May or June, I should think."

May or June. It took three to four weeks to recover from a TRAM flap procedure. This meant my new body wouldn't be ready in time for the summer sailing season. My vanity genes kicked in and I shrugged. "Might as well get it over with!"

"Good girl!" She laid a reassuring hand on my shoulder. "You won't be sorry. See you in two weeks."

Out in the reception area, I pushed my folder through the glass window that separated the cashier from the patients. I wrote a check for the day's visit, cringing at the amount, and hoped that Blue Cross/Blue Shield wouldn't give me any grief about the claim. After I paid, the cashier directed me to Cindy, who handed me a preprinted instruction sheet. On my way to the elevator, I scanned it. On Monday I'd stop taking aspirin because it thins the blood; a week later, I'd report to the hospital. Nothing for breakfast, the instructions said, not even black coffee. I pushed the elevator button. No coffee. Bummer. Maybe there was still time to change my mind.

I sat in the doctor's parking lot with the engine running, turned the heat to high, and considered where to go next. If I turned right, I could go home, have a late lunch, and continue making cold calls to people who might or might not have been patients of Dr. Sturges's. If I turned left, I could drive to Georgina's, like I promised Daddy. Either way, I figured I was in for some abuse. People on the other end of the telephone can always hang up in your ear, but if I showed up on the doorstep at Georgina's and rang the bell, I would be a little hard to ignore. I desperately needed to talk to my troubled and troublesome sister. If Dr. Sturges's self-help group met at All Hallows, Georgina almost certainly would have been involved. And if so, she might be able to tell me a lot about the other patients.

I turned left.

Thirty minutes later, I had parked on Colorado Avenue and was standing on Georgina's front porch, mashing on the doorbell with my thumb and admiring the stained glass in her neighbor's dining room window. I pressed the bell again and could hear it echo from somewhere at the back of the house. Nobody home. I checked my watch. Three o'clock. I found myself hoping Georgina was out consulting a new therapist, but she was probably at the grocery store or taking the boys to a Cub Scout meeting. I sat on the porch steps, the concrete cold as ice through my slacks, and considered my options. I could wait here for Georgina, freezing my tush, or do a little retail therapy and get something to eat. I wasted a couple of hours at the Towson Town Center, annoying shopkeepers at the White House and Hecht's by trying on clothes without actually buying anything, then, because Café Zen was on Belvedere only a couple of miles away, I took myself there and dawdled over a delicious veggie stir-fry. At six, I returned to Colorado Road, but before I laid so much as a toe on the porch, I knew no one was home. The curtains were still drawn, no lights shone from behind them, and Scott's SUV wasn't parked anywhere on the street. *Shit!* If I wanted to find out more about the group at All Hallows, I'd have to try the direct approach. It was Wednesday. In one hour it would be seven. The hell with Georgina. I'd simply join the group myself.

I remembered that All Hallows stood on the corner of West Melrose and Roland. I parked on Melrose and approached the building from the front. The double wooden doors were painted bright red. I jiggled the knob, but they were securely locked. I followed a concrete sidewalk around the side of the church to where another set of double doors led into a passageway that connected the south door of the church with the parish hall. I pulled on a brass handle and was relieved when it opened easily. Since I knew the church itself was locked, I turned right and passed through another doorway into the parish hall. It was so dark where I stood that I couldn't even read my watch, but at the other end of the room slivers of light outlined three evenly spaced doors, all closed. I selected the one on the far left, pulled it open, and found myself in another dimly lit hallway, wondering vaguely if I hadn't been walking around in circles. Making an educated guess, I turned left and strolled along the corridor past a number of offices with their doors closed. From an office near the end of the corridor, however, light spilled and I could hear a radio playing softly. Civilization!

When I appeared in his doorway, the occupant looked up, startled, his eyes round and gray over the tops of his glasses. Lionel Streeting, the Senior Warden. Since I'd last seen him at that organ concert, he'd traded in his slimy silver suit for one in gray-green polyester. Still a sartorial disaster.

"May I help you?" Lionel closed the folder he was studying and stood, checking me over, taking in my gray slacks, white turtleneck, and dark blue car coat. I must have passed inspection, because he nodded almost imperceptibly.

"I'm looking for the self-help group that's meeting here tonight," I said.

Streeting had been standing, rigid as a telephone pole, behind his desk, but he oozed around it, stopping just in front of me. "And you are . . . ?"

"Hannah Ives."

"Pleased to meet you. I'm Streeting." The hand he extended was cold and slightly damp.

"They're in the fellowship hall in the church basement." He touched my elbow. "Here, let me show you."

I preceded him out the door while he held it open with the flat of a broad, hairy hand. "I didn't mean to interrupt your work," I apologized. "Please. I'm sure I can find it myself."

Streeting turned out his office light and pulled his door firmly shut behind him, checking to see if it was locked. "No, it's no trouble. No trouble at all." He leered at me, revealing long, impossibly white teeth. "Always like to be helpful." At the end of the hall, he flipped a light switch that illuminated a stairway. "This way." He bowed slightly and made a gallant sweep with his arm, indicating that I should go down ahead of him. I shuddered. Lionel gave me the willies. Particularly as I had no idea where he was taking me.

"I'm new to the group," I said. And just in case he had mischief on his mind, I added, "They're expecting me."

I had reached the bottom step. Here the hallway smelled damply of cinder blocks and new paint. Marbleized tiles like black bowling balls covered the floor. Lionel did a little quick step to catch up with me. "I suppose you heard."

"Heard what?"

"About the tragedy. Terrible. Terrible." He wagged his head from side to side, his eyes clamped shut. "The woman who ran the group was murdered last week."

"Really?" I stopped dead in my tracks and turned to look at him. "How perfectly awful! Is the meeting off, then?"

"Oh, no. No, no. I don't think so. You'll find some of the ladies already here."

"Does the church sponsor the group?"

"We give them a place to meet, but we do the same for the Girl Scouts, Alcoholics Anonymous, and a mystery writers' critique group, so we can't be accused of playing favorites." He chuckled dryly.

We were passing the church kitchen, whose stainless steel counters and appliances gleamed. I paused for a moment to consider a series of bulletin boards, where pictures of missionary couples and of members doing an inner city neighborhood cleanup were posted. Nearby, on a wooden rack, name tags of church members had been slipped into slots labeled with letters of the alphabet. In the C's I touched my sister's name tag.

Lionel noticed. "Our church organist," he told me.

"Oh?" Good. He didn't recognize me, then.

"Damn fine organist, but she plays too loudly." He pointed to his right ear with a crooked index finger. "Used to come to these meetings regularly, but I haven't seen her around for a while."

"Maybe she felt she didn't need the support anymore."

"Maybe."

I followed Lionel through another set of double doors into a narrow corridor lined with choir robes hanging on hooks. It opened into a brightly lit fellowship hall. Tables, their legs folded flat against their undersides, lay stacked one upon another at the far end of the room. At the other end, near a stage hung with limp, gold-trimmed maroon curtains, sat six women in folding chairs arranged in a circle. Two of the chairs were empty.

An attractive African-American woman in an electric blue business suit stood slightly apart from the others. Her eyes were swollen as if she'd been crying. I imagined she was grieving about the doctor, but she could just as easily have had a fight with her husband. Or suffered from allergies.

Lionel coughed discreetly and the chattering stopped. "Ladies!"

All seven heads swiveled in our direction. Lionel cleared his throat. "Ladies, this is Hannah Ives. She's interested in joining your group."

A tall woman with long, thick salt-and-pepper hair set against dark olive skin, heavily made up to mask old acne scars, rose to greet me. "Welcome, Hannah. I'm Joy Emerson and this is Toni, Claudia, Suzanne, Mindy, JoAnne, and Gwen," she said, pointing at each of the women in turn.

I wondered if JoAnne was the J in J. S. Riggins, but nobody was offering any last names and I couldn't very well ask.

"My friend, Georgina, told me about the group."

"Really?" Joy extended her hand in my direction, palm up, indicating that I should take a seat. "I don't believe she's here tonight."

"No," I said simply.

I grinned and pointed at Toni. "Let's see . . . that's Toni and Claudia and Mindy—no, Gwen . . . Oh, Lord. I hope there won't be a test in the morning!" I shook my head and plopped myself down into an empty chair next to Suzanne, the woman in the blue suit who was now repairing her makeup, applying glossy red lipstick to her mouth with a narrow brush.

Toni, who had been busily stuffing her purse under her chair, looked up. "It won't take you long to get to know everyone."

I was aware that Lionel, who had been loitering near the door to the kitchen, had finally left the room. When he was out of sight, Joy returned to her seat, sat down, and leaned forward, a hand on each knee. "I'm not a therapist, but I'll be facilitating the group for the time being, Hannah. Georgina may have told you about our therapist . . ." She paused and took a deep breath. "Dr. Sturges was murdered. I still can't believe it."

I nodded, not looking directly at anyone. "I read about it in the paper." To my right, JoAnne—or was it Mindy?—gulped and fumbled in her purse, finally producing a tissue with which she dabbed delicately at the corner of each eye.

Joy shook off her melancholy as if it were an old shawl and chirped, "Perhaps introductions are in order." A lopsided grin creased her elaborate makeup. "I'm the adult child of an alcoholic," she confessed. "My mother." She turned to her left. "Mindy?"

Mindy, an attractive brunette with pale, Irish skin, picked nervously at the sleeve of her sweater and said, "I'm trying to overcome my addiction to cigarettes."

As we went around the circle, I met a drinker, a compulsive eater, a battered wife, a cutter who couldn't control the urge to mutilate her body, and individuals in various stages of depression. As it got closer and closer to me, I started to panic. I hadn't even decided what my problem was going to be.

"I'm Suzanne and I'm an alcoholic." Suzanne sat directly on my right.

Fish or cut bait, Hannah! You're up! I sat there, tongue-tied. Fourteen eyes were focused on me. Except for the cancer, I was fairly normal. Maybe a tad on the thin side after all the weight I lost during chemo. "I'm bulimic," I blurted.

Joy plopped back in her chair and everyone seemed to relax perceptibly. I felt as if I'd passed some sort of test. "What we do here every week, Hannah, is support each other in our healing," Joy explained with a sympathetic smile. "We're all at different stages in our journey. Sometimes the path to healing is rocky and hard, but you'll discover that the only way out is through."

I nodded, trying to dredge up everything I had ever read in the popular press about bulimia in case I was called upon to perform.

"Today, we are going to be dealing with anger." Joy surveyed the group, her dark eyes alighting on each of our faces for a moment.

A plumpish woman I took to be in her mid-thirties,

with her dark hair tied back in a low ponytail, raised a tentative hand.

"Claudia?"

Claudia rummaged in the colorful fabric-covered gym bag at her feet and withdrew a photograph in a simple black frame. "I want to show you something." Her voice quavered and she crushed the picture to her bosom so that no one could actually see it. After a few moments, she tipped the photograph away from herself slightly, looked at it one last time, then passed it to Suzanne. "This is the child my father was having sex with thirty years ago. That precious little girl with the flowered Easter hat, lacy dress, white anklets, and Mary Jane shoes. Me."

Suzanne studied the picture for a few moments, then solemnly handed the photograph to me. I felt like Alice, stepping through to the other side of the looking glass.

"One night my father came into my room, slipped his hand under my nightgown . . ." Claudia's voice broke and she began to sob. "After that, the world was never the same. How could he do that to me? I loved him! I trusted him!"

Joy's voice was soothing as molasses. "Relax, Claudia, and let the memory come."

"The next morning I told my mother, but she didn't believe me. She slapped me halfway across the room and called me a liar. Said I was a wicked little girl. Mothers are supposed to protect their children! Oh, God, oh, God!" She rocked back and forth, tears streaming down her face and landing, unchecked, on her blouse.

The picture of Claudia had stopped with Gwen, who returned it to the sobbing woman, holding it faceup on her outstretched palms. "It's not your fault, Claudia."

Claudia retrieved her picture and gazed at it again, her cheeks streaked black with mascara-laden tears. She caressed the face of her childhood image. "I was a smart little girl. I should have figured out how to avoid it."

"You were just five years old then, Claudia. You didn't have the power to protect yourself." Gwen caressed the other woman's cheek.

With loving care, Claudia laid the picture on the floor next to her chair. When she looked at us again, her face was flushed and her eyes mere slits. "I'm so angry at him for doing this to me! He screwed up my whole life!"

Gwen wrapped her arms around Claudia in an expansive hug. Toni stood and did the same. Everyone began chanting variations on a theme of "It's not your fault." I sat motionless, silently observing.

Joy approached and touched Gwen on the shoulder. Gwen and Toni stepped back, leaving Claudia exposed, her head bowed, looking sad and vulnerable. Joy handed Claudia a soft towel she'd produced from somewhere. "Here," she said. "Pretend your father is sitting in that chair and show him how angry you are."

Claudia held the towel by both ends and, in a practiced motion, twirled it into a tube. "I *hate* you!" she screamed, slapping the empty chair with the towel that cracked over it, like a whip. "How could you do this to me?" *Thwack!* The chair shuddered with each blow and inched across the floor away from her.

All of the women were standing now, cheering Claudia on.

"Hit him, Claudia!"

"Show him who's boss!"

"Kick him in the balls!"

"Kill the bastard!"

Claudia, red-faced, continued to flail at the defenseless chair. After a few minutes, she wound down and drooped, exhausted, the towel hanging limp in her hand, the tears dry on her face. Everyone leapt up and surrounded her like Teletubbies in a big group hug. Seeing me hesitating on the sidelines, Joy turned to me and cocked her head toward the huddle, indicating I should get into the supportive spirit of things. I strolled over and stood uncomfortably on the periphery, my arms draped loosely around Joy and Mindy. Half of the women were crying, and I was pretty close to tears myself. Eventually individuals began to peel away from the edges of the group, break up, and return to their seats. Claudia retrieved her chair, sat rigidly in it, her precious picture in her lap. "I love you," she told her image. "I'm so proud of you."

Then it hit me like a ton of bricks. That was the significance of the photograph in Georgina's bedroom! The children hadn't been playing with it, after all. Georgina had been using it in just this way, to handle her feelings of guilt over our father's alleged sexual abuse. As much as I wanted to wring her neck, I felt a twinge of sympathy for my sister. For whatever reason, perhaps what went on in this very group, Georgina really believed she had been abused.

"You are a *good* little girl," Claudia cooed.

"We talk to our inner child," Mindy whispered helpfully in my ear. "We let her know that we love her and forgive her."

For a minute, I thought I'd been beamed from Maryland to a commune in Malibu. People in Maryland didn't speak to their inner children. I wondered, vaguely, where I had stashed my love beads.

For the remainder of the session we listened to Toni

complain about her louse of a husband. She had been hoping to get him into therapy with Dr. Sturges, but just when he agreed to go, the doctor had died. "Now I have to start all over," she whined. "In the meantime, if he lays one finger on me," she waggled a finger for emphasis, "even one little finger, I'm going to have him arrested for assault and battery." I shared the opinion expressed by Mindy that Toni would be better off without the bum, then we surrounded Toni in a group hug.

I was thinking about the old saying—a little knowledge is a dangerous thing. Joy was not a trained therapist, after all. How much of what I was seeing tonight was Diane Sturges's and how much was Joy's interpretation of her former therapist's techniques? I recalled that party game where the first person whispers "I went to London to visit the Queen" in someone's ear and dozens of players later it comes out "Camels wear army boots in winter." It was scary. These women were still so profoundly under Diane Sturges's influence that she might as well have been controlling them from beyond the grave.

When I checked my watch again, it was nearly eight-thirty and I had just breathed a sigh of relief when Joy, the perfectly correct facilitator, turned to me.

"How can we help you, Hannah?"

I started tap-dancing. "Well, talking about anger, I'm here because I'm angry with myself for not being able to control my eating. I binge on ice cream and pizza, Little Debbie snack cakes, potato chips, any kind of junk food I can get my hands on." I paused and looked around the circle. "Then I throw it all up."

"First of all," Joy explained, "you need to understand and accept that it's not your fault. There's something in your past that's making you treat yourself this way." She aimed a long, manicured finger at my chest. "There's an unhappy child in there. Think about your history. Search your memory."

My homework was to buy a notebook. "The prettiest notebook you can find," advised Mindy. I was supposed to go to a quiet place where I wouldn't be interrupted and write a letter to the little girl inside of me.

"Even if you don't yet believe she exists, say that. Or you can say, 'I hate you! You got me into this mess!' " Joy instructed. "You can't begin to have a relationship with your child until you make contact with her. Writing to her is the first step." I gathered I would be first up at next week's meeting, so if I intended to come back, I'd actually have to give this writing nonsense a whirl.

The meeting ended with everyone standing in a circle, holding hands in silent prayer. *Lord, get me out of here,* I prayed.

In two minutes, He did.

On the way to my car, while wrapping my scarf around my neck against a chill mid-January wind, Mindy and Gwen caught up with me. Gwen had blond pigtails, wide blue eyes, and freckles. She looked like Pippi Longstocking. "Mindy and I usually go to Starbucks for coffee afterward. Would you like to join us?"

"Sure. I could use a tall cappuccino right now." The heck with the decaf, I decided. I'd have high-test.

"Do you know where it is?" Mindy wanted to know.

"Off Falls Road, over by Fresh Fields?"

"Right! We'll meet you there."

From the church, I turned right onto Roland, left on Lake, and proceeded cautiously down the hill to Falls Road. As I passed Coldbrook, I shivered. For all I knew, Dr. Sturges's ghost was still hovering about, unavenged, in the woods surrounding her house down at the end of that dark, silent street. I turned right on Falls and left almost immediately into the Fresh Fields parking lot, winding clockwise around the store until I came to Starbucks.

When I entered, Mindy and Gwen were already saving me a place in line. We picked up our coffees, and I watched Mindy doctor hers with two packets of brown sugar and a generous sprinkling each of cinnamon, cocoa, and vanilla. In spite of the season, Gwen had ordered a Frappuccino.

Feeling uncomfortably new-kid-on-the-block, I joined the two women at a small, round table.

"Where do you live?" asked Gwen.

"In Annapolis," I said without thinking.

"Annapolis. That's a long way to drive. Don't they have support groups in Annapolis?"

Mindy rapped the back of Gwen's hand with a black plastic spoon. "Don't be so rude, Gwennie. You're supposed to be welcoming!"

"No, no," I said, thinking fast. "It's a fair question." I set down my cup. "To tell you the truth, I just didn't know anybody in Annapolis to ask. And Georgina was so keen on your group that I decided to give it a try."

"Where is she, by the way?" Gwen pushed the ice around in her Frappuccino with a straw.

"I'm not sure," I said truthfully. "I stopped by her house, but she wasn't home."

Mindy studied me seriously over the rim of her cup. "Your bulimia?"

"Yes?"

"You force yourself to throw up all the time?"

"Uh-huh."

A looked passed between Mindy and Gwen. "You know what Diane would have said about that?"

"What?"

"Diane would have told you that's usually a symptom of childhood sexual abuse."

I nearly choked on my coffee. "No way!"

"Way!" said Gwen. " 'Don't vomit,' she would have advised you. 'Get that penis out of your mouth another way.' "

I stared at Gwen, hardly daring to breathe.

"Believe me, I know," offered Mindy. "I used to be anorexic." She ran her hands down her sides and over her hips. "You'd never know it to look at me now."

"I'll say." Mindy was the perfect size six most women were fruitlessly starving themselves for. "So Diane Sturges cured your anorexia?"

Mindy nodded. "We did it together."

"How?

"I'll have to go back to the beginning to explain. I started starving myself in college. I felt obese if I weighed more than one hundred pounds. I'd eat a cracker and a can of tuna. That'd be it for the day. I dated for a while, but I was terrified of sex. But you have to be a woman to have sex, don't you? So if you don't eat, you don't mature. No hips, no breasts, no period—no problem!" She turned her coffee cup around and around in its saucer. "I was raped by my uncle every summer from the time I was nine until I turned sixteen."

"She finally got the courage to confront him." Gwen looked at Mindy and smiled, obviously proud of her friend's accomplishments. "We couldn't have done it without Diane."

I turned to Gwen. "Were you anorexic too?"

"No. I came to Diane for help with my drinking problem. She made me see that my addiction was a way of coping with sexual abuse. I drank to keep the memories at bay, and when they did come, I drank to numb the feelings, to escape the pain. When I sobered up, those memories started flashing back at me like a slide show gone berserk. Diane saved my life and my sanity." Gwen covered her eyes with her hands for a few seconds, then turned her unflinching gaze on me. "I was raped by my father when I was three. He hurt me so badly I had to have stitches."

"My God!"

"We lived on a farm in Wisconsin. Isn't that a hoot? The land of purest milk and cheese. One time my father forced me into the barn and made me stick a nail into my doll, right between her legs where her vagina would have been. I had forgotten all this, but Diane helped me remember."

"Why would you *want* to remember? That sounds like a nightmare, Gwen. Are you sure that it really happened?"

Gwen twisted her straw into a spiral and wove it around her fingers. "Would anyone *invent* something that bad? Would anyone willingly go through all this torture?" She threw what was left of her straw onto the table. "I don't think so."

We sat in silence for a while, drinking our coffee while the staff behind the counter made noisy preparations for closing.

Suddenly Gwen turned to me and changed the subject. "How's Georgina? Have you talked to her recently?"

I shook my head.

Mindy and Gwen exchanged glances. "We haven't seen her since before Diane was killed."

"She's taking that pretty hard," I told them.

"She was abused by her father, too, you know," Mindy added.

I froze. "She mentioned something about that."

Gwen rested her elbows on the table, leaned forward, and whispered. "Her father gave her a knife and ordered her to dismember her favorite Cabbage Patch doll."

I started to feel light-headed. I wished the kid behind the counter had a good tot of rum I could slosh in my coffee. I stared at a poster on the wall and silently counted to ten. "Pardon me for saying this. Perhaps it just shows how naive I am, but don't you think it's a little strange that both you and Georgina have such similar memories about mutilating your dolls?"

"The faces of abuse are often very similar. Sometimes what you hear from other people in the group . . . it's like holding up a mirror to your own life." Gwen spoke slowly and distinctly, as if she thought I might have trouble understanding her.

"I'm sure I've never been abused."

Mindy raised an eyebrow and shot Gwen a knowing glance. She reached into her purse and extracted a silver case with the initials A.G. engraved on the lid, flipped it open, and took out a business card. "Here." She laid the card flat on the table and shoved it across to me with two slim fingers. "Call me. Anytime. I'll be there for you."

Gwen smiled at her friend, then turned to me. "Mindy's a wonderful mentor."

I sent a smile back across the table. "Do you do this for everyone, Mindy?"

Mindy started to answer, but Gwen cut her off. "No." She paused and at a nod from Mindy continued. "It's odd, but when we first joined the group we thought— this is *so* great! We'll have all these new friends to share our problems with. But it didn't happen that way."

Mindy shook her head. "No. Gwen and I have been best friends for years. We met at a good, old-fashioned tent revival, didn't we, Gwennie?"

Gwennie nodded.

"But we've never become close with any of the others," Mindy continued.

"Why?" I asked.

"I think it's because we sit in these weekly meetings, throwing up our lives, examining each other's vomit, so to speak. It's embarrassing. Once I ran into Toni on the street, and we simply ducked our heads and walked on."

"Why did you invite me here, then?"

"I think we have a lot in common, Hannah, and I want to help."

"I appreciate it, Mindy," I said, tucking the card into my shirt pocket. "But as I said, I'm certain I've never been abused. I would *know* if something like that had ever happened."

Gwen laid a hand on my shoulder. "Just listen to your Little Girl this week. See what she has to say."

"I'll do that," I promised. But as I left them in the parking lot and climbed into my car, I was confident that the only thing my Little Girl was going to tell me this week was that nice as they were, these ladies were freaking nuts.

chapter

11

THE FOLLOWING MORNING, AT O'DARK-THIRTY, AS they say in the Navy, I got up and drove Ruth to the airport. Ordinarily I would have parked in the short-term garage, shouldered half her luggage, and, after a pit stop at the Starbucks concession, accompanied her to the departure gate. But I was still PO'd with my sister for bailing out on us. Perhaps a little bit jealous, too. She was flying to Paradise, after all, leaving me in . . . well, the word "hell" came to mind.

Even though she was going halfway around the world, the embrace I gave Ruth was perfunctory. My heart thawed sufficiently to help pile a purse, which was almost as large as her small rolling carry-on, on top of her big suitcase. She smiled, waved, turned, and dragged the precariously teetering tower of bags away. "Bon voyage," I called after her. I stood by the open trunk of my car and watched until she and her luggage had been swallowed by the automatic doors.

On my way home, I remembered to stop at Hecht's in the Annapolis Mall to purchase two special bras that hooked in the front, something my plastic surgeon had recommended. At home, I scratched "bras, two" off my To Do list. I brewed a pot of tea and let it steep while I considered the other items on the list. Defrosting the ancient basement refrigerator could definitely wait; there was hamburger in there left over from midshipmen cookouts in 1997. And just the thought of cleaning the hall closet made me sneeze. I laid the list aside.

I decided to write to my Little Girl while last night's session was still fresh in my mind. I had found a suitable notebook at the mall and nearly bought it, before remembering that Emily had given me a notebook and a matching pen for Christmas several years ago, back when I'd been doing nonstop complaining about my boss and the other oddballs I had to work with at Whitworth & Sullivan. Emily thought it would help if I kept a diary. I recalled stashing the notebook in the living room desk, but when I looked, it wasn't there. Funny, I could see the darn thing in my mind's eye almost everyplace in the house. After a thirty-minute scavenger hunt that sent me wandering from my cookbook shelf to the basement office to my bedside table, I finally found it, under some sheet music in the piano bench.

"It needs to be pretty," Mindy had said. Well, this certainly qualified. Emily's gift was bound in pink-and-blue flowered cloth, with lace trim printed on. I took the notebook to the kitchen, poured my tea into a large mug, and sat at the kitchen table with the notebook lying open and accusingly blank in front of me.

What the heck was I going to say?

Hello, Little Girl, I finally wrote. *How are you?*

Fine, she said. *But a little hungry.*

My Little Girl wanted comfort food. Macaroni and cheese.

Hannah, you are not getting into the proper spirit of things. I tried again, casting my mind back to my childhood. How far back could I remember?

I slouched in my chair, thinking. San Diego, of course, when I was ten. Before that, Italy. Italy remained in my mind like an impressionistic painting, a kaleidoscope of happy, sunny images. The mountains, the sea. Marita, the maid, young and giggly, not many years older than Ruth and me. Her handsome boyfriend, Paolo, who won our hearts with his silly acrobatic tricks. Before Italy had been Pensacola and that wretched boy next door who always called me Hannah Banana. And before Pensacola? I sucked on the end of my pen, pushing the retractable button in and out with the tip of my tongue. Norfolk was a blur, yet some memories bobbed to the surface, clear and sharp. I remembered building a fort with Ruth in the woods behind our house. I remembered sending a dead raccoon out to sea on a makeshift raft, like a Viking funeral.

I shut my eyes. An image materialized behind my lids. An image of a backyard wading pool with me lying in it, my hair floating around my head, my eyes staring up into the bright summer sky. I was swishing my head back and forth, feeling the sticks and lumpy lawn under the thin vinyl bottom of the pool. Ruth on a nearby swing, laughing, her legs, ankles crossed, rhythmically slicing across the trees that framed my view of the Virginia sky. Daddy was nowhere in the picture. I knew he'd been at sea.

I remembered our pets. My mother favored orange tabby cats—Marmalade and Sunshine—and we'd once had a big, galumphing sheepdog named Snowshoes. Had I had a favorite doll? I didn't remember. *Hmmph.* If I couldn't remember my own doll, I doubted I could remember Georgina's. Besides, I never liked Cabbage Patch dolls; never understood the attraction of those little scrunched-up, withered-apple faces. Emily had been six when the Cabbage Patch mania swept the country. She called me the meanest mother in the world when I refused to scratch and claw my way through the lines at Toys "R" Us or buy a ticket on the Concorde and fly to Europe to buy her a Cabbage Patch Kid like everyone else's mother.

I sat up straight. *Wait a minute!* That had been the Christmas of 1983! Georgina had to have been, what, in her twenties? Cabbage Patch Kids had been fairly new then. Georgina couldn't have owned one much before then! Nobody could.

I padded downstairs to the computer and turned it on, fiddling with the mouse while I waited impatiently for Windows to load. When the desktop appeared, I clicked on the AOL icon and went to Lycos.com on the Internet. "Cabbage Patch Kids," I typed on the query line.

Almost three thousand hits. People all over the world were collecting the little tykes. One redheaded baby boy doll had been auctioned for three hundred dollars. Holy cow! Seeing stuff like that made me want to turn out the attic. There might be a lucrative market for those old fondue pots and lamps made out of wine bottles that I couldn't bear to throw away.

I paged down, clicking on various sites maintained by avid Cabbage Patch Kid collectors. Just as I thought. Even if Georgina had owned an original Xavier Roberts doll shipped straight from Babyland General Hospital in Cleveland, Georgia, instead of a later doll by Coleco, Hasbro, or Mattel, she was still way too old. Cabbage Patch Kids had been invented in 1978, when Georgina was twenty.

The sooner I talked some sense into my crazy sister, the better. I remembered what Ms. Bromley had said. Maybe this was just the kind of proof I needed to make Georgina see reason. I dialed Georgina's number, but no one answered. By now I was wondering if Scott had taken his family on a vacation without telling anybody. I left a message saying I would call back, then considered what to do next. I didn't feel much like talking to my Little Girl again, although I had to admit she'd been extraordinarily helpful about the Cabbage Patch Kid.

The pages from Dr. Sturges's appointment book lay where I had left them on the desk. *C. Cameron* was next on my list. I had jotted down a possible telephone number with an address on Keswick Road. I dialed the number, and when a woman answered, I went into my spiel. "Ms. Cameron, this is Betty Smith from the Baltimore Police."

"Yes?" She sounded meek, almost frightened.

"I'm following up on a few things from the other day."

Suddenly her voice became guarded. "Haven't I talked with you before? Your voice sounds familiar."

Strangely, she sounded familiar, too. Suddenly the faceless voice on the other end of the line acquired plump cheeks and a dark brown ponytail held back with a red barrette. Claudia from All Hallows! I tried to make my voice sound like a cross between Debra Winger and Lauren Bacall instead of the Minnie Mouse range I sometimes slip into when I get excited. "No, you talked with Officers Williams and Duvall."

"I could have sworn . . ."

I moved on quickly, not giving her the leisure to think. "Do you know of anyone who had a grudge against the doctor?"

"No one. She was helping us!"

"Irate husbands? Angry fathers?"

"How would I know that?" She became wary. "What did you say your name was?"

"Smith, Betty Smith. Baltimore Homicide."

"Look, Ms. Smith. I already told you. Dr. Sturges was the kindest, most generous woman I've ever known. I can't think of *anybody* who'd want her dead."

A gravelly voice in the background wanted to know how long she was going to be on the telephone and demanded lunch. "Look," she said, "I gotta go. Why don't you give me your telephone number and I'll call you back if I think of anything."

Oh, hell. The only Baltimore telephone number I knew by heart was Georgina's. I improvised a number recklessly and hung up, practically throwing the receiver into the cradle. I wondered whose number that was and hoped that Claudia would never have occasion to use it.

I added a line for Claudia Cameron to my list. Next to her name I wrote "Father?" After that evening at All Hallows, Claudia's description of her abuse made me wonder where *her* father had been on the afternoon of January 15. He could have just as much motive as our father for getting rid of Dr. Sturges.

I studied the names in the doctor's appointment book, looking for other possible matches with members of the group at All Hallows, but other than Claudia and JoAnne, none seemed likely.

I was so lost in thought that when the phone rang, I dropped my pen. I could see from the caller ID that Scott was on the line, calling from his cell phone.

"Hi, Scott."

"It's not Scott. It's me, Georgina."

"Oh, Georgina! Hi!"

"I hate it when you do that, Hannah. That caller ID of yours is spooky."

"It wasn't my idea. It was Paul's. He likes to know when someone is calling from the academy."

"Well, it's weird."

I guessed she was speaking from her car, because her voice kept fading in and out. I needed to find out, because I didn't want to say what I was about to say if she was in control of a moving motor vehicle. "Where are you?"

"In the backyard, picking up the kids' toys."

So far so good. "Georgina, I want to tell you something and I want you to think about it."

"How mysterious! What?"

"Cabbage Patch Kids were invented in 1978."

The line hissed and crackled for an eternity before Georgina spoke again. "So?"

"You were twenty years old in 1978."

"I honestly don't know what the hell you're talking about, Hannah."

"Just think about it, Georgina."

I wondered how I could ask this next question without letting on that I knew more than I ought to about her therapy group. And then I thought, so what if she knows? Maybe it would help the truth get through her thick skull. "When you weren't home last night, I went by the church looking for you."

"I wasn't there. Choir rehearses on Tuesday and I usually practice on Friday."

"But I ran into Lionel."

"Lucky for you." She snorted.

"Doesn't he ever go home?"

"From time to time. His wife's something of a battle-ax."

"Lionel told me about a therapy group that meets at the church and mentioned that you used to attend it."

"What a tattletale!" She sighed. "I did go for a while, but I was finding the private sessions with Dr. Sturges much more helpful. Besides, I was practically living at that church. I needed a break."

"Did you get involved with that group because it met at the church?"

"Quite the other way around."

"How do you mean?"

"I heard about the organ job from one of the members in the group."

I nearly dropped my cup. "So, how did you find out about the group itself?"

"Through the children's pediatrician, Dr. Voorhis. After Julie I was going through a spell of depression, and during one of Julie's well-baby visits, he recommended Dr. Sturges. In a way, that's why I called."

"Huh?"

"I think I've found a new therapist. Dr. Voorhis recommended him, too."

"That's great!" I said, hoping that it was. If the new therapist was from the same school as the old one, though, Georgina could be looking at years more of the same expensive nonsense.

"Scott's taking me to interview him tomorrow afternoon, but I need your help."

"Oh?"

"Could you watch Julie for me?"

"How about the boys?"

"They're in school. I'll only need you to pick them up if we're running late."

Tomorrow would be Friday. I would have to miss my morning at St. John's. I thought about telling her to get

a baby-sitter, but I didn't want to do anything to dis-
courage her from seeking treatment. Besides, I adored
my niece, and it wasn't Julie's fault her mother wasn't
always playing with a full deck. "OK, what time?"

The relief in her voice was apparent, even over the
bad connection. "Thanks, Hannah! I don't know what
I'd do without you. Can you come around ten-thirty?"

I said I'd see her then and hung up.

I sat there for a while, thinking. One woman had
found her way to Dr. Sturges's group via a notice in Fresh
Fields. Georgina got there through Dr. Voorhis. Some of
the women were undoubtedly church members. But
then I remembered something Mindy had said about a
tent revival. Tent revivals didn't sound very Anglican to
me. I wondered how Mindy'd gotten involved. I trotted
upstairs to the entrance hall, found my purse, and rummaged through it, looking for the business card Mindy
had given me.

Amanda Glover was CEO of a management consulting firm in Towson. After two intervening gatekeepers,
one of whom must have been paid extra for her melliflu-
ous British accent, Mindy came on the line.

"Hi, Hannah. I'm glad you called."

"Look, I'm sorry to bother you at work, but I was
wondering about something."

"What?"

"Who recommended Dr. Sturges's group to you?"

"Our pediatrician. Why do you ask?"

"I, uh, I just realized that I didn't know anything
about her, except what Georgina told me. I guess I just
wanted to make sure the methods she used with the
group were, well, orthodox."

Mindy chuckled. "You can be certain of that. Diana
was licensed by the state of Maryland."

"So," I asked, "is someone else qualified going to take over?"

"I should think so. Joy is trying to find another therapist by the end of the month."

"Who is your pediatrician, by the way?"

"Dr. Voorhis. You got kids? He's absolutely the best."

Bingo! Two votes for Dr. Voorhis. "If I were in the market I'd sign up right now, Mindy, but my daughter is twenty-two and lives in Colorado. I have a one-month-old granddaughter."

"No way! You? A grandmother?"

"Yup."

"Honestly, Hannah, you don't look old enough to be a grandmother."

"Sold my soul to the devil in exchange for eternal youth," I quipped.

There was a long silence, and when Mindy spoke again, her voice was cool and measured. "A word to the wise, Hannah."

I wondered how I had stepped on her toes.

"Don't mention the devil in group session."

"Sorry."

"You had no way of knowing. It's Gwen. Her parents were involved in a satanic cult."

I gulped. "The dairy farmers?"

"It takes all kinds." While I was digesting this, another line began to buzz, saving me from having to come up with a coherent reply. "Look, gotta go," Mindy chirped. "Thanks for calling. Will I see you on Wednesday?"

"Probably."

"Good!" She sounded like a cheerleader. "Keep journaling!"

"I will."

After I hung up, I stared at the wall for a while, then

looked at the yellow pad in front of me. I'd written *Dr. V* in big, square capital letters and drawn several circles around it. What connection did the pediatrician have with Diane Sturges? Not her husband. I'd read in the *Sun* that Sturges had been married to an architect. That certainly explained the geometric roofline and cantilevered wings of their fashionable Lake Roland home. Was Dr. Voorhis her lover? Or was it just a case of one medical colleague helping out another? I sat there, puzzling, idly drawing additional boxes around his name and decorating the results with superfluous circles and arrows. How was I to know that in less than twenty-four hours I'd be face-to-face with the man, under totally unforeseen circumstances?

chapter

12

AT A FEW MINUTES AFTER TEN-THIRTY, I FINALLY found a parking space for my car near the cul-de-sac at the end of Colorado Avenue. I strolled up the sidewalk on the sunny side, savoring the sensation of warmth against my cheek while the rest of me was freezing in the inadequate windbreaker I'd tossed over my jeans and T-shirt.

At Scott and Georgina's, I reached over and unlatched the gate, then hurried up the walk that bisected the front yard. Ragged remains of summer flowers waved desultorily in the crisp breeze. I passed an overturned tricycle, probably Julie's, a basketball squashed flat, and a plastic softball bat that, judging from the crack along the seam, might have been used to squash the former.

I pulled open the screen door and rapped sharply with the knocker.

"Come in." Scott sounded so close, I thought for a minute that he'd hollered at me through the mail slot.

I turned the knob and pushed the door open with two fingers, nearly bumping into my brother-in-law, who was shrugging into a khaki trench coat. He snatched a wool golf cap from a hook near the door and laid it flat on his head, like a pancake.

Unlike the last time I saw him, Scott was positively charming. He had changed so much, in fact, that I wondered if he'd had a personality transplant.

"Thanks, Hannah. You are a gift from heaven." He kissed the air next to my cheek.

I cringed. After what he'd said about my parents the other day, I didn't feel like having anything to do with the jerk.

Scott waved vaguely. "The boys are at school and Julie's in watching TV."

"Fine," I snapped, and hung my coat on a hook next to Georgina's familiar green one. It swung in the breeze like a ghost, reminding me of the day I had found Georgina at Dr. Sturges's. I turned to face him. "And when may I expect you, Scott?" I hoped he'd notice my icy tone, but the man was oblivious.

"We'll pick the boys up at school and be back around four."

I looked around. "Where's Georgina?"

"I'm coming!" Georgina appeared in the door of the living room looking radiant. Her auburn hair was piled up on her head in an elaborate twist and her makeup was cover-girl perfect. I'd dressed in five minutes that morning and didn't dare pass a mirror for fear that I'd die of fright. Or shame.

I grabbed both of Georgina's hands in mine and squeezed. "It's *great* to see you looking so well, Georgina."

She smiled weakly. "I'm a mess, Hannah, but I'm hoping that this new doctor can help straighten me out."

I had to agree, Georgina *was* a mess. A beautiful

mess, like a freshly painted Victorian house consumed by termites and riddled with dry rot. I pulled her to me and hugged her hard. "God, I hope so, baby!"

"C'mon, Georgina!" Scott had opened the door. A cold breeze whistled up my pants legs and a dry leaf skittered across the hardwood floor.

Georgina grabbed her coat and handed it to Scott, who draped it carefully around his wife's shoulders. She stepped out onto the porch, turned her head, and graced me with a Mona Lisa smile. "Wish me luck!"

"Good luck." I waved and stood in the doorway until Scott started his engine. As I closed the door, I heard the SUV roar away.

"Hey, Julie!" I called. "Where's my favorite niece?" There was no answer, but I could hear the TV blaring. When I entered the TV room, Julie appeared flushed and listless, curled up on the sofa with Abby. The blue-gray afghan Mother had crocheted for Georgina two Christmases ago was tucked loosely around her knees. Sally Jessy Raphael was interviewing a former stripper. Clearly no one did any prescreening on the cable box in this house. I found the remote and clicked over to Channel 22. *Arthur* was just ending and *Wishbone* would be coming on soon.

Julie took her thumb out of her mouth and glared at me contemptuously. "I was *watching* that, Aunt Hannah!"

"That's a grown-up show, Julie. Not for kids."

"But it was in-ter-rest-ing," she whined, pronouncing every syllable. "That lady's a proseltude."

I tried hard not to laugh. "What does Abby like to watch?"

Julie lifted her toy rabbit and stared at her, nose to nose. "What do *you* want to watch, Abby?" Abby's whole body nodded, and Julie looked at me with serious eyes.

"Silly Jessy," she translated. "Abby wants to watch Silly Jessy." She clicked back to the network show.

I sat down on the sofa next to my niece. One of her taffy-colored ponytails had come loose; the other was bound with a fat green rubber band like the kind that holds celery stalks together in the grocery. I reached out to tuck her hair behind her ear and was surprised to find that she had a fever.

"Ow!" Julie's mouth was a rosy "O" that declined to release her thumb. "My ear hurts, Aunt Hannah."

"Well, no wonder. You had the TV up so loud." I grabbed the remote and punched the volume control until an advertisement for snow tires was reduced to a dull roar.

Julie laid her left palm flat against her ear. "It *really* hurts, Aunt Hannah." A big tear coursed down her cheek and dripped onto Abby's nearly bald head.

"Did you tell Mommy?"

She shook her head.

"Daddy?"

"Uh-uh."

A diabolic plan was beginning to take shape in my head. I, her concerned and compassionate aunt, would take Julie to the pediatrician. To Dr. Voorhis. I was ashamed of myself, but only for a moment. What is the greater good, I thought? And after all, even if the ear-ache was a false alarm concocted by a bored, neglected four-year-old, how could it hurt? I knew one way to find out if the child was faking. "I'm going to take you to the doctor, Julie," I said.

Julie wiped her nose with the back of her hand, leaving a shiny streak. Her eyebrows knit with worry, then she surprised me by saying, "OK."

I held out my hand. "Let's get your coat."

Julie squirmed off the sofa without using her hands, her thumb still in her mouth, Abby clamped under her arm as though it were in a vise.

While helping Julie into her jacket, I noticed my sister's key ring hanging on a hook near the front door. I had my own house key, of course, but was curious about one of her keys, a flat brass key to which was tied a white disk labeled "AH." All Hallows? Nowhere was the key stamped "Do Not Duplicate," so, thinking it might be useful someday, I tucked the key ring into my pocket, intending to get a copy made. I knew I could put it back before Georgina ever noticed it was missing.

A few minutes later, as I strapped Julie under the seat belt of my Le Baron, I wondered what I would say to the doctor. I should have called for an appointment, but had decided to chance it. They could hardly kick a sick child out of the office.

A quick look in the telephone book told me that Dr. Voorhis had his office at Greenspring Station near the intersection of Joppa and Falls Road. Soon Julie and I were zipping up 83. I made the complicated exit and parked in front of a fake Colonial Williamsburg complex of upscale shops and professional buildings. Julie's eyes, level with the window, caught sight of a shop. "Can I have an ice cream?"

"Later, love, after we see the doctor."

Hand in hand, we strolled into the building and checked the directory together. Dr. Voorhis's office was on the second floor. Once there, a receptionist dressed in a mint green suit with matching shoes and hose looked up when we entered. Julie's hand was clasped tightly in mine as she lagged shyly behind. "I'm sorry, I don't have an appointment"—I checked the nameplate on her desk—"Mrs. Care." I fought to control a laugh.

What a name for a nurse! "I'm taking care of my niece."
I dragged Julie out from where she was hiding behind
me. "Julie Cardinale. She's a patient of Dr. Voorhis's."

Mrs. Care's face brightened and she beamed in
Julie's direction. "Hi, Julie. It's nice to see you again."

Julie, her thumb still planted firmly in her mouth,
studied Mrs. Care through suspiciously lowered lashes
and gave no sign that she recognized the woman. Mrs.
Care returned her attention to me. "What seems to be
the matter with her?"

"She's got a raging ear infection, I'm guessing. My
sister mentioned that she has had them before."

"The doctor's not in yet, Mrs. . . . ?" She raised an
inquiring eyebrow.

"Ives. I'm Julie's aunt."

Mrs. Care jotted my name down on her telephone
message pad. "As I was about to say, Dr. Voorhis has
been delayed at the hospital, but I expect him any moment. If you and Julie will just have a seat in the waiting
room, I'll let you know just as soon as he comes in."

Julie and I planted ourselves in a couple of overstuffed chairs by the window and spent the next ten
minutes thumbing through an old *Smithsonian Magazine*, learning about what was in the Smithsonian's "attic." Julie's thumb never left her mouth. It must have
been shriveled up like a prune by then. Another patient,
a girl I judged to be about fourteen whose mother was
nowhere to be seen, worked diligently on her math
homework. Two mothers with infants sat opposite us,
and a little boy about Julie's age hid behind his mother's
chair and peeked out at Julie from time to time.

I expected to see the doctor when he walked through
the front door, so I was surprised when Mrs. Care announced that the doctor would see Linda Parsons now.

Dr. Voorhis must have had a private entrance. The older girl slammed her math book shut, stuffed it into a tattered bookbag, and disappeared through a door behind the receptionist's desk. Julie and I had made it completely through two more *Smithsonian*s and a *Highlights* magazine before it was our turn.

"Ordinarily I'd take Julie right into the examining room," Mrs. Care said as she escorted us to the doctor's private office. "But since you aren't the child's mother, I suspect he'll want to talk with you first." We sat down before a desk completely clear of papers except for one file precisely in the center, a brass lamp with a black shade, a crystal clock, and a pen and pencil set—I tilted my head to read the inscription—presented to the doctor by the Baltimore Rotary Club.

I held Julie on my lap, her legs dangling between my knees as she scissored them rapidly back and forth. My eyes drifted from the desk to the credenza, where a picture of a man I took to be Dr. Voorhis was posing, Hemingway-esque, with a swordfish three heads taller than he was. Next to it sat an Oriental vase, and next to the vase, in a silver frame, stood an eight-by-ten photograph that stopped my heart. I had never seen her alive, but recognized her picture from the newspaper. What was a photograph of Diane Sturges doing on Dr. Voorhis's credenza? Adrenaline rushed into the space under my rib cage, hard and cold.

I twisted my neck until the tendons twinged, to study the wall behind me. Dr. Voorhis's diploma from Johns Hopkins hung front and center on the wall, flanked by other certificates and photographs. Holding Julie on my hip like a baby, I stood up and turned to study the photographs more closely. Dr. Voorhis shaking hands with Governor William Donald Schaefer. Dr. Voorhis receiving an award from Mayor Schmoke. From the formal pictures, I realized where I had seen his face before—in a photo on Diane Sturges's desk that terrible day I had rescued Georgina. *Well, well, well.* That was a fact to chew on.

Then another photo made it all perfectly clear. Dr. Voorhis and a woman I took to be his wife were posed on the deck of a cruise ship, a young girl sandwiched between them, her golden hair cascading over her shoulders. Even then, Diane had been a beauty.

But why would Dr. Voorhis be recommending his daughter? Didn't that constitute some sort of ethical conflict? *No, silly.* Doctors can't *treat* their own family members. I supposed they could recommend them as professionals to anybody they wanted.

"Put me *down*, Aunt Hannah. I am not a baby." Julie squirmed in my arm. It was like trying to hold on to a cat in a bag. I lowered her into the chair. Julie had taken her thumb out of her mouth long enough to reposition Abby under her arm, when Dr. Voorhis breezed in behind us, his white coat open and flapping behind him, revealing khaki trousers, a light blue shirt, and a dark blue tie.

"Morning, ladies." He stood behind his desk, opened the file folder, turned over a few pages, and studied them through a pair of black reading glasses perched dangerously near the end of his long nose.

He whipped off the glasses and looked up. "Well, Julie Lynn, what seems to be the matter with you today?"

Julie unplugged her thumb and pointed to her ear. "My ear hurts."

"Well, we'll just take a look at it, then." He beamed a five-hundred-watt smile in my direction. "And you are?"

"Julie's aunt." I was thinking fast. "My sister, Georgina, is unable to care for her children right now. She's too upset over the recent death of her therapist."

It was cruel, bringing that up. I expected his face to crumple, his eyes to fill with tears which he would fight, bravely, to hold back. As soon as the words were out of my mouth, I watched the doctor's face, but nothing twitched or blinked. There was absolutely no sign of recognition.

Julie was ignoring us, marching Abby up and down the arm of her chair, humming loudly. "My sister's at home," I lied. "Under medication."

Dr. Voorhis nodded. "Ordinarily, since I don't know you, I'd want to speak to Julie's mother, but since little Julie here seems to make a habit of attracting those big, bad earache bugs . . ." He patted Julie on the head. "I think Dr. Vee will know just what to do." The smile ratcheted up to a thousand watts. "You remember Dr. Vee, don't you, sweetie?"

Julie, both arms firmly wrapped around Abby rabbit, nodded.

Dr. Voorhis extended his hand. "Follow me, young lady." Julie reached out and he covered her tiny hand in his, holding her up as she hopped off the chair. I followed them down a short corridor and into an examining room. Dr. Voorhis lifted Julie onto the examining table, where she sat, her legs dangling over the side. "Will you take off your T-shirt for Dr. Vee?"

Julie nodded, her mouth clamped shut. I held Abby while Julie lifted her T-shirt and, in one smooth cross-armed movement, popped it off over her head, setting her ponytails *sproing*ing.

Dr. Voorhis was washing his hands. "Help her off with her jeans, will you please? I'll need to check her lymph glands."

Julie cooperated while I unzipped her jeans. When I pulled them down over her hips, though, I nearly died. Julie had apparently dressed herself that morning—out of the ragbag. The underpants she wore had a hole the size of a quarter in one side, and the elastic waistband had long ago died. To keep her underwear from falling down, Julie had gathered the fabric together at the waist and secured it there with a large blue diaper pin. Dr. Voorhis shot a questioning glance in my direction. I decided to pretend I hadn't noticed. He checked Julie's glands for swelling, examined her wrists and ankles, looked down her throat, and warmed the end of the stethoscope under his arm before laying it against her bare chest.

Julie, who had been silent up until now, staring at the acoustical tiles in the ceiling, suddenly revived. "Oh, Doctor." She heaved an exaggerated sigh. "I'm so tired! I didn't sleep a wink last night."

Dr. Voorhis had finished with the stethoscope and tucked it into his pocket. He strapped a light to his head, took Julie's chin in his hand, and used an otoscope to peer into her ears.

"You see, my parents were having a party," Julie continued.

Voorhis stepped back to look at the child. I didn't believe for a minute that Scott and Georgina had been celebrating the night before, but didn't want to contradict her. I held my breath, but was entirely unprepared for what Julie said next.

"And everybody was wearing sheets."

"Julie!" I aimed an unconvincing smile in the doctor's direction. "Kid's got an active imagination."

Dr. Voorhis looked skeptical, and I could see my suitability for taking care of my sister's child being severely questioned. "How long have you had this earache, Julie Lynn?"

Julie focused her wide, innocent eyes on his. "Today," she said. She pointed a chubby finger at me where I sat with white-knuckled fingers practically squeezing the life out of her rabbit. "Abby's got an earache, too."

"Really? Well, let's see." Dr. Voorhis took Abby from my hand, lifted each floppy ear, and examined it with his otoscope. "Tsk, tsk, tsk. Your bunny's got a bad infection, Miss Julie." He looked at me. "Ear infections are particularly bad in rabbits. So much ear."

I warmed up to the pediatrician. I'd never seen one work so well with children. My daughter Emily's pediatrician had been a competent but humorless man who never liked coming to the office on Sundays, which was the only day that Emily ever seemed to get sick. Dr. Voorhis sat at a small table in the corner of the examining room, made several notations on Julie's chart, then pulled a prescription pad toward him. "I'm prescribing an antibiotic for Julie," he told me. While he scribbled, I helped Julie dress, vowing to find her some decent underpants the minute I got her home, even if it meant doing a load of laundry myself.

I took the prescription slip from Dr. Voorhis and tucked it into my purse. "I'm hoping my sister will be feeling better soon." I lifted Julie from the table and set her feet firmly on the floor. "I've got enough worries of my own right now." In the hallway, I turned to face him. "I understand you recommended Dr. Sturges to my sister."

He nodded. "I did."

"My sister really grew to depend upon her." Astonishingly, there was still no mention of his relationship to the woman. I could have been talking about the weather. The man must have been seriously into denial.

"Well, good-bye." He crouched in front of Julie, balancing on the balls of his feet. "Take your medicine, Ms. Julie." He shook her hand solemnly. "And take care of that rabbit." He handed Julie a slip of paper torn off his prescription pad. "Here's some medicine for Abby, too."

I paid the receptionist the ten-dollar co-pay required by my brother-in-law's health plan, then left the office with Julie skipping cheerfully next to me. When I tucked her into the seat belt, she still had the paper the doctor had given her clutched in her hand. "Abby's got a persipshun! Abby's got a persipshun!"

"Can I see?"

She thrust the paper under my nose. In large block print, Dr. Voorhis had written, *Abigail Lapin. One carrot. Three times a day.*

JULIE AND I DROVE DIRECTLY TO BASKIN-ROBBINS
on Smith Avenue. While we waited for her prescription
to be filled at the pharmacy next door, I treated her to
that ice-cream cone I had promised. I watched, with affection, while Julie strolled up and down in front of the
display case, her brow screwed up in concentration as
she tried to make a selection from among all the tubs of
flavors behind the glass. No one else was in the store,
and the youngster behind the counter had been well
brought up, waiting patiently for his pint-sized customer to come to a decision. After several long minutes,
Julie pressed an index finger flat on the glass and announced, "That one. Chocolate. And put sprinkles on
it." She glanced up at me sideways through fringed
lashes. "Please?" I smiled and nodded. When the clerk
handed Julie her cone, I ordered a rum raisin for myself.

While we sat in the store, licking our cones, Julie
mused, "When I get old, I'm going to get a job."

I ran my tongue around the perimeter of my cone,

catching early drips. "That would be nice. If you worked here, you could eat ice cream all day."

Julie shook her head, setting her ponytails dancing. "Nuh-uh. I want to be a doctor."

"Like Dr. Voorhis?"

"Nuh-uh. I want to take care of sick animals."

"Then you want to be a veterinarian."

She nodded, her tongue still glued to the chocolate cone. "Yeah. A vegetarian. Mommy says we can have a dog when she gets better."

I admired her optimism, but was saddened to think that it might be a long time, then, before the Cardinale household ever acquired a pet. I looked at Julie's wide, innocent eyes peering over the top of her cone and swallowed around the lump that had suddenly developed in my throat. "What kind of a dog do you want, Julie?"

"A big, huggy dog," she said. "Not little and skinny like Wishbone on TV."

I thought of Snowshoes again, for the second time in as many days. "When your mommy was a little girl, Julie, we had a big fluffy dog named Snowshoes." I held my hand out about three feet from the floor. "He was this tall."

"I want a dog like Snowshoes," she said, cautiously nibbling the rim of her cone.

We enjoyed our ice cream, discussing dogs and cats, most of which she had seen on TV, except for a neighbor's cat, a sleek white animal named Sir Francis Drake who enjoyed visiting the Cardinale garden on sunny afternoons. "Queen Isabella died," Julie said, matter-of-factly.

"Queen Isabella?"

"She was the lady cat married to Sir Francis," Julie explained.

"Oh." I squashed my ice cream down into the cone with the flat of my tongue. "That's too bad."

"Mommy says that happens. Animals die." She looked up at me. "People, too."

"That's true, Julie."

"Mommy's doctor died, and now she cries all the time."

"I know."

"Maybe if we get a dog, Mommy will stop crying."

"I certainly hope so, Julie."

Until then, I had been reluctant to bring up the party Julie told the doctor about, but it had been preying on my mind. I decided to ask.

"Was Mommy happy last night? At the party?"

"Mommy said it was Daddy's party and we had to go to bed." She glanced at me sideways and a sly grin crept over her face.

"But you didn't go to bed, did you, Julie?"

"Nuh-uh. Sean and Dylan and me, we watched from the top of the steps."

"What did you see?"

"Just a bunch of grown-ups with sheets on, drinking wine."

"Are you sure about the sheets?"

She nodded. "Mommy had a pink one."

"What were they doing in the sheets?"

"Singing funny songs. And dancing."

I was having a hard time picturing my introverted sister and her straightlaced husband cavorting around their living room wearing sheets.

"What else were they doing?"

Julie shrugged. "It was really boring. Dylan let me play with his Game Boy. Do you have a Game Boy, Aunt Hannah?"

"I have a computer."

"Game Boys are fun," she announced before polishing off the flat waffled bottom of her cone and licking her fingers. "I want to have a Game *Girl*!"

I dipped a napkin in ice water and dabbed at the sticky brown residue remaining on her lips and chin. I wished I could ask more about the party, but realized that Julie had probably told me all she knew. "Time to go, Miss Game Girl. Your prescription must be ready by now, and I also have another errand to run."

She hopped off the stool. "OK."

First we stopped at the hardware store, where I had a copy made of Georgina's church key. All the while I was paying at the pharmacy for Julie's antibiotic and driving back to my sister's home on Colorado, I puzzled about the party Julie had described. Julie was the most pragmatic child I knew. If she said it happened, it happened. But perhaps it had happened in a fever-induced dream. No matter how I looked at it, it just wouldn't compute.

Back at the house I sat Julie on the kitchen table and gave her a generous spoonful of a viscous pink medicine that the pharmacist said was supposed to taste like strawberries, but, judging from the grimace on Julie's face after she swallowed it, probably didn't. Upstairs, I settled Julie into bed for a nap and read her the first few chapters of *Muttketeers!*, a Wishbone adventure book. By the time I got to " 'All for one and one for all,' the musketeers and D'Artagnan shouted together," Julie was asleep, with Abby rabbit nestled in the crook of her arm. I laid the slim paperback next to her hand and slipped out of the room.

Remembering my promise to do something about the laundry, I visited the bathroom used by the children and dumped the overflowing clothes hamper out on a spread-out towel. I gathered up the corners of the towel like a hobo's bundle and headed for the basement. With both arms full, I had to flip the light switch up with my elbow and make my way cautiously down the wooden stairs.

Georgina's washer and dryer sat in a dark corner of the basement, near the furnace. I batted my hand around over my head until I made contact with the cord that turned on the overheard bulb. When light flooded the area, I could see I had my job cut out for me. Piles of laundry were already stacked up in front of the washing machine, and the dryer's door yawned open. Clean, dry clothes spilled out onto the door as if someone had been pawing through them, looking for something. I tossed my bundle on top of the accumulated pile and leaned over the dryer, pulling out items, mostly towels, and folding them up on top of the machine. That done, I lifted the lid on the washer. It was full of damp laundry still stuck to the sides of the drum by the spin cycle.

I reached into the washing machine and started extracting items and shoveling them into the dryer. A sheet. Several washcloths. A towel. Another sheet. And another. *My God!* The load was almost entirely sheets. With my heart pounding in my ears, I checked out the pile of laundry that had been waiting to go into the washer. More sheets. Hardly daring to breathe, I counted them. My sister (or someone) had been in the process of washing twenty-three sheets. Some were twin size; some doubles; and many bore the telltale stains of red wine. Julie hadn't been imagining things, after all!

I leaned against the washing machine and tried to catch my breath. Surely there was a logical explanation. If so, I couldn't imagine what it could be.

I loaded the children's clothes into the washer, scooped

some detergent out of the box and sprinkled it over them, twisted the dial to regular wash, and got the machine going. Other than incredible sloth, what could explain the presence of so many dirty sheets? The washer began vibrating against my back as I pondered. Visions of Georgina and Scott frolicking around their living room with their sheet-clad friends while the children were consigned to bed made my blood run cold. I thought about what Gwen had said about satanic cults. *Oh, my God!* Had the children witnessed some sort of diabolical ritual?

Normally I would have stuffed the clothes into the machine, tossed in a handful of detergent, and gone upstairs. But for some reason, I stayed there with my troubled thoughts, mesmerized by the rhythmic *ja-jung, ja-jung* of the washer and enjoying the warm, gentle vibrations against my back. The washing machine entered its first spin cycle, making so much noise in combination with the dryer that I didn't hear my brother-in-law until he had come all the way down the basement steps and was standing behind me. "You didn't need to do that," he said.

I nearly leapt out of my Nikes. I pressed a hand to my chest, hoping to keep my heart from bursting out of it. "You scared the hell out of me, Scott!"

Scott's face crinkled into a grin. "Sorry." His arm swept the room. "You didn't have to do the laundry. Taking care of Julie was enough." Beneath the light from the unshaded overhead bulb, Scott looked older than forty-five. His prominent brows shaded his eyes, causing dark half-moons to appear under his lower lids.

"The children were out of clean underwear," I said. "You should see what Julie wore this morning. Straight out of the Salvation Army reject bin."

Scott's face grew serious. "I'm sorry about that. Georgina . . ." He shrugged. "Well, you know."

I nodded. "That's OK. I don't mind doing the laundry. Not a bit."

"Thanks, Hannah." He bent over and began sorting through the pile of laundry at his feet.

It was this touch of domesticity that moved me. I found myself warming to my brother-in-law, although I wasn't so blind as to discount entirely the possibility that I was being manipulated again. I couldn't stand not knowing. "Scott, you have to tell me one thing."

He glanced up from where he had been separating dark green towels from the light-colored sheets. "Yes?"

"What's the story with all the sheets? You have *months'* worth down here. I don't even own that many sheets."

I studied his face, looking for any signs of panic or alarm, but he simply grinned.

"It'll sound kind of funny, but the truth is, we were having a party."

"A party?" I gawped.

"I thought it would cheer Georgina up. Last month I talked her into serving as rehearsal accompanist for the amateur theater group I'm involved with. She may have mentioned it."

I shook my head. "Nope."

"So when they were looking around for a place to hold the cast party, I volunteered."

"A party I can understand, Scott, but sheets?"

He broke into huge, rumbling laughter, throwing his head back with his mouth open so wide I could see his fillings. "Oh, Hannah, whatever must you think? Didn't I mention the play? It's *A Funny Thing Happened on the Way to the Forum*."

Even in the uncertain light, relief must have flooded my face, because Scott crossed the room and slipped his arm around my shoulders. "Toga! Toga! Toga!" he chanted, inches from my ear.

I slumped against him, weak with relief. "When Julie told me about the party, Scott, I have to confess I was more than puzzled."

"I think the party did Georgina good, but it's hard to say. At least she *smiled* at me for the first time since Diane Sturges died." Scott indicated the laundry. "Georgina had put everything on hold." He cast me a glance heavy with meaning. "I mean everything! But, after the party, she seemed almost normal. She even agreed to look for another therapist."

Until he reminded me, I had nearly forgotten the reason for my niece-sitting gig. "And did she find one?"

Scott shook his head. "We didn't think the guy she saw today was a good match. But she's got an appointment with another therapist early next week. It won't be long."

I yanked the cord that turned off the light immediately over our head. "Togas, huh?" I remembered a similar party at a co-op dorm on East College Street, a dilapidated pile that in later years I swore had been used as a set for the movie *Animal House*.

"Togas." He led the way back up the basement steps, then turned to look down at me, standing four steps below. "Why? What did you think?"

"Scott, you really don't want to know."

ON SATURDAY, MY PARENTS ARRIVED EARLY, NOT TOO long after lunch. Distressed at how washed-out and tired my mother had appeared when I last saw her, I had called and invited them over for dinner. After depositing Mother with me, Daddy and Paul disappeared almost immediately, heading for Galway Bay, the pub around the corner, to bend an elbow over a beer or three and trade corny jokes with Fintan, the owner's irrepressible brother. Mother and I adjourned to the kitchen where she sat bolt upright in a chair, her hair, closer to the color of apricots in the artificial light, curling damply and in sharp contrast against her pale cheeks.

"Thanks for having us over, Hannah. If you hadn't asked, I would have hinted. I just couldn't face cooking today, and I know your father is getting tired of carryout."

I was making lasagna from scratch, a favorite recipe that used meatballs instead of crumbled hamburger. I dumped a cup of seasoned bread crumbs mixed with Parmesan cheese into the ground round, added an egg, and began kneading the mixture with my bare hands. "We'll have salad with this, and garlic bread."

"Sounds delicious. What can I do to help?"

I held up a hand, gooey with meat mixture. "Absolutely nothing. Just sit, drink your tea, and keep me company." I pinched a bit of the mixture from the bowl and began rolling it between my palms, forming a meatball about three-quarters of an inch in diameter. "And I'll tell you the story of Julie and the Sheets." I tossed the meatball into a hot frying pan, pinched off some more of the meat mixture, and began shaping another.

"Julie and the Sheets? Sounds like a rock band. I can't wait."

By the time I finished my tale, eight more meatballs were sizzling in the pan and my mother was sprawled in her chair, convulsed with laughter. "Scott is such a *stick*! Just the picture of him romping around, draped in a sheet . . ." Mother wiped her eyes with a napkin. "That's just too funny!"

"And Julie tells me Georgina wore pink. Even in her selection of recreational toga wear, your youngest daughter remains resolutely fashion-conscious."

The smile slid from her face. "What are we going to do about Georgina, Hannah?"

I dropped another meatball into the frying pan. "I honestly don't know, Mother." I didn't dare share the information I had learned posing as a police official to make highly illegal telephone calls. She would have scolded. But I did mention my visit to the therapy group and my conversation afterward with Gwen and Mindy. Mother seemed enormously cheered when I told her about the Cabbage Patch doll. "I'm sure it will sort itself out," I said. "Georgina is interviewing new therapists as we speak. Diane Sturges was just one bad apple in a very large basket of good ones. Surely she'll find somebody competent."

"I hope you're right." She stirred her tea. "Want to know what I've been doing since Tuesday?"

I turned my head and raised a questioning eyebrow.

"I've been surfing the Internet."

"You? No way."

"I went over that information you got from L. K. Bromley and started hunting on the Internet for information on childhood sexual abuse." She leaned forward in her chair. "It's all very distressing, I'm afraid. While I have no doubt that there are adults out there who were sexually abused as children, people who may well have wiped the memory of abuse clean out of their minds, I'm equally convinced that Georgina's memories are totally false."

"We all know she wasn't abused, Mother, so the memories *must* be false. And if so, we have to ask ourselves: Where did they come from?"

"That damn therapist," my mother said. "Over the past few days I've read articles about hundreds of young women like Georgina, and I think I can see how it happened."

I turned my back to the stove. "How?"

"Well, a patient comes in with a list of symptoms. If the therapist believes in recovered memory and tends to see sexually abused children around every corner . . ." She extended her hands, palms up, and shrugged. "I rest my case."

I remembered my conversation with Mindy and Gwen, about our present condition being the result of some dreadful, long-hidden event in our past. I paraphrased Gwen. "I see your point. If I'm an alcoholic, I must be trying to drown the evil memory. If I try to slit my wrists, it's because I hate myself for allowing Uncle Hugo to take advantage of me."

"Exactly. And Georgina's a textbook case."

"How so?"

"She's depressed. Reason unknown."

"If I were married to Scott, I'd be depressed, too."

"Hannah, mind your manners."

"Sorry. Go on."

"It's all so scriptlike. She had stomachaches. Recurring nightmares. She wet her bed until she was ten."

"What does that say about sexual abuse?"

"If the bed is wet, who'd want to crawl into it?"

"Oh, gawd, Mother. That's gross."

"Your sister took an overdose of sleeping pills at fourteen—"

I spun around, the lasagna forgotten. "What? You never told me that!"

"You were away at college." She moistened her lips. "It was exam time and I didn't want to worry you, honey."

"Jeez, Mom. What else haven't you told me?"

She ignored my question. "The point is, it all fits a pattern. It's a red flag that screams 'child abuse.' " Her violet eyes widened. "Even if it didn't happen."

"So what else did you learn online?" I returned to rolling up the meatballs.

"That there are parents in easy reach of my modem who've been falsely accused of abusing their children." She pushed her cup, still full of tea, away. "I can't tell you how much comfort it gives me to know that there's a logical reason behind Georgina's delusions—that those

memories were planted there by an irresponsible therapist. I'm confident that over time, she'll come to realize
this and change her story."

I hoped my mother was right. I turned my attention to
the simmering sauce, tasting it with a wooden spoon and
adding a slug of Tabasco. I was rolling up the last of the
meatballs when the telephone rang. "Could you get that,
Mom? My hands are a mess."

Mother pushed herself out of her chair and moved
to the telephone with uncustomary slowness, as if every
bone in her body hurt. She reached for the receiver.
"Hello?"

Her face transformed itself from blank indifference
to surprise, then to shock. "I beg your pardon?"

I looked up from the sizzling meatballs. "Who is it?" I
whispered.

Mother listened a few more seconds, then slammed
the receiver into its cradle. She returned to her place at
the table and sat down with an audible *plop*.

"Who was it?" I asked again.

"I don't know! He frightened me, Hannah. It was a
man's voice, but he didn't identify himself. He just
growled into the receiver, 'We know who you are. Cut
it out or you'll be sorry.'" She studied me seriously.
"He thought I was you. Then he said, 'Leave Diane
Sturges's patients alone.' What did he mean by that,
Hannah?"

I pumped some soap onto my palm and washed the
meat off my hands in the sink, keeping my back to my
mother until I figured out what I was going to say. I felt
like a high school kid trying to decide how much of
the fun at a slumber party I was going to tell her about.
Mother had enough on her mind without my sharing
with her everything I'd been up to. I turned to face

her. "After I found out Georgina had been involved with that therapy group at All Hallows Church, and I talked with some of the women . . . maybe I upset someone."

"Who the hell was *that*, then?" She gestured toward the telephone. "It certainly wasn't a woman!"

"I don't know." I sat down next to her, drying my hands on my apron. "It could be the husband of one of the women. A father, maybe." I tried to make light of the situation. "It could even have been Scott, I suppose, disguising his voice."

"It wasn't Scott. I would have known Scott."

"I know one way to find out." I crossed to the telephone and pressed the review button on our caller ID. "Damn. Unknown. The bastard was blocking his number." I reached out and patted her hand. "It's nothing to worry about. Somebody's nose is out of joint is all."

She grasped my chin and turned my head so that she could look directly into my eyes. "Speaking of noses, are you sure you aren't poking yours in somewhere it doesn't belong?"

"Yes, Mother," I lied.

"You don't have a good track record on minding your own business, as I recall."

"No, Mother."

I rose and picked up the loaf of French bread from the counter and set it on a cutting board in front of her. I handed her a serrated knife. "Here. Would you slice it for me?"

"Be happy to. On the diagonal?"

I nodded. Mother began carefully slicing the bread while I returned to the stove and moved the meatballs around the pan to keep them from burning. I had just put the lasagna noodles on to boil when I heard the front door slam. "Finally! Our menfolk are home from the perilous hunt." I rested the spatula on the edge of the pan. "We're in the kitchen," I shouted.

But it wasn't Paul or my father. I knew it when I heard the surprise in my mother's voice. "Well, hello."

I paused in my stirring and turned around. Georgina stood in the doorway between the kitchen and the dining room, her green coat unbuttoned, revealing a scoop-necked T-shirt tucked into a pair of slim blue jeans. "I . . . I didn't expect to see you here," she stammered.

Mother laid the knife down carefully next to the cutting board. "But I'm glad you're here, sweetheart. I've been wanting to talk to you."

"Well, I don't want to talk to you, Mother. And you can stop sending me those articles."

I looked from my mother to my sister. "What articles?"

Georgina answered, "Those damn false-memory articles." She stood in the door and seemed prepared to stare Mother down.

"You were such a wonderful, happy child until all this happened, Georgina. You've been brainwashed by that therapist. *She* planted those awful memories in your head."

Georgina threw her purse down on the floor. "For the love of God, Mother. You don't understand anything! Why would my therapist put ideas into my head? Why would I have gone into therapy if I hadn't been abused? I didn't need a therapist to convince me I'd been abused, for Christ's sake, I went to therapy for help *because* I had been abused!"

Mother gazed at the spectacle of her youngest daughter with sad eyes. A tear rolled down her cheek.

Georgina, who must have noticed our mother beginning to cry, ignored it. "And that part about my having been a happy child is a crock! I wanted to *die*, Mother!"

She slumped back against the doorjamb. "Sometimes I just wanted to die."

Mother rose from her chair, supporting herself by holding on to the table. "Why did you tell the police that your father abused you, Georgina? I just want to understand."

"Because he did!"

"How can you *say* these terrible things about your father? He never harmed a hair on your head." She turned to me. "Tell her, Hannah!"

But Georgina didn't give me the chance. "You can believe that lie if you want to, Mother. But it happened. I was molested. And your denial is not going to change that fact!"

Mother took a step toward my sister, her arms outstretched. "Georgina . . ."

But Georgina backed away. I stood there, helpless, wanting to intervene but not knowing what to say. When Georgina spoke again, her voice was laced with venom. "The day I came home from the hospital after getting my tonsils out, Daddy came into my room, ripped the covers off my bed, and raped me."

Mother fell back against the table. "Oh, my God!" Mother's eyes were pleading. "How can she say that, Hannah?"

"Georgina!" I grabbed her arm and squeezed it, hard. "Stop it! Can't you see how much you're upsetting her?"

"She's upset! Ha!" Georgina leaned toward Mother, pulling away from me. "You were supposed to protect me, Mother, but you didn't. You just stood by and let it happen. You had to have heard my screams."

Mother's eyes had not left my face. Suddenly she moaned and slipped to the floor.

"Mother!" I let go of Georgina, rushed to Mother's side, and knelt down. Perhaps she had fainted. I grabbed Mother's hand and rubbed it briskly, trying to coax some warmth back into it. "Mother!" The tips of her fingers were blue, and so were her lips. What was happening?

"Oh, God, Georgina. Call nine-one-one! I think she's having a heart attack." I desperately tried to remember what I had learned in CPR. I felt for a pulse in my mother's neck. At first there was nothing, no movement at all under my fingers. Then I felt a flutter. Then another. But Mother remained unconscious, and her hands were cold, so very cold. I looked around the kitchen for something to throw over her. Georgina hadn't moved, but was backed up against the wall, her eyes wild with panic.

"Give me your coat, Georgina." Georgina seemed frozen. "Give me your coat!" I screamed. "And call nine-one-one. Now!"

Georgina snapped out of her daze, slipped out of her coat, and threw it to me. I laid it over my mother, tucking it around her sides to separate her body from the cold floor. Behind me I could hear Georgina, stirred to action at last, giving our address to the operator. In less than two minutes, I heard the reassuring wail of an ambulance coming from the fire station a short distance away.

When I looked again, Georgina was sitting on the floor under the telephone, her knees to her chin, rocking back and forth, wailing. I kept checking Mother's pulse, praying that her heart would keep going until the ambulance arrived. "Mother," I crooned. "Hang in there. You're going to be all right. The ambulance is coming. I can hear it now."

"It's all my fault!" Georgina wailed behind me. Great sobs racked her body. She buried her face against her knees. "She's going to die, and it's all my fault!"

I had to agree that it was Georgina's fault, but I didn't see how it would help the situation to tell her so. I stroked my mother's cheek and continued to speak soothingly to her. The world had telescoped to just me and my mother on a cold kitchen floor. "They're coming, Mother. You're going to be fine."

I turned to Georgina. "Go open the front door." She raised her head and looked at me, streaks of mascara running down her cheeks. "Now!"

Georgina crawled to her feet and scrambled out of the room, wiping her eyes with the back of her hand. I heard the front door open and, a few seconds later, the thump of heavy shoes clumping across the dining room.

Two paramedics burst into the kitchen carrying a stretcher on which were balanced several pieces of boxlike equipment. I stood and moved away from my mother's side. "I think she's having a heart attack," I said. "She's got a pulse, but it's very weak and irregular."

I stood by, helpless, while the older of the two took her pulse, nodded to his colleague, and with swift efficiency, hooked Mother up to one of the boxes—a heart monitor. He flipped a switch and studied the digital display for a few moments. "V-tach," he muttered. "We need to shock her out of it, pronto!"

I was aware of Georgina behind me when I heard her ragged breathing. We watched silently while the paramedic ripped my mother's shirt open and tore it away from her chest. A single button popped and rolled away across the floor. I followed it with my eyes until I lost it under the refrigerator.

The younger paramedic, his hair cut in a blond buzz, squeezed gel from a tube onto a pair of electric paddles, then rubbed the paddles together vigorously. He laid them against my mother's bare chest.

"Clear," the older one shouted.

Mother's body arched and fell.

He consulted the monitor, then shook his head. "Again. Clear." I watched the electricity course though my mother once more.

What he saw on the monitor this time pleased him. "Better," he said. He looked up at me. "We'll need to take her to the hospital and get her stabilized."

I nodded, numb. "Can I go with her in the ambulance?"

The blond one nodded.

While they bundled Mother onto the stretcher, I turned to Georgina. "Go around the corner to Galway Bay and find Daddy and Paul. Tell them what's happened. Ask them to meet us at the hospital."

Georgina nodded, mutely, picked up her coat from the floor, and disappeared through the back door. I trailed after the stretcher as the paramedics carried it through the dining room, into the hall, and down the front steps. Outside our house, the ambulance had drawn a small crowd. A clump of tourists clustered across the street on the sidewalk in front of the William Paca House, gawking. I barely noticed. I climbed into the ambulance and held my mother's hand, still cold, as the ambulance screamed down Prince George to College Avenue.

Everything was a blur after that. I remember the bright lights of the emergency room as they wheeled Mother through the automatic doors and away from me. I remember a nurse asking me questions. Name. Address. Next of kin. I didn't break down until they asked for her social security number. "How the hell am I supposed to know that?" I shouted at the nurse. She handed me a tissue and waited, her fingers poised patiently over her keyboard, until I had calmed down enough to continue. "My father will be here soon," I assured her. "He'll know."

After about ten minutes, Daddy burst through the door with Paul at his heels. An orderly was just passing, an instrument tray covered with green surgical cloth in his hand. Daddy grabbed his arm. "Where is she?" he demanded. "Where's my wife?"

"Daddy!" I ran to his side. "They're taking care of her in there." I pointed toward one of the emergency cubicles. "She's got an irregular heart rhythm, Daddy. Ventricular tachycardia, someone said."

Daddy rushed off in the direction I had pointed, but Paul hurried after him, stopping him short with a hand on his shoulder. "George, come on. Let's sit down. I'm sure they're doing everything they can."

Daddy shrugged Paul's hand away. "I need to see her. She needs to know I'm here."

Paul approached the nurse I had just been speaking to. "This is Captain Armstrong. His wife's just been brought in. Can he see her?"

The nurse looked up from her computer screen. "I'll find out for you." She tapped a number into the telephone, whispered into it, listened for a while, nodded, and hung up. "Please have a seat. Someone will be out to see you in a few minutes."

"Oh, God!" I threw myself at Paul and melted into the circle of his arms. "That sounds bad, Paul."

He led me to a chair, then sat down next to me. Daddy refused to sit. Straight-backed and sober, he continued pacing. "Tell me what happened," Paul asked me. "Georgina was hysterical. I couldn't get a sensible word out of her."

So I told him.

"That little bitch," he said.

"It's not her fault. She's confused."

"That's no excuse for what she just did to your mother."

A doctor wearing a blue shirt and a red tie under his lab coat pushed through the swinging doors. Daddy ambushed him. "How's my wife, Doctor?"

The doctor took my father by the arm. "Let's sit down, shall we?"

I gripped Paul's hand in terror, knowing the news couldn't be good.

"Your wife's got an enlarged heart, sir. She's very weak. We'll need to keep her here for a while and start her on some medication to stabilize her heart rhythm."

"Will she be all right?" I asked.

"It's too soon to tell. There appears to be considerable damage to the heart muscle, but with rest and medication, there's a chance she'll recover."

"What are you doing for her?" Paul inquired.

"We've started her on amiodarone and wheeled her down to the coronary care unit."

"When can I see her?" Daddy demanded.

"Shortly. Be patient. I'll send for you."

As I watched my father's face, the last word that came to mind was "patient."

The next time we saw Mother, she lay on a bed in the coronary care unit in a small glassed-in cubicle near the nurses' station. An IV disappeared into her arm, a monitor beeped next to her bed, and oxygen hissed through a tube into her nose, but she was awake.

"Hannah . . ." she whispered.

Daddy took up a post next to his wife and held her hand.

"They say you're going to be fine, Mother."

"What a liar!" Mother managed a weak smile.

"Your heart's enlarged," I told her.

"I guess this means I have to give up cigarettes again."

I looked at Paul. "All is not lost. The woman still has a sense of humor."

A nurse appeared. "I'll give you five more minutes. But she really needs to rest."

"Can I stay?" My father's face was lined with worry.

The nurse softened. "Of course. I'll just bring you a chair."

I kissed my mother good-bye, hugged my father, and walked down the corridor to the snack bar, where Paul bought us each a coffee. I was halfway through it before I thought to ask. "Where's Georgina?"

"Frankly, my dear, I don't give a damn."

I knew Paul was just trying to cheer me up, quoting Rhett Butler like that, but suddenly it all came crashing down on me. My mother's health; my father's reputation; Georgina's mental state; my own upcoming surgery; and the mess I had left in the kitchen back home. The floodgates opened. I put my head down on my arms and began to sob. I felt Paul's hand, soft upon my back, his gentle breath against my ear. "Hannah, Hannah, it's going to be all right."

"No, it isn't," I wailed. "It's all turned to shit! And on top of everything else, I've ruined the lasagna."

THE NEXT WEEK WAS A BLUR. JUST WHEN WE THOUGHT everything was going well, Mother's heart went wild again and she had to be shocked back to life. Soon after that, her doctor transferred her by ambulance from Anne Arundel Medical Center to the coronary care unit at University Hospital in Baltimore. I spent my mornings at St. John's, trying to lose myself in the worlds L. K. Bromley had created. The afternoons were spent visiting my mother. Daddy was at her side day and night. Nobody had seen Georgina.

All day Monday I tried to contact Ruth in Bali. The only thing I remembered about the resort was that it had "Ubud" in the name, but I recalled that she had found it on the Internet, so it wasn't long before I came up with a list of possibilities. When I finally found the hotel where "Missy Gannon" was staying, she had already left on a bus trip to Mount Batur and Uluwatu Temple, but a woman with a voice like temple bells promised to deliver my message as soon as the tour group returned.

Needless to say, I didn't make it to All Hallows on

Wednesday. I telephoned Mindy and told her why. She made sympathetic noises and hoped I'd be back the following week. I said I didn't know. I was supposed to be having surgery myself.

"Nothing serious, I hope."

"Oh, no," I lied. "Just routine." I hadn't mentioned the breast cancer before, so I thought it'd seem a little strange to bring it up now.

Frankly, I didn't know what to do about the reconstruction. With Mother so sick, no one could fault me for canceling. But after they moved her to Baltimore, her condition stabilized and it looked like she might be coming home before long.

Paul encouraged me to go ahead, effectively erasing his prior claim of impartiality. Maybe he'd been looking at the photo of me in the yellow bikini, too. "Your mother couldn't be in better hands," he said reasonably. "There's absolutely nothing you can do for her that isn't already being done."

"But I won't be able to visit her in the hospital," I complained.

"Why don't you ask her what she thinks," he suggested.

So I did. Mother let me know in no uncertain terms that she'd be seriously annoyed if I didn't go through with my surgery. "It's the next step in the healing process, Hannah," she said.

The nurse had propped Mother up in bed so that I could comb her hair. I took the brush, eased the tangles out of the back where the hair had become matted from rubbing against the pillow, and fluffed up the flyaway wisps that framed her face. "Are you sure?"

"Absolutely." She touched my cheek. "You've been looking forward to this for so long. You *must* go ahead with it now."

"You won't miss me?"

"Of course I'll miss you, sweetheart. But, trust me, you'll never forgive yourself if you don't follow through with your plans. And neither will I if you let my little"— she raised the arm that was connected to the IV—"my little inconvenient illness stand in your way."

So on Thursday I returned to Anne Arundel Medical Center, where they x-rayed my chest, drew my blood, had me pee into a plastic cup, and pronounced me fit for surgery the following Monday.

That night, Ruth called collect. Through a poor connection that echoed everything I said into my ear two seconds after I had said it, I explained the situation. When she heard the news, she panicked. She'd book a flight right away; but who would arrange it? Her ticket was nonrefundable; what would she do? She had paid for everything in advance; how would she get her money back? The waiting list for the workshop was two years long; when could she ever come again? I had to put Paul on the phone to calm her down. Eventually we decided that since Mother's condition had stabilized, Ruth would stay in Bali for the time being. She gave us the number of the hotel's fax machine and we promised to send her daily progress reports.

I spent that weekend in Baltimore, reading to Mother from *Queens' Play*. Escaping to sixteenth-century France with Dorothy Dunnett's dashing Scotsman, Crawford of Lymond, was just the diversion we both needed. On Sunday afternoon I laid aside the book, smoothed back her hair, and kissed her forehead, leaving her sleeping peacefully. *Take care of her*, I prayed. *Please take care of her until I get back.*

And I checked myself into the hospital, as planned.

chapter

16

IT MUST HAVE BEEN THE CLATTERING OF THE BREAK-
fast carts and a gnawing hunger that awoke me. Gradually
I became aware of my surroundings. First the sheets and
lightweight blanket in which I was cocooned; the pillow,
just one, so my head was lower than I was accustomed to;
the walls, illuminated by the light slanting in from the
hallway; a TV mounted high on the wall. Katie Couric was
interviewing a dark-haired woman, her mouth working
silently.

I looked toward the window and saw that it was still
dark. They'd taken my watch, so I didn't know what
time it was, but if *The Today Show* was on, it must be at
least seven. They'd taken my jewelry, too, but I wouldn't
let them touch my wedding rings, so they'd taped them
to my finger with adhesive tape.

In a chair in the corner, a shadow stirred. "Honey?"
Paul must have stayed with me all night. I turned my
head on the pillow to face him.

Paul unfolded from the chair and crossed to my bed.

He took my hand where it lay on top of the cover and covered it with both of his.

I started to shiver. "I'm cold."

"It's just something in the medication they gave you." He leaned over and covered me with his body, his arms parallel to mine, his lips against my neck. Paul's face was hot and his ear was cold, as if he'd just come in from outdoors.

"Morning." The word stuck in my throat. "God, I'm thirsty!" I pointed toward a cup on the windowsill. "That coffee?"

Paul smiled. "Was. I finished it last night."

"Damn." I grumped.

He reached out and drew a finger across my forehead. "You couldn't have it anyway, sweets. You're NPO today. Nothing by mouth."

Speaking of mouth, it was dry as a desert. I felt as if my last meal had consisted entirely of sand. "That's cruel and unusual," I muttered. I listened forlornly as the food cart rumbled past my door without stopping. Pancakes this morning, from the smell of it. And bacon. I nearly wept.

A nurse appeared, a relentlessly cheerful grandmotherly type I hadn't seen before carrying a blue foam plastic tray. "Good morning, Mrs. Ives!" Paul straightened and stood by the side of the bed, but didn't let go of my hand.

"Time for a shave!" She set the tray on my bedside table, waved Paul back into his chair, and pulled the privacy curtain around my bed, all in one smooth motion. She helped me out of my nightgown, then tucked a disposable plastic sheet under my side to protect the mattress before lathering up my chest and abdomen with a warm, soap-filled sponge, applied in vigorous circles across my skin. As she worked, she kept up a steady stream of conversation about her daughter, an amazing woman who had dedicated her life to the eradication of yellow fever. The razor slid smoothly over my chest, the excess water trickling down my side in a cooling stream. After both areas were clean as a whistle, she helped me into a hospital gown and Paul was allowed back into my chamber. "As if you hadn't seen me naked before," I scoffed.

"I'm sure they have their procedures, Hannah. Wouldn't want to upset the apple cart."

A few minutes later, a young man in white appeared to insert an IV in my arm. As skilled as he was, my stomach revolted at the procedure. I had to swallow repeatedly and think happier thoughts to keep from barfing . . . as if there was anything in my stomach to throw up anyway. Soon the needle was taped into position on top of my hand. I didn't know what was in the IV, but it crept coolly up the veins in my arm. I thought about all the convicts on death row. This is how executions start.

I began to shiver, and Paul rang the nurse for another blanket. As he tucked it around me, I said, "I'm frightened, Paul. I keep thinking about them cutting me open. I imagine how I'll look, spread out and naked. I picture them making the incision, the blood welling up, the surgeons pawing through my insides."

Paul rubbed my arm, the one without the IV in it. "You've been watching too much TV, not to mention being cursed with a vivid imagination." Paul seemed to sense the source of my fear. "Don't worry, Hannah, you'll be fine. Think of it this way—in a few minutes you'll drift off to sleep and when you wake up, it will all be done."

Something good was in the IV. I was barely able to keep my eyes open. I laid my palm flat against my chest, feeling with my fingertips the familiar ridged scar under the thin cotton gown the hospital had provided. "I hope it will be worth it."

The nurse peeked around the curtain. "Why don't you go get some breakfast, Mr. Ives?"

"I'd rather stay, if you don't mind."

"Suit yourself." She grinned. "The cafeteria's no great shakes anyway."

An hour later, when they wheeled me and my bed to the elevator, Paul walked alongside, still holding my hand. They allowed him to stay for the short time I was parked in the corridor outside the operating room suite. Before they pushed me through the swinging doors, he laid a gentle kiss on my lips. I was barely awake, still savoring that kiss, when they transferred me, limp as a rag, to the gurney in the operating room. I remember someone strapping a blood pressure cuff to my arm, and then the sweet taste of garlic in my mouth. A clock on the wall was stuck at nine, and I drowned in waves of darkness.

I first awoke in the recovery room, but it's hard to be sure. Conversation whirled around me like autumn leaves in the wind. It registered in snatches. A date someone had for the movies that night. The creep some soft-voiced person was married to. The bargains to be had at somebody's close-out sale. Somewhere among the babble, I recognized my doctor's voice and struggled to open my eyes. Something puzzling about a purse. I did need a new purse, but what had Dr. Bergstrom to do with it? "The surgery went well," her voice told me, as reassuring as a mother, and then it, too, swirled away.

Then, I don't know how much later, I was back in my room. I recognized the flowers Emily had sent. A dozen red roses, with one yellow one from baby Chloe. My daughter was getting sentimental in her old age. I didn't see Paul.

When I woke again, the TV seemed stuck on the Discovery Channel. I watched a turtle lay eggs on the beach and cover them up with sand, then my eyelids slammed shut.

When I awoke, that same damn turtle was lumbering toward the water and God-knows-what was making a hideous noise like a vacuum cleaner under my bed. Something squeezed my legs, and I wondered, *What the hell?* but my mouth was so dry it came out *Whada ha?*

Paul's face appeared in my field of vision wearing what could be interpreted as a reassuring smile. Relief shone from his eyes. "Hi, love." He smoothed the hair from my forehead and kissed the spot he had cleared. I managed a lopsided grin. Then the vacuum cleaner cranked up again and something squeezed my legs.

I tried to raise my head, but it felt as if it weighed fifty pounds and belonged to someone else. "Whah?" I nodded toward my feet.

Paul lifted a corner of the blanket, revealing plastic sleeves resembling water wings encasing my legs. "It massages your legs," he explained. "Keeps blood clots from forming."

"Oh," I mumbled. "That's good." The compressor cycled off and the cuffs deflated.

"The operation went well," Paul told me. "Very well."

I was afraid to look. With difficulty I raised my head until my chin touched my chest. A lovely mound of bandages gave shape to my hospital gown. I reached up to touch the mound on the right but was caught up short. My arm was attached by a tube to another machine with dials, buttons, and a bright digital display. "What's this?"

Paul lightly touched the tube leading into my arm. "I don't exactly know, honey."

A new nurse materialized in the dark at the foot of the bed. "It's an I-Med pump, hon. It delivers your pain medication." She fiddled with the dial, then handed me a button on the end of a long cord. "Just press this with your thumb when you start feeling pain."

Since my abdomen had been burning for the past ten minutes, I pumped the button. In seconds, the pain was reduced to a dull throb.

"It's morphine," she said.

I twisted my face into a maniacal grin that might have been mistaken for a look of pain. She patted my leg sympathetically and laid another gadget that looked like a TV controller next to my hand. "Push this if you need anything. It'll ring for me." I wondered what would happen if, in my confused state, I started ringing for the nurse and pumped myself full of morphine instead. I held up the morphine button. "What if I keep pumping?"

"Sorry, hon. We thought of that. It delivers a measured dose and it's on a timer." She tucked the covers around my hips. "Wouldn't want anyone to overdose."

"What a party pooper! Just when I thought there might be a silver lining in all this."

The nurse fussed with my ice water pitcher, set it on my bedside table, then breezed out of the room.

After she left, Paul dragged his chair closer to my bed. The legs made a screeching sound on the linoleum. The dinner cart rattled by, leaving an aroma of overcooked broccoli and fried chicken in its wake. My stomach revolted. "Oh God, I'm going to throw up." Saliva filled my mouth and I swallowed repeatedly, fighting the sensation, trying to keep everything down, although what there could be to throw up after not having eaten for a whole day I couldn't guess.

A plastic, kidney-shaped basin appeared under my chin, but I only heaved wretchedly, spitting up a trickle of yellow bile until I fell back on my pillow, exhausted. My nose was stopped up so I could hardly breathe. Tears slid sideways down my cheeks and into my ears. "Oh, Paul, I'm so tired."

Paul laid a damp washcloth on my forehead, momentarily making me forget the cuffs pumping up and down relentlessly on my legs.

"Here, dearie." The nurse reappeared and pressed a small pillow into my hands. "Press this against your stomach if you have to throw up, cough, or sneeze. It'll support the incision and help lessen the pain."

I placed the pillow against my stomach and held it there with both hands while I retched miserably and fruitlessly into the basin. Chemo redux. I remembered proclaiming to Joy's therapy group that I was bulimic, and decided that anybody who'd purposely stick a finger down her throat to make herself feel this way had to be crazy.

The nurse wiped my chin with a tissue. "This is another reason we don't want you to eat anything before surgery, dear."

I flopped back on the pillow and pushed the hand holding the basin away from my face. "I think I'd feel better if there was something down there to throw up other than major organs."

"How about sucking on some ice?" A spoonful of crushed ice touched my lips with healing coolness. I moved the chips around in my mouth with my tongue, enjoying the clicking sound they made against my teeth.

Paul bathed my brow again with a cloth soaked in cool water. I pumped the morphine button a couple of times and closed my eyes.

"She's asleep, Mr. Ives. Why don't you go get some dinner?"

"I heard that," I whispered. "Cappuccino. Yes. I'd love a cup."

Why Dr. Voorhis had wandered into my hospital room, I couldn't imagine. Maybe I was hallucinating. I'd done it before. Once upon a time I'd been so sick with the flu that I imagined Immanuel Kant perched at the foot of my bed, a wizened mouse of a man, explaining the whole of *Critique of Pure Reason* to me. Even more amazing, I understood him.

Dr. Voorhis's ghost wore brown, the color of the leaves that had formed his daughter's final bed. Her face floated up, golden hair fanned out around it, like a pillow. Her face, then his face. The same gray-blue eyes. Dr. Voorhis's mouth moved, but I couldn't hear what he was saying. Kant had, at least, been audible. No sense being rude, even to a specter. "Hi," I croaked.

Dr. Voorhis's features warped and slid, his round eyes became slits, his smiling mouth twisted into a leer, like a fun house mirror. I turned my head to see whether Paul had noticed the man, too, but his chair was empty. Oh, yeah, dinner. Paul had gone to the cafeteria to get dinner. I turned my head to the door, expecting to discover that Dr. Voorhis had vanished, but the apparition had moved to the side of my bed, next to the I-Med machine. He reached out and placed a hand on my knee. I felt the coldness of his touch even under the blanket.

"What . . ." *What are you doing here?* I wanted to say. *You practice in Baltimore.* But my lips were numb and my tongue seemed to fill my mouth. If Paul showed up, would Voorhis go *poof*?

The hand crept up my thigh. Blood pounded in my ears so loudly it drowned out the sound of the air compressor under the bed. Gasping, I patted around the top of the blanket, feeling for my call button to summon the nurse. *Where the hell is it?*

I touched something hard and cold. I wrapped my fingers gratefully around it and pushed the button, but only succeeded in turning up the volume on the TV. I dropped the remote and heard it clatter to the floor. *Oh, God, where was that call button?* I'd never needed it before. Paul had always been here for me.

My eyes locked on Dr. Voorhis and I watched, hypnotized, as he reached into an inside jacket pocket and pulled out a narrow package, about the size of a pen. The package crackled as he opened it, like cellophane. I was feeling along the aluminum bed rail, hoping to find the call button cord wrapped around it, when I heard something go *snap!* like a toothpick breaking.

I located a button at the edge of the mattress and pumped with my thumb for all it was worth. But it must have been the morphine control, because Dr. Voorhis's face shimmered before me, like a mirage on a hot summer day. His gray hair lengthened and curled softly around his ears; the black-rimmed glasses melted away; and his mustache morphed into the smiling, glossy pink lips of my nurse. "How are we doing, hon?"

I was dizzy with hyperventilation. *Thank God!*

The nurse picked up my wrist between her thumb and forefinger and, with her eyes on her wristwatch, took my pulse. "Goodness! Your heart's going a hundred miles an hour!"

"Nightmare," I mumbled.

Trussed up, tethered to tubes and wires, including a catheter and a tube snaking out of my chest, I was completely helpless. "What's this?" I touched the smooth, round surface of a blue plastic object lying just under the edge of my blanket.

"We call it a purse. It collects the fluid draining from your chest."

I managed a weak smile. "Not exactly Gucci, is it?"

"No. That drain will stay in for a few days, but we may be able to take the catheter out tomorrow, once you get up on your feet."

"On my feet? So soon?" I couldn't believe it. I felt like I'd been hit by a two-ton truck.

"The sooner you're up on your feet, the sooner you're out of here."

Paul materialized at the foot my bed, holding a Styrofoam container with a straw in it. "I thought you might like a Coke." He raised a questioning eyebrow at the nurse.

"That's fine," she said. "We'll be starting her on solid food in the morning."

Food. Yuck. My stomach roiled. The nurse cranked up the back of my bed and tucked a pillow under my shoulders, making it easier for Paul to hold the cup under my chin. I never remember a Coke tasting so good. I drifted off to sleep after that, with Paul holding my hand.

When I awoke, who knows how much later, Paul was sprawled in his chair watching the news. His deck shoes sat side by side on the windowsill, next to an arrangement of red and green carnations looking for all the world like Christmas leftovers. "Paul?"

He padded to my side in his stocking feet.

"Stay with me, Paul?"

"Don't worry, love. I'll be right here."

I had been lying flat on my back. When I tried to turn my body in his direction, a searing pain shot across my abdomen. I sucked air in through my teeth. "Oooh!" I pumped on the magic button and waited the few seconds it took for the pain to be reduced to a dull throb. Wonderful machine! Whoever invented it deserves to be a millionaire. Afterward, I tried unsuccessfully to stay awake, gazing at Paul through eyelids at half-mast. "Night-night," I said, and he faded away completely.

The next morning, well before dawn, I was awakened by a new nurse, intent on recording my temperature and blood pressure. "How did we sleep?" she asked, sticking a plastic thingamabob in my mouth.

"Fitfully," I mumbled around the thermometer. I raised my leg a few inches off the sheet. "Hard to sleep with these things pumping up and down on your legs every few seconds, not to mention that rogue Hoover howling away under the bed."

"She must be feeling better. She's getting cheeky," Paul remarked from his place by the window. He had shoved two chairs together and was using them as a bed. He pushed one away with his foot, stood up, and slipped into his shoes. "While you're busy here, I think I'll get some coffee."

"Bye!" I chirped. "Bring me a cappuccino!" I turned pleading eyes to the nurse. "I can have a cappuccino, can't I?"

She shrugged. "Don't see why not." She waved Paul out the door, then pulled the privacy curtain around my bed. "Which do you want me to get rid of first? The catheter or the water wings from hell?"

"The catheter, please!" She busied herself with the tube and I breathed a huge sigh of relief when it was removed from my nether region. A minute later I felt like a new woman when the inflatable cuffs were history as well. I bounced my legs up and down on the mattress, enjoying my freedom.

The nurse handed me a pair of paper slippers. "Here. Let's put these on and we'll take a short walk."

I nodded at the IV apparatus, still attached to my arm. "I suppose that comes along with me."

"For another day, at least." With a hand under my back, she helped me into a sitting position. I teetered for a few minutes on the edge of the bed, fighting waves of blackness, with my feet dangling over the side. She slid the slippers onto my bare feet. She steadied my elbow and, with the other hand stabilizing the IV apparatus, helped me wriggle off the bed.

My favorite blue velour bathrobe hung on a hook by the door. I couldn't imagine how I was going to put it on with my arm attached to enough equipment to man the space shuttle, until the nurse slipped the plastic IV bag off its hook and passed it through the sleeve of the robe, my arm following. "Clever girl," I remarked.

The floor was cold under my feet as we shuffled out the door and walked down the hall toward the nurses' station. I must have been a pathetic sight pushing my IV machine along in front of me with my "purse" pinned to my hospital gown and banging against my side with each deliberate step. At the nurses' station, we turned and headed back to my room. The nurse accompanied me to the chair that had been so recently vacated by my loyal husband and helped me sit down in it. "Sit here while I change your bed."

I watched as she stripped the sheets from my bed, snapped some clean ones open over it, and expertly began making up the bed. "I'm going for a clean blanket," she said, indicating a light brown stain on the one I had been using.

"Sorry." I felt myself blush. "I must have nodded off with a Coke in my hand."

She was a long time coming back. When I got tired of waiting, I got up and slid my feet around the room, admiring the flowers my friends and family had sent. Emily's roses were beginning to open. I buried my nose in one of the blooms and inhaled deeply, reminding myself of the rose gardens my mother had planted in every house we had ever lived in. The red and green carnations, I saw, were from Scott and Georgina. I wondered if the children had picked them out. There was even an arrangement from Whitworth & Sullivan. That touched me. My old boss, Fran, must have sprung for it. I couldn't imagine Cooper, Whitworth & Sullivan's office manager—cum—drill sergeant, coughing up the cash. Especially for an ex-employee he'd so recently had the pleasure of laying off. Steadying myself with a hand on the bed, I inched along it until I reached the bedside table where I'd piled the books I hoped to get to during my hospital stay. Paul's selection, the latest mystery by Kate Charles, imported from Britain, teetered on top. As I reached for it, I knocked the whole damn pile onto the floor. *Klutz!* Holding on to the IV apparatus, I bent my knees and sank slowly to the floor.

Next to the books, on a floor otherwise so spotless you could eat off of it, lay a purple plastic cap, like the top of a ballpoint pen, only smaller and narrower.

I picked it up and was examining it closely when the nurse returned. "What on earth are you doing on the floor?"

"Picking up my books." With both hands on the IV pole, I struggled to stand. "What's this?" I held the purple thing out.

She answered at once. "The protective cap for a hypodermic syringe. Where did you find it?"

"On the floor."

She studied me curiously, her head cocked to one side. "That's odd. You weren't scheduled for any additional medication." She spread the blanket over the clean sheets on the bed and began to tuck it in, making neat, square corners. "I'll have to speak to housekeeping. Somebody's been careless with the sweeping again."

I curled my fingers around the pole so tightly that my fingernails cut into my palm. Somewhere midway between the incision on my abdomen and the new breast taking root on my chest, a cold knot of fear began to grow. When Paul returned carrying a paper cup from the Seattle Coffee Company, I was already tucked up in bed, shivering, the blanket wrapped tightly around me. I wrapped my hands gratefully around the cup and felt the warmth spread up my arms, but I doubted it would melt the iceberg taking up residence in my gut.

"Paul?"

"Yes?"

"Look what I found." I reached into the pocket of my robe and pulled out the mysterious piece of plastic.

"What is it?"

"A syringe cap. I found it on the floor this morning."

"So? This is a hospital, Hannah."

I shook my head, trying to clear the cobwebs out of my brain. "While you were gone, I thought Dr. Voorhis came into my room."

Paul set his coffee on the bedside table and turned his full attention on me. "The pediatrician? Why would he come all the way down from Baltimore just to visit you?"

"At first I thought I was dreaming. But now I think maybe I wasn't. He had a hypodermic with him. What if he injected me with something?" My imagination was running wild. "What if he's given me AIDS?"

Paul was incredulous. "Your first instinct was right, Hannah. You were having a nightmare."

"Then how do you explain this?" I held the purple cap between my thumb and forefinger and extended my arm. "I'm sure I heard a snap when Dr. Voorhis twisted this off the needle."

"Look at me, Hannah!" His face was inches from mine. "You're talking to a man who sat here all night while you moaned and groaned and talked a blue streak."

"I did?"

"You did."

What was I going to say? Paul knew about my crashing the therapy group, of course, and about my trip to Dr. Voorhis's office with Julie, but I hadn't told him about my interviews with Voorhis's daughter's former patients.

"Well . . ." I set my cup on the bedside tray next to the breakfast I was no longer hungry enough to eat. I considered confessing to my crimes, but decided this wasn't the time or the place. Once too often before, I'd stuck my nose where it didn't belong. The last time I'd nearly drowned and taken Paul's sister along with me. "Maybe you're right," I said at last. "Perhaps I *was* dreaming."

But the syringe cap, tucked deep into the pocket of my robe, remained a tangible reminder of what might have been. Apparitions don't touch you, after all. And they certainly don't smell like Old Spice.

WHOEVER SAID THAT LAUGHTER IS THE BEST MEDI-
cine didn't have a row of surgical staples marching
across his belly. Well-meaning friends would invariably
try to cheer me up with jokes and convoluted shaggy-dog
stories, the kind that always seem to be streaking their
way around the world on the Internet. "Stop!" I'd yell,
the therapeutic pillow pressed firmly against my stomach to keep it from hurting like hell whenever I laughed.

I'd been recuperating at home for nearly a week, installed on the sofa in the living room, when Ms. Bromley
brought me all twelve episodes of *Fawlty Towers* on tape.
I cheerfully accused the mystery novelist of trying to
kill me.

Otherwise, I was bored out of my skull with nothing
better to do than brood over what might have been a
botched attempt on my life. To humor me, Paul had
called Dr. Voorhis's office and learned he was attending
a medical conference in Pebble Beach, California; that
didn't stop me from insisting that he double-lock the
doors behind him whenever he left the house.

Friday morning, thank goodness, he stayed home. I was touched when he cut my peanut butter sandwich into four narrow strips like I used to do for Emily. I dipped a rectangle into a mug of tomato soup that I was steadying with two fingers on the arm of my chair. I watched the bread wick up the soup, then popped it into my mouth. I wiggled my fingers in Paul's direction, but all I could see was the top of his curly gray head behind *The Baltimore Sun*.

The sports page spoke. "What are you up to today?"

"Boring, boring, boring." I dipped another piece of sandwich into my soup. "I can't wait to get these stitches out." I squirmed around on the sofa to face him. "They're beginning to itch like crazy."

Paul peeked around the page. "That's a sign it's healing."

"And I've got cabin fever. Big time. I'm even missing Ruth and her holistic homilies."

Paul laid the paper on his knee and held it there with the flat of his hand. "She'd probably wave one of those useless crystals over your chest." His smile changed to a worried frown. "I wish there was something I could do."

I fussed with the afghan that covered my legs and folded my arms over my chest before remembering that that wasn't a good idea. "Ouch!"

"Careful, honey."

"I want to *do* something, Paul. Something more exciting than walking back and forth to the bathroom."

"You're a clever girl, my love. You'll think of something." The corners of his mouth held the promise of a grin as he shook his head back and forth and returned to the paper. I watched while he breezed quickly through the basketball section and got to the page where they listed the local college scores.

Looking at him, I had a sudden inspiration. "Be my Marta Hallard," I blurted.

"Your what?" The pages rustled.

"My Archie. My Lewis."

Paul peeped around the newspaper. "What the hell are you babbling about?"

"Sidekicks," I said. "Marta Hallard was the woman in *Daughter of Time* who helped Alan Grant solve the mystery of the princes in the tower while he was laid up in the hospital with a broken leg."

"I get it. Archie is Nero Wolfe's general factotum. And Lewis is that guy on Inspector Morse."

"Right. In *The Wench Is Dead*, Morse is in the hospital and Lewis does the investigating."

"I think I hear my mother calling," Paul teased.

"No, honestly! I want you to find out something for me."

Paul covered his face with the newspaper and groaned. "I'm not listening."

"C'mon. It's a piece of cake. All you have to do is check out Dr. Sturges with the Maryland Board of Physician Quality Assurance."

"That's a mouthful! What is it? Some sort of Better Business Bureau for doctors?"

"Exactly. Find out if there were ever any complaints against her."

"And you think this quality-assurance bunch is going to tell *me* anything?"

"Of course they will. You're a consumer."

"Jeez, Hannah."

"And while you're at it, check out Dr. Voorhis, too."

"And what's in it for me?" His face was split by the crooked grin I loved so well.

"A night of wild, passionate sex." I ran a hand lightly over my bandages. "On account."

Paul crossed the room, leaned down, and planted a highly satisfactory kiss squarely on my lips. "Temptress."

"Is that a yes?" I asked when I could breathe again.

"It's a maybe."

Ten minutes later, Paul went to meet a mid for extra instruction at the academy, leaving me ensconced on the living room sofa, fully provisioned with the remains of my peanut butter sandwich, an empty mug with a disgusting red map coating the inside, a portable phone, and the remote control. I polished off the sandwich and considered what to do next. Under normal circumstances, to distract myself, I'd clean something, like a closet or the refrigerator; the basement if I were really desperate for diversion. But I wasn't supposed to be doing anything requiring stairs for at least a week, and it would be another four weeks before I could do any heavy lifting. My To Be Read pile had dwindled to just one book, a science fiction novel with a lurid cover that I decided I didn't want to read anyway, no matter how many weeks it had been on *The New York Times* Best Seller List.

I lay on the sofa and stared at the ceiling. There was a crack in the plaster that ran from the chandelier to the corner of the room nearest the dining room. Funny I hadn't noticed it before. I thought about manicuring my nails, painting them bright red. I would do my toes, too, I decided. But no, the nail polish was upstairs, and besides, with the stitches, I couldn't bend over far enough to reach my toes. I sighed and aimed the remote at the TV, clicked, and began grazing through the channels. I watched Vanessa fantasize about Jake while Giovanni had Vanessa on his mind. On another channel, Kevin proposed to Amber before going into a sudden seizure. Two channels further on, Rick considered whether to tell Ethan and Charity how Tabitha switched Ethan's sperm test results. And I thought my life was complicated. In a minute we'd have a little soap opera right here on Prince George Street: Hannah, paralyzed by boredom, tries to explain to Paul why she threw a brick through the television. Suddenly I wanted my folder, my notes, Dr. Sturges's appointment book pages, and the collection of other items that Paul jokingly calls my Junior Detective's Kit. But it was downstairs in the office, so I watched Margo consider how to report Caitlin as an unfit mother, then decided the hell with both of them. Stairs, schmairs. How hard could it be?

I flung aside the afghan and shuffled toward the hall in my bare feet. I took the stairs one at a time, slowly, leaning against the wall about halfway down to catch my breath. By the time I reached the basement I had to rest on the bottom step. Where was that blessed I-Med machine when you needed it? Tears of frustration stung my eyes when I realized down was easier than up. I might not be able to make it back upstairs on my own steam. When Paul came home he would find me still sitting there, weeping. Maybe he'd yell.

When the pain subsided and I could move again without wincing, I eased myself over to the desk and found my Junior Detective's Kit was just where I'd left it. I lowered myself carefully into the office chair and rolled it over to the desk, where I could flip through the pages of my notepad and review the list of patients I had talked to. Wandowsky and Riggins. Check. I'd eliminated Jacobs and Cameron and several others. To see if there was anybody I'd missed, I leafed through Diane Sturges's appointment book pages again.

One name had appeared once, early on, so I hadn't paid much attention to it—S. Gloden. Odd name, Gloden. I played with it, pronouncing the name over and over with different emphasis. *Glod*-en. *Glow*-den.

It was Paul's habit to leave the computer on, so I wiggled the mouse until the screensaver on the monitor faded away, then clicked onto the Internet. At the Lycos white pages, I tapped "Gloden" into the search box. Nothing. *Gloden?* Maybe it was a typo for Logen, or . . . of course!

Golden!

I tapped in "Golden" and "Baltimore," then used the pull-down menu to select "Maryland." I tried, in turn, various zip codes corresponding to the neighborhoods around All Hallows, and on the third try came up with a winner. A Stephanie Golden lived on North Charles Street. Before I could talk myself out of it, I logged off the Net, picked up the telephone, and called her.

After four rings and no answer, I expected an answering machine to kick in, but in the middle of the fifth ring, someone picked up. "Hello?"

If this was Stephanie, she sounded a lot like my grandmother Reid. "Stephanie?"

"Yes?"

The almost familiar voice gave me such a warm, fuzzy feeling that I thought twice about pretending to represent the police department. It would be like lying to my grandmother. "Ms. Golden, my name is Hannah Ives. Can I talk to you for a minute about Diane Sturges?"

"Are you from the police?"

I decided if I talked fast enough and sounded ditzy enough, maybe Stephanie wouldn't wonder where I had

gotten her name. "Lord, no. That's why I'm calling *you*.
I was a patient of Dr. Sturges and the police came to see
me yesterday. They said they were talking to all of Diane's patients, but I'm not so sure I believe them. They
really scared me. They seem to think *I* had something to
do with her death." I paused and heaved an exaggerated
sigh. "Did they talk to you?"

"Oh, yes. And I gave them an earful."

She seemed more than happy to give me an earful,
too. Stephanie had been Diane's patient for two years.
"Before I went to Diane, everybody—my husband, my
kids, my coworkers—thought I was a basket case." She
snorted softly. "I was a poster child for ACOA, trying
to be everything to everybody. The little engine that
could."

"What's ACOA?" I asked.

"Adult Children of Alcoholics." I wrote "ACOA" on
my notepad and wondered if I fell into that category,
too. I had rarely seen him falling-down drunk, but
Daddy certainly didn't have his drinking anywhere near
under control. Especially not these days.

"Is that what led you into therapy, the fact that one of
your parents was an alcoholic?" The thought made me
nervous.

"I think so." She paused to consider. "When Diane
came along, I was a hungry pup, ready to suckle on any
breast that came my way." Stephanie giggled. "So I got
on with Diane right away. It wasn't long before she became my mentor. She was going to help me kick butt."

"I can understand the need to take charge of your life.
Mine seems to be swinging completely out of control."

"Mine, too, but I'm better able to handle it now. As
I think back on it, though, I was probably just going
through menopause, but Diane made me believe that

something terrible had happened to me, something so terrible that I couldn't remember it."

Where had I heard that before? "Are you saying there was nothing seriously wrong with you?"

"Nothing that a few hormone pills couldn't cure."

I paused to organize my thoughts. "Diane and I hadn't come along that far before she . . ." I faked a sniffle. ". . . before she died."

"You were new to the group?"

"Very. Now I'm wondering if it wasn't all for the best. I would have *hated* going to therapy if all I was going to do was be forced to think about terrible things!"

"I *did* hate going to therapy. With a passion. It was painful and tough, but in a way, that's what made it so attractive. I thought if I could just make it to the other side, I would really have accomplished something. I'd be free! Maybe I'd be on the *Tonight Show* with Jay Leno."

"So you joined up."

"Yup. I bought a ticket on that pop psychology train and hopped right on. Diane was my fairy godmother, holding one hand for the journey while I was writing checks with the other."

I laughed out loud. "You sound very cynical."

"Well, it took me a while to realize that she was simply fleecing the flock."

"How so?"

"It's simple math, really. Fifty dollars a month for the group sessions at the church and a hundred dollars for each one-on-one. Multiply that times the number of patients . . ." She paused as if performing the calculations in her head. "Well, you do the math!"

I was. By my reckoning, Diane Sturges had to be pulling in at least $160,000 per year, even allowing time out for vacations. "Not much of an incentive to help patients get well and move on, is it?"

"No. And Diane often made me feel as if I wasn't doing my homework." Somewhere on Stephanie's side of the telephone, a teakettle screamed. She must have been talking on a portable phone, because I heard footsteps and the teakettle was choked off in mid-shriek. "I wanted so much to produce something for her that sometimes I'd make things up. But it was never enough. One time when I was being nonproductive, she fell asleep." Stephanie apologized for the clattering crockery and made herself tea. "It was the same during group. I was beginning to crack under the peer pressure."

"I felt a lot like that myself when I couldn't get my Little Girl to talk to me."

"Tell me about it! On the other hand, if I became rational, she'd sometimes scold me, telling me it was my job to *feel*, not to *think*." Stephanie paused and took a deep breath. "I finally had enough."

"So what did you do?"

"I told her that just because those other ladies had been abused, didn't mean that I had. For two years I'd been walking on eggshells, terrified that I'd remember the incident with a capital *I* at any time. What if it happened while I was driving? Or in the grocery store? Or in church? Or holding my grandbaby? I'd wake up in a cold sweat at four in the morning and ask myself, 'Stephanie! Are you about to remember?' "

"Did you? Remember, I mean."

"No. Nothing ever came into focus for me, and I finally realized that there had been no incest. None at all. I told Diane I thought everyone in the group was only interested in helping me solve my problems because they were working so hard on trying to solve their own."

"When did you last see Diane?" I asked, although I already knew what her answer would be from the information in front of me.

"The Tuesday before she died. I tell you, Hannah, when I heard about it on the news, I felt terrible, thinking that I might have been responsible."

"Responsible? Why on earth?"

"They said a fall from the balcony, so naturally I thought . . ."

"Suicide?"

"Uh-huh."

"Why suicide?"

"I can't tell you for sure. It's just a feeling I had. You should have seen the look on her face when I told her that I'd come to the conclusion that I hadn't been abused at all. I had expected an argument, but she just sat there quietly, as if I weren't even there. Then she ended my session twenty minutes early and said she wouldn't even charge me for it."

"How odd."

"That's what I thought."

"I have to say that you seem fine now. Very confident."

"It's ironic really, that I started using the tools she gave me to begin seeing the light."

Thinking about Georgina, I said, "Some of us didn't get that far."

"I know."

We promised to meet for coffee sometime, but I think we both knew that after we hung up we'd never talk to each other again.

I returned to my folder, wishing that Georgina, like Stephanie, would finally see the light.

Before Mother's heart attack, I had rummaged through back issues of the *Sun* until I found Diane Sturges's obituary. The clipping stared up at me now. Where had she come from? Born in Providence, Rhode Island, in 1966, she'd moved to Baltimore, but it didn't say when. In 1983 she graduated from the Garrison Forest school and attended college and graduate school at Johns Hopkins. The obituary said she was survived by her husband, Bradley Sturges, a Washington, D.C., architect, and her father, Dr. Mark Voorhis. Nothing new there. I sat back in my chair and studied Diane's picture, looking so much like that other woman in the photograph in Dr. Voorhis's office. Wait a minute! What about a mother? For the first time in many months, I longed for the reference section of the Whitworth & Sullivan library, where I could instantly lay my hands on reference books like the *AMA Directory of Physicians* whenever I wanted them. I consulted the computer, but the darn book didn't appear to be online, so I reached for the telephone instead and called the public library on West Street. They didn't have a copy. I shuffled things around on the desk, searching for the Naval Academy phone book, then called the Naval Academy library. The nice gentleman who answered the reference line apologized profusely and told me they didn't have the book either. *Pooh!*

I stared at the monitor for a while, then had a sudden vision of Penny Evans, Whitworth & Sullivan's workaholic reference librarian, who was probably plowing her way through a pile of reference questions the height of the World Trade Center right then, not that anyone would appreciate it. Want something done, they say? Ask the busiest person you know. That was Penny.

Amazingly, I hadn't forgotten Whitworth & Sullivan's telephone number. I was so proud after punching in all the numbers correctly that it was a big letdown to get

Penny's voice mail. "If you're there, Penny, grab the AMA directory and call me back," I recorded, then hung up in a grumpy mood.

I rearranged my papers, putting them in a semblance of order, then played a game of computer solitaire. Suits of cards were cascading down the screen in victorious waves when the phone rang.

Penny hadn't changed a bit. The same chirpy voice. "Hi, Hannah. You can't imagine how surprised I was to get your call. How the hell are you?"

"Hanging in there, Pen. Just had my reconstructive surgery, so I'm stuck at home and feeling kind of punk."

"Jeez. My aunt had that done, so I've got some idea of how you must feel."

"Uncomfortable as hell and twice as bored."

"So, you decided to call me up for entertainment?" She burst into song, a hilarious off-key rendition of "Let Me Entertain You." When I cheerfully protested she said, "I could use some diversion anyway. Fran's got me working on the use-tax statistics."

I groaned. "Poor you."

"Keeps me off the streets. And speaking of off the streets and out of trouble, how about you, Hannah? Last time I heard, you'd been in some sort of boating accident and two people had drowned."

"Too true, I'm afraid." I thought about those desperate moments last spring when someone I'd grown to care about had betrayed me, nearly costing Connie and me our lives.

The ring of another telephone on her end filled the awkward silence. "Sorry."

"Do you need to get that?"

"No. I'm not officially here. Say," she chirped in a

let's-change-the-subject tone of voice, "what do you want me to do with this AMA directory I've lugged all the way over to the phone?"

I could picture Penny, standing at the waist-high desk with the receiver tucked between her ear and shoulder, her left earring unclipped and resting on the counter in front of her. "I'd like you to look up somebody for me, a Doctor Diane Sturges."

"Sure." I heard pages flipping. "Russell, Stanley, Sturges. Diane, did you say?"

"Yup."

"Got a Charles Sturges, but no Diane."

Feeling foolish, I remembered what Mother had said about Diane not being a real doctor. "How about a Doctor Mark Voorhis?"

"OK. Underwood, Victor . . . here we are, Voorhis. He graduated from John Hopkins in sixty-one, did residencies in Oklahoma and St. Louis. It lists an office address in Baltimore." She rattled it off, but I didn't need to write it down. It was the Greenspring Center where I had taken Julie.

But I was interested in the time before Baltimore. He must have practiced somewhere. "Where did he go after his residency?"

"Doesn't say. There's nothing between St. Louis and his present location in Baltimore."

"Damn."

"Wait a minute." The receiver banged in my ear and I could hear Penny shoving books in and out on the metal shelves. In a minute she was back. "We're in luck. He's gotten himself listed in *Who's Who*. Got a pencil? Here we go. Voorhis. Between sixty-nine and seventy-nine he was practicing at the Morgan Clinic in Waterville, Illinois.

The next year, he shows up in Baltimore, practicing in pediatrics. Looks like he's been there ever since."

I did a quick calculation. Diane would have been about thirteen when he picked up sticks and headed east. "I wonder why he left Illinois?"

"Beyond the scope of this book, dah'link."

"Do you suppose Waterville has a newspaper I could check?"

"Hold on a sec." I heard the thud of the heavy book closing before I got an earful of the white noise that told me that Penny had put me on hold. While I waited, I pulled out Paul's Rand McNally road atlas and looked up Waterville, a little town off I-74 about halfway between Bloomington and Peoria. I fiddled with my notes and the pages from Dr. Sturges's appointment book, making experimental probes under my bandages with an index finger in an attempt to quell the itch. I'd found a particularly satisfying spot and was scratching away when Penny came back on the line. "Hannah? I'm looking at the Nexis listing. There's the *Waterville Gazette*, but it's only been online since ninety-two."

"Rats."

"But I did a quick check, and they've got the microfilm at the Library of Congress."

Great. The Library of Congress. Usually the thirty-five-mile drive between Annapolis and Capitol Hill wouldn't have fazed me. But for the next several weeks of my recuperation, that microfilm might as well have been on the moon. "Say, Pen, in light of my present delicate condition, I don't suppose you could . . ." I ventured.

"Sorry, Han, but why do you think I'm burning the proverbial midnight oil? I'm outahere on the red-eye special tonight. You know how hard it is for Ken and me to get our schedules together. I finally talked him into a couple of weeks at my brother's place in Tahoe."

"Lucky you," I said, but truthfully, I couldn't think of anything I'd like doing less than skiing. My son-in-law, Dante, had talked me into taking a skiing lesson while I was out in Colorado meeting my new granddaughter. After tumbling downhill in a pinwheel of skis and limbs and nearly being beheaded by a novice on his virgin Boogie board run, I didn't take much to the sport. I maintain that one should grab a bathing suit and head Caribbean-ward in winter. I thought about my new breast quietly taking root under the bandages. Maybe next year.

I thanked Penny profusely and was about to hang up when I remembered what had started me thinking about Voorhis's background in the first place. "Penny, do me one more favor. Does *Who's Who* say anything about a wife?"

Penny sighed heavily. "*Now* you tell me. I just closed that book, Hannah."

"I'll be forever in your debt."

Pages rustled. "It says he married a Fiona Shenker in 1965."

I scribbled the name down.

"And someone named Loraine Hudson in 1986."

"Thanks again, Pen."

"Anything else you want to know? His mother? Father? Shoe size?"

I chuckled. "No, I think that's it. You're the best!"

I hung up and pouted. It would be weeks before I'd be well enough to drive into D.C. and look at that microfilm. I played another game of solitaire, lost, then drummed my fingers on the mouse pad. I was not noted for my patience. I could just hear Mother say, "Hold your horses, Hannah. Those microfilms aren't going anywhere." She'd be right, of course. Mother was usually right. She would have warned me about going against doctor's orders and walking down the stairs, and she'd have been right about that, too. I sat in my chair, longing for my pain pills, and waited for Paul to return home and rescue me.

WHEN MARK VOORHIS CAME UP SQUEAKY CLEAN with Maryland Q and A, I wasn't surprised. With Voorhis's spotless reputation and charming bedside manner, which I had experienced firsthand, I hadn't really expected Paul to uncover any dirt about the pediatrician. But Diane was another matter. I was sure that her controversial techniques must have disagreed with somebody, so it was a surprise when she, too, came up with a clean bill of health. Paul didn't find her listed with Maryland Q and A, of course, since she wasn't an M.D., but he'd thought to check the state licensing boards. None was aware of any complaints against the woman.

I thought about what Stephanie had told me about her final session with Diane. I wondered what Stephanie had said that upset the therapist enough to cut the session short. Stephanie had been talking about her fear of memories coming back full-blown. What had Diane remembered? Something terrible in her own past? I was convinced that the answer lay in Waterville, Illinois.

Paul needed only minimal arm-twisting before agreeing to go to the Library of Congress to look through the microfilm of the *Waterville Gazette*. "Who am I this time?" he teased. "Marta or Lewis?"

"I'm rather partial to Lewis," I said.

Paul tipped my chin up and kissed me. "You know who gets my vote?"

"Who?"

"Jimmy Stewart."

"Why Jimmy Stewart?"

"Because in Hitchcock's *Rear Window*, old Jimmy had Grace Kelly do his legwork."

"Get out of here!" I bopped him over the head with my pillow.

The rest of the day crawled by. At one o'clock I made the first of my twice-daily calls to Mother in the hospital and we compared health notes. Lately she had been making an effort to sound chipper when we talked, but I could tell it was all an act. Even though I kept our conversations short, toward the end her voice would fade and she'd hand the phone off to Dad, who rarely left her side. I'd ask the inevitable—how's she doing—and we'd have strained, one-sided conversations where he'd try to answer my questions without upsetting Mother, who, knowing her, would be pretending not to listen.

"She's not much better, is she?" I'd ask.

"You could say that."

"But not worse?"

"That's right."

"What did the doctor say?"

"Good to hear you're on the mend." A glib non sequitur signaled that I'd better ask for details another time.

"Thanks, Daddy. I'm still sore and positively itching

to get out of the house, but I see the doctor on Friday. If it's OK with her, Paul says he'll drive me up to visit Mother this weekend."

"So soon?" His voice brightened. "She'll be really glad to see you." He took a deep breath. "And me, too, of course."

I could hear muffled conversation in the background. "What's that?"

"Your mom says don't rush it."

"Don't worry, I'm not."

Paul returned home around six-thirty, bearing a bag of Chinese carryout. All day I'd been on my own in the food department, which meant whatever I could scrounge from the refrigerator. Lunch had been leftover spaghetti zapped in the microwave and a sorry-looking bowl of Caesar salad. Paul barely had time to lay the cartons out on the kitchen table before I tore the lid off the hot-and-sour soup container and began slurping down steaming mouthfuls between demands for a full report on his research.

"Tell me what you found out." I opened a waxed-paper envelope and munched on one of those crunchy noodles designed to throw on top of the soup.

Paul speared a dumpling with his chopsticks. He waved it at me and I watched it wobble, fall, and splash into the dipping sauce, decorating the tablecloth with mahogany speckles. He picked it up with his fingers. "Eat your tofu," he said. "Then I'll tell you."

"Sadist." I popped open a carton of steamed rice and inverted it over my plate. When I lifted the carton away, it left a rectangular block, which I draped with spicy green beans.

"Nope. Masochist. That drive to D.C. is hell. Can't

understand how you put up with it for so many years."
The last dumpling disappeared down his throat.

"I imagine we needed the money," I teased. "Remember Emily? And all those paychecks I signed over to Bryn Mawr?"

"There was that," he admitted.

I laid down my chopsticks, sat up straight in my chair, folded my hands primly in my lap, and said, "OK. Out with it."

"I guess I've tortured you long enough." He leaned forward with his arms resting on the edge of the table. "OK, here's the scoop. The *Waterville Gazette* comes out every Thursday. It's a provincial rag reporting on local politics, school and church events, much like our *Chesapeake Times* down in Pearson's Corner."

I remembered the *Chesapeake Times*. Once upon a time I'd made headlines there, when I discovered the body of a murdered teenager floating in an old cistern. I picked a green bean up with my fingers and nibbled it slowly while Paul continued.

"Because Dr. Voorhis left Waterville sometime in 1979, I began looking in the December issues and worked backward. In November, there was an announcement that two doctors, a married couple, had bought the Morgan Clinic. And that led me backward to an even more interesting article."

While I held my breath, Paul shoved his chair back and reached for the battered briefcase he'd propped against a table leg. He extracted a sheaf of papers from the side pocket and held them out to me. "Here are photocopies of everything I found."

I snatched them from his outstretched hand. "You sweetheart!"

"They're roughly in order."

My heart began to pound as I shoved my plate away, flicked some grains of rice onto the floor, and arranged the photocopies on the table in front of me. The one on top showed a simple invitation-style announcement bordered with a Greek key design. It introduced Drs. Warner and Millicent Rickert to the Waterville community and invited patients to look to the clinic for all their medical needs. The next photocopy was from the society page. It described a farewell party held for Diane Voorhis at the Waterville Country Club, sponsored by someone in the Junior League, the mother of one of Diane's little friends. The article was dry and about as interesting as reading the stock market quotes—I mean, who *cares* what kind of flowers decorated the tables—until the final paragraph:

> Diane, 13, will be relocating to Baltimore, Maryland, where her father, Dr. Mark Voorhis, is going into private practice. Fiona Voorhis, his wife of fifteen years, a popular member of the Junior League and an active member of St. Anthony's church, died in August.

I sensed Paul staring at me. I whistled and looked up. "What did she die of?"

"Read on, McDuff," he said with a twinkle.

Since everything seemed to be arranged in reverse chronological order, I dived straight to the bottom of the stack. Under a picture of an attractive woman bearing an uncanny resemblance to Diane Sturges was the headline: LOCAL WOMAN FOUND DEAD OF CARBON MONOXIDE POISONING. I checked the date. On a Tuesday night in August of 1979, Fiona Voorhis had been discovered dead in her car, a Volvo station wagon, when her husband returned home following his rounds. He told police he had heard the engine running, but by the time he opened the garage and pulled his wife from the car, it was too late.

"Where was Diane?" I asked Paul.

He laid a finger on a photocopy featuring several pictures of a barn fire. It was from the following week's paper, and it carried more details. The night her mother died, thirteen-year-old Diane had been attending a church camp in nearby Durham. *Poor thing*, I thought. *No wonder she was so screwed up, losing her mother like that. And so young*. The police had found a suicide note, but its contents had not been revealed. Family friends had reported that Fiona had been recently despondent. Again, no cause for that depression was given. The final article dealt with the inquest. Fiona Voorhis's death was ruled a suicide. I counted on my fingers. Five months later, Dr. Voorhis had sold his practice and he and his daughter were on their way to Baltimore. I wondered why.

I turned the photocopy over, as if expecting something to be printed on the back of it. "That's it?"

Paul nodded. "Isn't that enough?"

I paged through the articles again. "I would give my eyeteeth to know what was in that suicide note."

"I don't suppose we'll ever know."

I had to agree with him. "It's an odd thing, though."

"What's odd?"

I shuffled through the photocopies. "Did you notice that the *Gazette* reports on everything under the sun— birthday parties for two-year-olds, high school dances, junior varsity basketball scores, the weekly menus at the school cafeteria . . ."

"And your point is?"

"There was a farewell party for Diane, but none for the good doctor."

"Maybe he didn't want a party. He was the grieving widower, don't forget."

I ignored him. "Makes me wonder all the more about that suicide note," I said. "The earlier articles hint at something more—that she was found dead under suspicious circumstances—but the reporter writing about the inquest doesn't even hint at anything suspicious or unusual."

"Let's ask Dennis."

Paul's suggestion surprised me. I'd thought about Dennis, too, but was glad that Paul had been the one to bring it up, not me. Perhaps his sister's boyfriend, being a policeman, could find out something about the case, maybe even learn the contents of the suicide note. "*You* call him," I prompted.

"Why me?"

"I'm always asking him for stuff. He already thinks I have a screw loose. The request might sound more reasonable coming from you."

"I doubt it." Paul stood, came around behind my chair, and rested both hands on my shoulders. "He'll just think I've joined the Hannah Club." He kissed the top of my head. "But since you're an invalid and completely at my mercy, I'll give it a shot."

Surprisingly, Paul reached Dennis at home. Widowed a little over a year, Dennis Rutherford divided his time between the Chesapeake County Eastern District police station where he worked and Connie's farm. From my one-sided vantage point, pinned by pain to my chair and listening to Paul as he wandered around the kitchen with the portable phone pressed to his ear, I gathered that Dennis had reluctantly agreed to make some discreet inquiries, but that he wouldn't guarantee to share the results with me. Paul promised to meet him for a beer and a long-overdue chin wag, or whatever male-bonding activities men get up to over beer when their womenfolk aren't around. "There!" He laid the phone on the table and turned to me. "Satisfied?"

I aimed my sweetest smile in his direction. "Very."

Paul covered his eyes with both hands. "Aieeee! It's the saccharine death ray!"

"And only one of my extraordinary talents not presently under reconstruction."

Paul circled the table, leaned down, and brushed his lips against the back of my neck. "Dennis also thought you'd like to know that the Baltimore police still don't have enough evidence to charge your father with anything."

I relaxed against him. "That's good news." I reached back and caressed his cheek, enjoying the prickly feel of it against my skin.

"It's after eight. Can I help you upstairs?"

I took the hand he offered and pulled myself up unsteadily. "Thanks." I had expected to hobble upstairs on my own—I was doing much better at stairs these days—but Paul surprised me by scooping me up as if I were a blushing bride. I wrapped my arms around his neck. He was panting slightly but trying not to show it when he arranged me gently on the bed in our room.

I laid the back of my hand dramatically against my forehead. "I feel like a heroine in a romance novel, a fragile lily doomed to expire from consumption." I faked a dainty, ladylike cough.

He tucked the comforter around my legs and began to chuckle.

"What's so funny?"

"I'm just remembering something. When I was a kid, my dad loved opera. Long before there was a Kennedy Center, we'd take the train up to New York to hear the Metropolitan Opera. Saw Leontyne Price in *Aida* once."

"You never told me that!"

"Never came up before."

I wondered what there was about *Aida* to make somebody laugh. "Correct me if I'm wrong, but isn't *Aida* a tragedy?"

"Uh-huh."

"Then what's so funny about going to the Met?"

Paul parked himself on the edge of the bed. "Well, I'd been to a lot of operas—*Don Giovanni, The Magic Flute, La Bohème*—but in all that time, I'd never seen a thin soprano. The first time I saw *La Bohème*—I must have been about ten—I goggled at the bloated diva who was practically bursting out of the seams of her Mimi costume and couldn't figure out what all the fuss was about."

I must have looked puzzled.

Paul crawled onto the bed next to me, fully clothed. He plumped up a pillow and sandwiched it between his head and the wooden headboard. "If you recall, Mimi's dying of consumption. I figured if she wanted to eat herself to death, that was her problem!"

I bent double with laughter, pressing the comforter against my abdomen. "Oh, help! You are a bad, bad boy!"

His arm encircled my shoulders and I leaned my head against his chest. "I certainly hope so," he whispered into my hair.

EVER NOTICE HOW YOU CAN GO FOR DAYS AND DAYS and nothing much happens? Get up, eat, sleepwalk through the day, eat, go to bed? Then all of a sudden— *bah-bing*—everything seems to happen all at once.

It began on Lincoln's Birthday, the day I saw my plastic surgeon. This miracle-working woman, whose office was decorated with her own paintings and sculptures, had created another masterpiece. My breast. A beautiful, healthy pink mound that stood tall and proud upon my chest. I was thrilled to be the owner of a boob that I didn't have to take out of a drawer every morning.

While the doctor warned me to examine myself often for telltale signs of rejection, I stood in front of the mirror, half listening, wearing not much more than a goofy grin and admiring my newly matched pair. I was enormously pleased; so pleased that after I left the office, I had to control an irrational desire to show off Dr. Bergstrom's remarkable handiwork to everyone I met.

I fantasized strolling up Maryland Avenue from shop to shop. "Look at this," I'd say to Jehanne, the curly-headed *barista* at Seattle Coffee. And she'd go, "Why, Mrs. Ives, wherever did you get that?"

I had permission to drive again, too. After we returned home from the doctor's, I left Paul happily puttering in his basement workshop and celebrated my new freedom with a trip to the grocery store. I wandered up and down the aisles as if greeting old friends—the coffee bins, the dairy case, the gourmet food counter—then carried some English muffins, cheddar cheese, and a carton of half-and-half through the checkout, managing to keep my shirt on the whole time.

My second solo outing caught me totally by surprise. I had spent the early part of Friday afternoon getting my prescribed exercise by strolling along the Naval Academy seawall, a bulkhead of heaped-up boulders and concrete that edged the academy shoreline from the Visitors' Center all the way to Hospital Point. I began my walk at the end of the seawall nearest the Visitors' Center, stopping to enjoy a panoramic view of Annapolis harbor. In Feburary only a few hearty cruisers and die-hard sailing liveaboards were anchored in the scenic harbor. In summer, though, it would be a different story; boats would be anchored wall-to-wall, and you could practically walk to Eastport without getting your feet wet. I smiled. Eastport. Home of Severn Sailing Association, the school where Paul had spent many dollars and hopeless hours trying to turn me into an accomplished sailor.

I had stopped to rest at the submarine memorial near Trident Light and had just parked my buns on the topmost step, when the cell phone in my parka chirped. Ruth was calling from a pay phone in the Los Angeles airport to tell me she was on her way home. Worry and guilt had gradually eroded her ability to concentrate on her spiritual growth. She'd left Bali after discovering an escape clause in the travel agency's contract that allowed partial refunds for bona fide medical emergencies.

Seven hours later, I met Ruth at BWI, gave her a hug, told her she'd need to heft her own luggage into my trunk, and drove her straight to University Hospital in Baltimore.

Mother was overjoyed.

Ruth was in tears.

I paced. I couldn't keep my shirt on, quite literally. "You gotta see this, Mom." I drew the privacy curtains across the glass partitions that separated Mother's room from the adjoining ones. I unbuttoned my shirt and unfastened my bra. "Tah-dah!" I flashed my mom. "What do you think?"

Mother beamed. "Beautiful, Hannah. A work of art."

From a bedside chair Ruth studied my chest with interest. "Weirdest show-and-tell I've ever seen."

"I don't think I've ever been so proud of anything in my whole life," I declared while reassembling my clothing. "It's a shame I can't show off Dr. Bergstrom's work to everybody."

"Speaking of everybody, where's Daddy?" Ruth wanted to know.

Mother managed a grin. "He'll be back in a bit. He went home to bathe and change his clothes after I complained that he'd been wearing the same olive-green trousers for the last three days and I was sick of looking at them."

Ruth brought Mother up to date on her abbreviated trip while I listened jealously. Morning walks to the rice paddies, meditation, herbal steam baths—it sounded positively divine. After an hour, Daddy joined us, smelling like Ivory soap and having changed into a pair of freshly pressed khaki pants and a red plaid shirt. His hair was still damp. I listened impatiently while Ruth repeated it all for him, but Mother didn't seem to mind. She smiled and asked questions as if it were the very first time she'd heard about colonic hydrotherapy.

Ruth's Conduit Street cupboard had never been so thoroughly bare, so I made her come to our house for dinner. Carryout was on the menu again, a particular specialty of mine. Ruth happily joined Paul and me in the kitchen, where we heaped our plates high and dug in.

That was where Connie and Dennis found us a few minutes later, our teeth sunk into slices of garlic bread and our forks fully draped with spaghetti puttanesca from Cantina d'Italia.

I wiped tomato sauce off my chin. "Hi, you guys."

Dennis removed his leather jacket and draped it over the back of a vacant chair. "Got something you've been waiting for, Hannah." He laid a photocopy of a fax on the table. "It's from the Waterville police department. Came in today."

"You are amazing!" My dinner was forgotten. "But how are you able to show this to us?"

Dennis pulled a chair out for Connie, waited until she was seated, then sat down himself. "It was all part of the official court proceedings. Although Mrs. Voorhis's note was never made public, the gist of it certainly leaked out."

Connie wriggled out of her jacket, leaned forward to snitch a strand of spaghetti from my plate, and continued, "Small wonder, when you read what it says."

I picked up the photocopy with both hands and held it in front of me. Paul leaned sideways and craned his neck to get a better view.

In a neat, looping hand, Fiona Voorhis had written:

I can't go on living. Truthfully, I have been dying for years, a little bit every day, sick with the knowledge of what Mark has done to our daughter; hating myself for the part I played in his abuse out of simple ignorance and denial. Will anyone listen to me now?

Underneath, on the same piece of paper, was the photocopy of another note. Fiona had left a message for her daughter, too.

My darling Diane. Someday you'll understand. Forgive me. I love you. Mother.

A dozen words that thirteen-year-old Diane Sturgis must have memorized and carried about with her in her heart.

Finally, all these years later, Diane had understood.

IT HAD BEEN TWO WEEKS SINCE DENNIS FIRST SHOWED us Fiona Voorhis's last sad letters. Connie sat across from me at my kitchen table with a half-eaten piece of apple pie in front of her. "You did *what?*" Her voice cut through the air like a saw hitting a nail.

"I sent him a note."

"What kind of note?"

"I got to thinking about that dumb movie *I Know What You Did Last Summer.*"

She closed her eyes. "I can't believe what I'm hearing."

"So I sent him a note saying, 'I know what you did.' And I stapled it to a clipping from the *Sun* about this guy who's on trial for abusing his daughters."

"Hannah, are you nuts?"

"It was anonymous. He won't know who sent it."

Connie laid down her fork and relaxed into her chair. "So what's the point?"

Connie was going to *hate* what I was about to tell her. "Well, I suggested he meet me at All Hallows to talk about it. At seven tonight."

I was right. Connie half rose from her chair with a murderous gleam in her eyes, then sat down abruptly.

"The way I figure it, Connie, if he's guilty, he'll turn up just to see what I know. If he's not guilty, he'll ignore it. Tear up the note and throw it away."

"What reason would he have to show up? You can't prove he abused his daughter."

"*I* know that, but he doesn't." I avoided her eyes. "I lied. I told him I had evidence he might be interested in."

Connie's silver earrings bounced against her neck. "Oh, Lord! And I suppose you'll want me to go along with you on this?"

"Well, yes. Why else would I tell you?"

She frowned. "Dennis isn't going to like this."

"I don't suppose he will, but I'm counting on you to get him to come along."

"What!" Connie spluttered, her face an alarming shade of pink.

"Don't blow a gasket, Connie."

"Easy for you to say. I'm panicking. You are dangerous to know."

"I've got it all figured out. Georgina told me about the sound system they use at All Hallows to record the sermons. It's installed in the fellowship hall somewhere, underneath the sanctuary." I had been trying to remember if I had seen an AV closet the night I crashed the therapy session. It might have been behind any one of several closed doors.

Connie avoided me by closing her eyes and resting her forehead on the palm of her hand.

"If Voorhis shows up in the sanctuary, I'll get him to confess and we'll have it all on tape," I argued.

"Hannah, I told you. Dennis will have no part of this."

"Why not?"

"It's got to be illegal, for one thing."

"That's just on TV." I leaned over and tried to look up into her eyes. "Look, I swear to you. Dr. Voorhis came to my hospital room. I was *not* imagining it. And don't forget what Dennis found out about Fiona Voorhis."

"Hannah, have you ever stopped to consider that Fiona Voorhis might have been deranged?" Connie skewered me with her eyes. "Just like a certain sister-in-law I could mention."

"I agree. Any one of these facts taken separately mightn't amount to much, but put it together with what Stephanie Golden told me about her last session with Diane Sturgis and it all adds up."

"To what?"

I felt for the plastic syringe cap, still in my pocket. Whenever I began to doubt myself, I'd wrap my fingers around that solid object and know I was completely sane. "It adds up to the fact that Voorhis killed Diane when she confronted him about his abuse. What's more, he knows I know it."

Connie studied me seriously. "Consider this. If Voorhis really visited your hospital room, then the man is dangerous."

"Exactly! That's why I need Dennis. If things get dicey, Dennis will leap out of the woodwork and make an arrest."

"Dennis can't do that! It's not his jurisdiction. You'll have to pull your own chestnuts out of the fire this time, Hannah."

Connie was remembering how Dennis had raced to the rescue the last time I had a showdown with someone intent on murder. Now I'd stuck my neck out again.

"Well, it's too late now. Voorhis must have my envelope. If he comes, he comes."

"Why don't we just stake out the church, hide in the bushes or something, and see if he shows up?" Connie didn't give in easily, but I was heartened to hear the "we."

"That won't do any good. *We'll* know, but where's the proof?" I shook my head. "Nope. We've got to get him to admit to everything on tape."

Connie was close to tears. "What a mess."

I smiled crookedly at her. "But, as you say, he won't show up and we can all go out afterward for pizza and talk about how crazy Hannah is."

Connie cocked her head to one side. "How are you going to get into the church? It's Friday, for Pete's sake."

I reached into my pocket and pulled out the second object that I kept there. "I've got a key."

"How on earth . . . ?"

"I slipped it off Georgina's key chain the day I was watching the kids. I had it duplicated."

"Is there anything you haven't thought of?" Connie sounded disgusted.

"Well, I'm not exactly sure how I'll set up the recording equipment because I've never seen it, but I'm counting on the church warden being there. He usually is. And he's such an old maid, he'd never refuse a policeman's direct request." I paused to see if she took my point. When she didn't say anything, I drove it home. "That's why I need Dennis."

"Dream on, Hannah. Dennis could never afford to be involved in an unauthorized taping outside his jurisdiction." She raised an eyebrow. "What do you need the church warden for?"

"Lionel Streeting? He's got the key to the AV room."

"I'm surprised you haven't had that copied, too," Connie muttered.

I made up my mind. "Look, we can do this without Dennis. I'll talk to Streeting myself. He's seen me, but he doesn't have a clue who I really am. I'll just *tell* him I'm from the police."

"And when he asks to see your badge?"

"I'll cross that bridge when I come to it."

In the end, we didn't need the key. When we got to All Hallows, the door to the parish hall was unlocked. Since Dennis wouldn't be involved, I hadn't dared tell Paul what I was up to, and in the absence of Dennis, Connie had finally agreed to come along, reluctant to leave me on my own. Following the same route as on my previous visit to the therapy group, Connie and I made our way along the darkened corridors.

"Do you suppose Lionel is here tonight?"

"If the door's unlocked, he must be. We can always check his office."

When we found it, the door to the Senior Warden's office was closed, but a light had been left on inside that spilled out over the transom.

I rapped on the door, but there was no answer.

"Wonder where he is?" whispered Connie.

I shrugged and led Connie down the stairs that would eventually bring us to the fellowship hall.

Suddenly she grabbed my arm and jerked me to a halt. "What's that?"

"What?"

"That sound."

We stood in silence, listening. Somewhere nearby, someone was whistling the theme from the movie *Titanic*. "Must be Lionel," I whispered back.

"I think we should get out of here, Hannah!"

"Shush. We can handle Lionel."

We followed the sound of the whistling to an area near the church kitchen where we found the door to the ladies' room propped open with a wooden wedge. The whistling emanated from inside. "Mr. Streeting?" I warbled.

The whistling ceased. Lionel emerged, blinking furiously, a roll of toilet tissue in each hand. "What do you want?" he asked. Then, recognizing me, added, "Mrs. Ives, is it? You've got the wrong day for therapy. That's Wednesday."

"I'm not here for therapy, Mr. Streeting. We're private detectives." I turned to my sister-in-law. "This is my partner, Connie Ives."

Connie's mouth flopped open and shut. Lionel's eyes narrowed suspiciously. "I thought you were here for therapy the other night."

"No, sir. I'm sorry if I misled you, but we're investigating the murder of Diane Sturges. Our client is one of her patients."

Lionel stared, his eyes enormous behind his glasses, the rolls of toilet paper quite forgotten. A war between propriety and curiosity must have been going on inside his head. Curiosity won out. He tucked the toilet paper under his arm. "What can I do for you, then?"

"You can help us set a trap for her killer."

His eyes widened. "A trap? How?"

"We have reason to believe that the killer will show up in the sanctuary tonight. Our plan is to trap him into a confession and record it on tape." Talking like that, I hoped I wouldn't get cited for overacting.

Lionel wagged his head back and forth. "I don't know. That sounds pretty dangerous."

I grasped his arm and pulled him aside, speaking to

him softly in what I hoped was a conspiratorial way. "He's also a pedophile, Mr. Streeting. We must get that man off the streets."

Lionel appeared to be wavering, but suddenly his eyes narrowed. "Wait a minute! Everyone knows about that Monica Lewinsky thing. Isn't it illegal to tape-record somebody without his knowledge?"

Of course it was. Everyone living in the state of Maryland during the whole unfortunate scandal knew that.

My mind was working fast. I remembered that Linda Tripp had recorded her conversations with Monica over a telephone. She'd also turned her tapes over to a New York City literary agent—how selfless, how patriotic—not to the police. I reminded Lionel of this.

I could see him taking it in. "I see, not quite the same thing, then, is it?"

"No, sir."

He chewed on this for a while, running an index finger absentmindedly around and around the inside of one of the toilet paper rolls. "I see your point, Mrs. Ives," he said at last. "How can I help?"

"We know you record the sermons each Sunday, Mr. Streeting. Is it possible to set that equipment up now?" I pushed up the sleeve of my sweater and checked the time. "It's just now six o'clock. If anything happens, and I've no guarantee that it will, we'll need to be ready to record around seven."

Suddenly noticing the toilet paper, Lionel blushed to the roots of his five-o'clock shadow. He waved a roll in our direction. "I was just checking the rest rooms for . . . well, you know."

Connie stepped forward. "Please go ahead and finish up, Mr. Streeting." She nodded toward the fellowship hall. "Then we'll need to stake out the sanctuary. Is this the way, sir?"

"Yes, yes. Just give me a minute." He disappeared into the ladies' room.

"Stake out? Sir?" I silently mouthed to Connie.

She shrugged. "In for a penny, in for a pound."

Before I could comment, the light in the rest room snapped out and Lionel reappeared, empty-handed. He kicked out the wooden wedge and pulled the door shut behind him. "Follow me, ladies."

Lionel led us down the corridor, past the kitchen, and into the deserted fellowship hall. I noticed that the chairs we had used during therapy had been folded and stacked neatly in a corner. In their place, long tables had been arranged, their tops covered with paper table-cloths taped down at each corner with red Mystik tape. "The monthly potluck supper," Lionel explained. He stopped. "Here we are."

"Here" was a solid wooden door with "Janitor" painted on it in three-inch-high block letters.

Streeting extracted a wad of keys from his pocket and unlocked the door, opening it to reveal a small, tidy room furnished with a metal desk and a gooseneck lamp. On a bookshelf behind the desk sat a professional-size cassette tape deck, an ancient reel-to-reel tape recorder, an amplifier, a tuner, several microphones, and assorted rectangular boxes labeled "Sony."

I peeked into one of the boxes and took out a blank cassette tape.

"We record sermons for our shut-ins," he explained.

I nodded and handed him the tape. "Can you set it up to record?"

"Certainly. Certainly." Lionel mashed a red button

on a wall-mounted power strip, causing all the equipment to spring to life. Digital displays glowed orange and green; red gauges oscillated wildly as if a radio were playing silently. He fiddled with some dials, flipped up a toggle switch, then slipped the tape I had given him into the drive.

"How do you activate the system?" I asked.

"I do that from here." He rested a hand on each hip, elbows pointing out. "I call it my command center." He pointed to a chair. On a shelf directly behind it sat a pair of identical speakers a few feet apart and angled in slightly. "I come down during the church announcements and turn it all on. Father Wylands always says a prayer before the sermon, so when I hear, 'Let us pray,' I push the record button and let 'er go."

I nodded, pretending to be impressed, but I was thinking how much easier it would be if the whole shebang could be operated by Father Wylands from a switch in the pulpit. But in that case, Lionel the High Lord of Toilet Paper and Everything Else would have one less excuse to hang around the church at night. "Can you show me the sanctuary?"

Leaving his equipment turned on, but carefully locking the door behind him, Lionel led us to a small door set in the wall. Surprisingly, it led to a spiral staircase about two and one half feet wide. He flipped on a light and began to climb, motioning for us to follow. "Careful!" he called down over his shoulder.

We wound around and around as we ascended, and I was thanking my lucky stars I wasn't any wider in the hips or especially prone to dizzy spells. At the top, we emerged through a door in the wall of the chancel just to the right of the altar. The door would be hidden from the congregation by the carved wooden bulk of the organ. "This is how our organist gets from the front of the church to the back balcony without interrupting the service." Lionel gestured toward the balcony, several hundred feet away. "The choir sits up there."

I wondered how Georgina managed to play the organ and conduct the choir at the same time, separated as they were by what seemed like half the length of a football field. Lionel must have read my thoughts. "There's another organ in the balcony, Mrs. Ives. Not a fine pipe organ like this one, of course." He stroked the wooden case lovingly. "But adequate." He polished an imaginary fingerprint off the case with the sleeve of his jacket.

"And the microphones?" Connie inquired. "Where might they be?"

Lionel snapped out of his reverie. "Ah, yes. The microphones. Let me show you. We have several."

The pulpit at All Hallows was also carved of dark wood, but much more elaborately than the organ. I counted twelve full-length statues of the Apostles around its base. An eagle, its wings spread out to hold whatever papers the priest preached from, decorated the top. Three short steps led from the chancel up to the pulpit. Lionel tiptoed up the steps, opened a small gate, then stepped inside the pulpit. "One mike is here." He pointed to a lavalier-style microphone that hung from a hook just inside the gate. "Father Wylands just clips it to his robe before he begins, although why he needs a lavalier mike, I couldn't say. It's not as if he ever *goes* anywhere while he's preaching." He stepped out, closing the gate behind him.

I noticed the long cord attached to the microphone and asked, "Aren't these microphones usually wireless?"

Lionel smiled down at me condescendingly. "Well, yes. But Father is hopelessly old-fashioned . . . and frugal. We'll use these until they wear out, I'm quite certain."

He waited until I had backed down the steps out of his way, then swanned after me, crossing the chancel to a lectern, also made of wood, but of a much plainer design. "We've a stationary microphone here," he explained. "It's so the readers can be heard by the congregation. Some of the women—" He stopped, looked from Connie to me, and evidently decided that whatever he had been about to say about women as readers wouldn't sit well with a pair of female private detectives. Instead, he pointed to a toggle switch mounted on the underside of the lectern. "But if I flip this switch here, the lectern can be patched into the recording system as well."

Connie had been observing this performance in silence. "Any other microphones?" she asked. "Like in the back?"

Lionel shook his head. "No, no. That's it."

"How can we be sure they're working properly?" I asked.

Lionel's face assumed a pained expression, as if we were questioning his integrity. "They work every Sunday. I don't know why they wouldn't work now." I stood my ground and simply stared at the man until he felt compelled to fill the silence. "But perhaps we should test it."

"Yes," I said. "Perhaps that would be best. Connie?"

Lionel bobbed and weaved his way back toward the spiral staircase with Connie at his heels. I checked my watch. Six-fifteen. In forty-five minutes we should know one way or the other about Dr. Voorhis.

I was standing at the lectern looking out over the empty pews and trying to calm my jittery nerves when Lionel materialized behind me. "Mrs. Ives?"

When I could breathe again, I said, "Yes?"

"When I get everything ready to go, I'll send the other Mrs. Ives up to tell you. Then you just speak into the microphones in a normal voice."

"Like this?" I leaned close to the microphone and intoned, " ' 'Twas brillig, and the slithy toves . . .' "

He raised both hands, palm out. "Not *that* loud, Mrs. Ives."

I straightened and took a step backward. "Like this? '. . . did gyre and gimble in the wabe.' "

He smiled a thin-lipped smile. "Much better." He executed an elegant about-face. "About five minutes," he called over his shoulder, and disappeared back down the rabbit hole.

" 'All mimsy were the borogoves,' " I continued, addressing the board on which the numbers for the hymns for the Seventh Sunday after Epiphany were displayed: 119, 123, and 128. I recognized 128—"We Three Kings." I tried out the tune with "and the mome raths outgrabe," but it didn't fit.

"Very enlightening." The familiar voice of Dr. Voorhis, smooth as satin, came at me out of nowhere.

"I haven't gotten to the best bits," I said into the shadows. I tried not to think about the Jabberwock, especially the bit about the vorpal blade that went snicker-snack.

Voorhis emerged from the baptistry alcove just to my left and stood squinting up at me in the dim light.

"You're early," I said, stating the obvious.

"I like to be prepared." It was a statement of fact, cool and dispassionate. "I knew who you were, you see."

"How? My note was anonymous."

"When you telephoned Claudia pretending to be from the police, Claudia was concerned. She called me. I simply dialed the number that had appeared on her caller ID. Need I tell you that it didn't ring at the police department?" I remembered, sheepishly, the threatening call my mother had answered on my phone. "I was going to pay you a visit in Annapolis, but then your note arrived." His teeth, long and narrow, flashed white. "This arrangement is much more convenient."

I wondered how long he had been standing in the alcove, listening. If he knew about the microphones, my proverbial goose would be cooked. "I didn't hear you come in."

"There's a side door, Mrs. Ives." He gestured toward the baptistry behind him. "It responded conveniently to manipulation by credit card."

"I see."

Voorhis took a tentative step forward, then paused in the side aisle, blocking my view of a marble memorial shelf on which someone had placed a vase of fresh flowers. "You said you had something to discuss, Mrs. Ives. So, here I am." He waved a ringed hand. "Discuss."

My fingers found the toggle switch on the lectern. Praying it wouldn't respond with a telltale click, I turned on the microphone. I steadied myself with both hands gripping the lectern. "The very fact that you're here, Dr. Voorhis, answers one question."

"And that is?"

"That you sexually abused your daughter, Diane."

"Abuse?" His hand rested on a pew. I could see the glint of a stone in his Johns Hopkins ring. "What nonsense! I loved my daughter, and she loved me. She was my joy, and I hers. Our times together were . . . special."

My stomach lurched, and it was all I could do to keep from throwing up. I could tell by the expression on Dr. Voorhis's face that he actually believed what he was saying.

"But she was only a child!"

He shook his head. "You don't understand. I didn't abuse Diane." He addressed me as he would a difficult and not very intelligent child. "Mrs. Ives, Mrs. Ives. How can it possibly be abuse, when she enjoyed it, too?"

My head reeled. I tried to imagine what I would do if I caught Paul fondling Emily. I felt like flying across the sanctuary and tearing this creep's face off with my bare hands, slowly, strip by painful strip.

"Your wife found out about it, didn't she?"

His silver eyebrows nearly met. "My wife?"

"The first Mrs. Voorhis. She couldn't live with that knowledge, could she?"

"What do you know about that?"

"I can read old newspapers, Dr. Voorhis. I know about the suicide note."

Suddenly I began to panic. What if the lectern mike wasn't patched in? What if Lionel had actually thrown the switch when he was showing it to us earlier? What if I had turned it *off* instead of *on*? I would have to lure the doctor closer to the microphone in the pulpit.

I stepped out from behind the security of the lectern feeling small and vulnerable. Dr. Voorhis stood only twenty feet away.

"You don't know anything, Mrs. Ives. My wife was deranged. That note you refer to was full of delusional crap."

"If it was all crap, why did you leave Waterville?"

"Small town. Smaller minds. There were some who believed the lies Fiona told about Diane and me. She was a disturbed woman, Mrs. Ives. Very disturbed." He took another step in my direction and I retreated, inching toward the pulpit as casually as I could without alarming him.

"But Diane came to believe it, too, didn't she, Dr. Voorhis?"

Since our conversation began, the doctor's attention had never wavered from my face, but he stared at me then with frightening intensity. "It's a dangerous thing when a doctor wanders down a pseudoscientific path and suddenly begins to believe all the garbage she's been peddling."

"Tell me, what happened the afternoon she died?"

We stood face-to-face, separated only by the three steps that led from the sanctuary up to the chancel. "She said she had something important to ask me." He smiled, remembering. "Diane was always asking me for advice about something—taxes, investments. So when I got to her office I was completely blindsided. To put it simply, she attacked me. She held me responsible for her mother's suicide, for having to leave her friends in Waterville." He stroked his tie. "Seems I'd ruined her life. Balls! She was a successful student because of me. She became a respected therapist because of me!"

"Why did you kill her?"

He thrust a hand into his jacket pocket, and I held my breath. *Did he have a gun?*

"I didn't mean to," he said at last. "It was an accident. Diane threatened to ruin my career. I tried to talk sense into her, of course, but I'd never seen such hate! After all I'd done for my daughter, she was out to ruin me." He touched a spot on his cheek, as if it were still tender from a blow. "She came at me, swinging with both fists. Then she started screaming. She was hysterical. I just wanted to calm her down, for Christ's sake. Somehow we ended up on the balcony. . . . I'm not sure what happened next. She just tumbled over the railing." Voorhis's dark wool suit, so well-tailored only minutes before, suddenly didn't seem to fit correctly. "I loved her so much . . ."

"You have a curious way of showing it."

"Ah, yes. The abuse. That's a laugh!" He paused, one hand still in the pocket of his jacket. "She started it, you know. When she was three. She loved to take a bath with her daddy. Then when she was five, she kept crawling into my bed, begging for a back rub. At first it was just cuddling. But then . . ." He lounged against the first pew, lost in thought. "Such a sexy little girl. So provocative, I couldn't help myself; no man could. You should have seen how she dressed in junior high—those skintight miniskirts and low-cut tank tops. Half the time she didn't even wear a bra. I *begged* Fiona to do something about the way Diane dressed, but she didn't. Oh, Diane knew what she was doing, all right."

"That *is* sexual abuse," I insisted. "No matter what her age, no matter what your relationship with her was, you had all the power. And if you used that power to pressure your daughter into a sexual relationship, your wife was right. Diane was being abused."

I studied his face, searching it for signs of understanding. "Dr. Voorhis, even if Diane walked into your bedroom stark naked and came on to you, as a responsible adult you should have said, 'Whoa. We've got a problem here.' You were her *father*! Why didn't you get her some professional help?"

He looked confused. "One night not long after Diane turned fourteen, she asked me to stop. And I did. It was over."

That may have settled the matter for him, but not for me. "But, Dr. Voorhis . . ."

He advanced. "How can I make you understand?"

I retreated. I raised my hand as if to steady myself

against the pulpit, but I was carefully feeling around for the microphone cord. If Voorhis got any closer, I planned to grab the microphone and scream the church down. I know it sounds insane under the circumstances, but I almost smiled, imagining Lionel sitting down below in his headphones, fiddling with his dials. I would rupture his eardrums for sure.

"That day in her office, she said she hoped I'd get AIDS or Alzheimer's disease. She told me she'd dance on my grave the day I died." Tears glistened in his eyes and he seemed somewhere far away. "She was Daddy's special little girl."

My searching fingers found the microphone cord, and as I began to curl them around it, Dr. Voorhis suddenly snapped to attention and took another step toward me. "As much as I loved her, I couldn't afford to have this become public knowledge."

I stalled for time. He was so close that I could tell that the paisley swirls on his tie were actually multicolored fish. "You got away with it before, in Waterville," I said. "You could get away with it again."

"Ah, but that was a very different time and place, Mrs. Ives. Very different. Nowadays, a man can be branded guilty of sexual abuse on the flimsiest of evidence—branded with an indelible A, if you will, that all the evidence to the contrary cannot erase. No, I can't afford to have even a hint of this known. I work with children, Mrs. Ives. It would ruin me."

His voice was steady and so calm that I was totally unprepared for what came next. Voorhis's arm shot out and circled my neck in a dangerous embrace, slamming my forehead against his chest. I managed to grab the microphone cord, but it dangled loosely from my hand.

Voorhis reached around me with his left hand. I felt

it slide slowly, almost sensuously down my arm until his hand reached mine and he was able to prize the microphone from my fingers. His arm tightened around my neck, like a vise, and my nose was squashed flat against his tie. I could barely breathe, let alone scream.

A sudden jerk nearly snapped my neck. Voorhis had yanked the microphone cord from its socket. Seconds later, he looped the cord around my neck and was using both hands, those hands that should have been dedicated to healing, to draw the cord tight. I couldn't speak, swallow, scream, or breathe. I clawed at the ever-tightening cord, but couldn't get my fingers under it.

I aimed a knee at his groin. A yelp told me I'd made contact with the target, but the pressure around my neck only increased. Voorhis's face, inches from my own, remained impassive. Except for a thin sheen of sweat across his brow, he could have been preparing his taxes or waiting in traffic for a light to change. The space behind my eyes turned red with the pulsing blood inside my head, then black, as waves of darkness washed over me. My knees buckled.

When you're dying, they say your life passes before your eyes. Not so. My last thought before I slipped into unconsciousness was Listerine. His breath smells of Listerine. Imagine! Remembering to use a mouthwash before setting out to kill somebody.

SUDDENLY I COULD BREATHE, AND THE PRESSURE on my neck was replaced by a heavy weight across my legs. Connie's face swam into view. She stood over me, a towering giant, Brünnhilde wielding a wooden pole. At the other end of the pole dangled the Maryland state flag. "Are you OK?" The flagpole clattered to the floor as she bent to help me up. But first she had to roll Voorhis away with a push of her foot.

Free of my attacker, I sat on the chancel steps, rubbing my throat. It hurt to swallow, and I was certain my voice box had been badly bruised. I looked at the doctor, whose head was gashed and bleeding profusely. "Is he dead?" I croaked.

"I doubt it. I just knocked him cold."

"Thank God you showed up! I wondered what had happened to you. Couldn't you hear what was going on?"

"Every word. Lionel switched on at the beginning of Voorhis's sad tale and recorded almost everything." She waved toward the hidden staircase. "I've been standing just inside the stairwell over there."

"No rush, I was just being strangled."

"Well, I didn't want to interrupt until he was finished confessing."

I rubbed my neck where the impression made by the microphone cord had bitten deeply into my flesh. "You could have made your presence known a tad sooner. I really thought I was going to die!"

Connie checked to make sure Voorhis was still out of it, then knelt in front of me. "As soon as he made a grab for you, I ran. I was going to jump him, but then I saw the flag and thought a piece of wood might be a more persuasive weapon than my bare hands."

Connie turned to Dr. Voorhis. She slipped out of her cardigan and used it to staunch the blood that was gushing from a wound on his scalp. When Voorhis began to move, his legs twitched, then he groaned. I grabbed the man's ankles with both hands and sat on his legs to keep him from getting away.

"It's a small cut," Connie announced, touching Voorhis's forehead with her fingers. "Might need a few stitches is all."

Voorhis stirred, his head flopped to one side, and he stared into the dark with unfocused eyes. "I'm sorry," he said.

I felt no sympathy for the bastard. "Sorry for what you did or sorry you got caught?"

"I've lost everything." He closed his eyes. "Fiona, Diane, Loraine . . ."

"Who's Loraine?" Connie wanted to know. She rolled up her stained sweater and slipped it between Voorhis's head and the cold stone floor. "Don't move," she ordered. "There's an ambulance on the way."

I was surprised. "Ambulance?"

"Lionel called nine-one-one," Connie said. As if

hearing a summons, the Senior Warden appeared from behind the pulpit. He studied the three of us. We must have appeared a strange triptych arranged up there between the pulpit and the lectern. With his hands clasped in front of him, Lionel glanced about as if looking for something to do. He picked up the lavalier mike from where it lay on the floor and returned it to its proper hook in the pulpit, not noticing the severed wire. A look of disapproval told me we were naughty children who had just messed up his sanctuary with a bit of roughhousing. He began to wring his hands like Uriah Heep. "I never . . ." he began. Then, "Nothing like this has ever . . ." He sputtered on for a few seconds, but failed to form a single coherent sentence. He pointed to the blood on the stone steps. "I'll just get . . . No, I suppose the police will be wanting to see that."

Suddenly, Lionel glanced over his shoulder toward the west doors as if something outside had attracted his attention. "I'll just see if they're here yet. They'll be wanting the door unlocked, I suppose." He stood for a few more seconds, rocking back and forth on the heels of his shiny vinyl shoes. "Shall I?"

Connie kept a firm grip on Voorhis's upper arm, while I continued to perch on his legs.

"Yes, Lionel. You go ahead and do that."

Encouraged, he turned smartly on his left toe and scurried down the center aisle, gradually disappearing into the shadows at the rear of the sanctuary, his keys jangling as he walked. The distinctive sound of a deadbolt lock being thrown echoed through the quiet sanctuary followed by a click. A soft light illuminated the west door.

I smiled at Connie. "Thank you," I said.

"I'm sorry I didn't believe you at first, Hannah."

"I do have an overactive imagination sometimes," I said, "but you have to admit that this time I was right on target."

A siren cut through the night, followed by the squeal of tires hitting the curb, hard. I heard Lionel say, "In there."

When Dennis and Paul burst through the door and came rushing down the aisle, I looked around for a place to hide. "Paul!" I turned to Connie.

Connie shrugged apologetically. "I know, I know. I said I wasn't going to tell them, but I lied."

Paul took the chancel steps in a single bound and was soon kneeling before me, my hands swallowed up in both of his. "Are you all right?" His eyes searched mine, as if the truth would be written there.

"I think so. Yes." I was stiff from sitting on Dr. Voorhis's bony shins. "Help me up."

While Paul pulled me to my feet and smothered me with attention, Dennis stooped over Connie, his strong hands gripping his thighs for balance. "What happened? I thought you said seven o'clock."

"Voorhis was choking Hannah, so I clobbered him with that pole." She pointed to the Maryland flag that lay on the floor several feet away. For Paul's sake, I was grateful that she didn't elaborate.

"He confessed," I told Dennis as I straightened to my full height. I adjusted my bra just in case my new breast had slipped sideways and tucked my shirt back into my trousers. "It's all on tape." Paul's arm slipped around my waist and pulled me close.

Meanwhile, Dennis was attending to Voorhis. The doctor stood unsteadily; he shook his head as if to clear it, then winced in pain. Blood stained the lapel and breast pocket of his suit.

"We'll see you get some medical attention, sir." After what the man had done, I couldn't believe Dennis was being so nice to him. I found myself wishing that they'd sew up that gash in his head with a dirty string and darning needle without the benefit of anesthesia.

"Can you walk?" Dennis asked the doctor.

Dr. Voorhis nodded. Keeping a firm grip on the doctor's upper arm, Dennis led him to a seat in a front pew, watched until he had sat down on the blue velvet cushion, then blocked any possible escape route with his body.

Lionel scurried up the aisle. "There's more police," he announced before disappearing again, only to return in thirty seconds to add that the ambulance had arrived as well.

"That will be Williams and Duvall." Dennis looked at me. "I gave them a call."

While the paramedics attended to Dr. Voorhis, Connie and I sat in a pew and gave our statements to Sergeant Williams. Officer Duvall scribbled down notes about what we told them in a small gray notebook.

Lionel disappeared down the spiral staircase and returned almost at once with something in his hand. He produced the cassette tape with a flourish usually reserved for magicians who pull rabbits out of hats. Sergeant Williams received it gratefully.

The paramedics had transferred Dr. Voorhis to a stretcher and began to roll him down the aisle. As they passed my pew, I held up a hand. "Just a minute. There's something I want to ask him." I leaned over the stretcher, feeling powerful for a change. "Tell me, Doctor, why did you come to my hospital room?"

Dr. Voorhis stared straight up at the ceiling.

"What was in that syringe?"

The doctor turned his head in my direction, slowly,

like a ventriloquist's dummy. His mouth moved. "I don't have the foggiest idea what you're talking about." He waved a hand. "Let's get out of here, gentlemen."

The last I saw of Dr. Voorhis was his smile . . . thin-lipped and sinister. I thought about that smile long after he was driven away in the ambulance, with Officer Duvall sitting by his side. I think about it today.

The five who were left stood on the porch of All Hallows and watched the vehicles disappear down Roland Avenue into the night. I shivered and held tight to my husband's hand. "What do you suppose will happen to him, Dennis?"

"I think after they get his head stitched and bandaged, he'll have had time to think. However good confession may be for the soul, I'll bet he'll have forgotten all about it on the advice of his lawyer."

"But we got it on tape!" Connie exclaimed.

Paul squeezed my hand. "Let's hope the lawyers don't figure out a way to suppress the tape as evidence."

Dennis stared in the direction where the ambulance had disappeared. A light snow had begun to fall. "With lawyers, anything's possible. Consider O.J."

"Let's not," I said.

"What next?" Paul was resting his chin on top of my head, and I could feel his chin move whenever he talked.

Dennis reached for Connie's hand. "I'm taking this lady home, and I suggest you do the same."

"Hannah?" Paul asked.

"Home." I turned to Paul and wrapped my arms around his waist, enjoying the solid, familiar feel and smell of him. I looked up into his face. "But first, we need to stop at Georgina's."

YOU CAN'T JUDGE A BOOK BY ITS COVER. THE PROV-
erb came to mind as Paul and I stood on the sidewalk in
front of Scott and Georgina's neat, middle-class home,
complete with white picket fence. Paul reached out to
open the gate, but I stopped him. "Just a minute." He
seemed puzzled, but waited patiently while I stood in the
cold night air admiring my sister's house. Golden light
shone through the lace curtains and cast warm rectangles on the porch. A TV murmured softly somewhere inside; a shadow, probably Julie, darted across the glass like
a nymph. It was a Norman Rockwell painting, the epito-
me of home and family. It was difficult for me to contem-
plate what *really* might be going on inside that house. I
sighed, and my breath came out in a white cloud.

"Hannah?"

I shivered inside my warmest jacket. "It's OK. I was
just thinking that appearances can be so deceptive."

"Do you want to come back later?"

"No. I need to let Georgina know that they've arrested Diane Sturges's killer."

"When she finds out who did it, do you think she'll welcome the news?"

I shrugged. "Only one way to find out."

Paul opened the gate and I passed through ahead of him. Once on the porch, we discovered that the screen door was locked for the night, so we rang the bell.

The porch boards vibrated as pint-size feet scrambled to answer. The chain lock rattled, the door eased open, and the serious blue eyes of one of the twins peered around it. "It's Aunt Hannah!" he shouted, throwing the door wide.

I could see from the pattern of freckles on his nose which twin it was. "Hi, Sean."

"We already ate dinner."

"We haven't come for dinner, Sean. We came to talk to your mommy."

"She's in the kitchen." Sean unlatched the screen door and backed away as we opened it and came through. At that moment, Dylan careened around the corner, chasing a ball. He fell on it, hugged it against his chest, and rolled over three times. "Hi! Wanna play soccer?"

"Me or your uncle Paul?" I asked.

Dylan scowled. "Girls don't play soccer." He looked at Paul for confirmation, then asked, uncertainly, "Do they?"

"I'm afraid they do, squirt."

"Oh." Dylan struggled to his feet, still clutching the ball. He aimed it at Sean, threw, and made a direct hit, thumping his brother soundly on the head.

"Ouch!" Sean whined. "You cut that out!" We were instantly forgotten as Dylan streaked around the corner into the living room with Sean in hot pursuit. Still wearing our coats, we wandered back to the kitchen.

The table held the remains of dinner. Julie sat in a chair, stirring a bowl of ice cream into chocolate soup.

Scott lounged at the head of the table, leaning on his elbows, sipping coffee. Two empty bowls, one licked clean, marked the places Sean and Dylan had recently occupied. Georgina stood at the sink, her back to us. A flowered apron was tied in a bow at her waist.

Scott's eyebrows disappeared into his hair. "Well, look who's here!"

With her hands still dealing with a greasy roasting pan in the sink, Georgina glanced over her shoulder. "Oh, hi."

I pulled out a chair and sat down. "Paul and I have news for you."

Scott set his mug down and stared at me curiously. "What news?"

Georgina turned, the picture of domesticity, wiping her hands on her apron. "Julie, are you going to eat your food or just play with it?" She must have suspected the worst. I could tell she was trying to get rid of her daughter.

Julie laid down her spoon, picked up the bowl with both chubby hands, tipped it toward her mouth, and slurped. When the ice cream was gone, she burped loudly.

Georgina snatched the bowl from her daughter's hands and banged it on the table. "That's enough for you, young lady. Go get ready for your bath."

Julie's chin was coated with chocolate. Scott held her chin and gently wiped it off with his napkin. "Off you go, missy."

Julie slid off her chair, ran across the room, and threw her arms around my knees. "Hi, Aunt Hannah." Traces of chocolate remained in the corners of her mouth as she grinned up at me.

I patted her head. "Did you save any ice cream for me, Julie?"

Julie shook her head solemnly. "Daddy ate it all up."

Scott smiled broadly at his daughter. "Bath. Go."

"Bye!" Julie scampered down the hall.

Georgina watched her go, then turned to stand behind Scott's chair, a damp dish towel draped over her shoulder. "What's wrong?" I could see the wheels turning. She thought something had happened to Mother.

"Why don't you sit down, Georgina?" Paul pulled out a chair and motioned her into it.

Georgina settled into the chair and turned her face toward us, lined with worry.

"It's what's right," I told her. "The police have arrested Dr. Voorhis."

"What?" Georgina shot a panicked look at Scott. "Why?"

"He killed his daughter, Diane."

"No!" The color drained from her face. Against the bright red and yellow flowers on the bib of her apron she looked pale. Scott reached out and gathered her hand into his.

"It's true. He confessed. He'd sexually abused her throughout her childhood, Georgina. When she confronted him about it, he panicked, they fought . . . and the rest you know."

"Then Daddy didn't kill Diane?"

"No."

"I was sure he'd done it."

"Daddy didn't kill Diane Sturges, and he didn't hurt you."

Georgina shook her head. "That doesn't change what he did to me."

I tried another tack. "Do you remember a woman named Stephanie Golden?"

Georgina nodded. "She used to come to the therapy group, but dropped out all of a sudden."

"Do you know why?"

"No."

"She told me she had come to believe that no matter what Diane Sturges seemed to think, she had not been sexually abused. When she mentioned this in therapy, something must have triggered a memory in Diane. Memories of abuse at the hands of her own father came washing over her. I think Diane realized then what a mistake she had made with some of her patients."

"Mistake?" Scott held tightly to his wife's hand.

"Georgina was never abused, Scott. Dr. Sturges just made her *think* she was."

"That's not true!" Georgina leapt to her feet, snatching her hand away from Scott's. "It happened! Why doesn't anybody believe me?"

"Georgina, you had a collection of symptoms that were similar to the doctor's own, which when put together in her own troubled mind screamed 'abuse.' But, they can also be symptoms of depression, Georgina."

Georgina pressed her back against the refrigerator door as if she were trying to merge with it, sobbing. "No, no!"

"Christ!" Scott was on his feet, too. "Can't you leave her alone?" He tried to gather his wife into his arms, but she pushed him away.

"I want you all to go away and leave me alone."

"Georgina, just do me one favor. Ask your new therapist about it."

Georgina stared purposely at a blank wall, her lower lip quivering.

At that inconvenient moment, the telephone rang. We all ignored it. I thought that the answering machine had picked up until Dylan poked his head into the kitchen. "It's Aunt Ruth," he announced. "She wants you, Daddy."

Scott took a long look at this wife, as if to reassure himself that she wouldn't disappear the minute he took his eyes off her. He raised a hand, palm out, in a hold-that-thought way, indicating that we were all to stay put until he had taken care of business. He reached for the extension which was mounted on the wall next to the refrigerator. "Yes, Ruth?" His face grew so serious that he had all of our attention. "I see. When?" He looked at me and shook his head. "Hannah and Paul are here. Sit tight, Ruth. We'll be right over."

"It's your mother," he said as he hung up the phone. His slender hands gripped the back of his chair. "She's had another heart attack. It doesn't look good."

Georgina's eyes grew wide and she slid down the refrigerator door until she was sitting on the floor just as she had done that day in my kitchen. "Mommy!" she wailed. "Mommy!" I didn't wait to hear any more. I raced out of the house with Paul on my heels.

I beat Paul to my car and had the engine running even before he folded his long legs into the passenger seat. We lost a few precious minutes turning the car around at the end of Colorado, where I used some language I bring out only on special occasions.

The light snow had turned to rain, transforming the streets into a glistening black ribbon that rolled out ahead of me. The traffic signal at Falls Road and the lights of the Texaco station merged into a kaleidoscope of colors, patterns that changed every time the wipers swept across the windshield in front of my face.

"Slow down, Hannah."

I accelerated through the intersection and swerved right onto the entrance ramp, then left, merging easily into traffic southbound on the JFX. "What if something happens before I get there?"

"Why don't you pull over and let me drive?" The last time he'd used that tone Paul had been disciplining Emily.

"No. I'm fine, really." I slowed to fifty-five and concentrated on the winding expressway, trying not to think about what life would be like without my mother. At the hospital, I screeched to a stop, wrenched my door open, and slid out, leaving Paul to deal with finding a space in the parking garage around the corner.

The revolving door spit me out into the hospital lobby, which was warm and dry. I brushed drops of water off my jacket and out of my hair and, ignoring the reception desk where I should have signed in for a visitor's badge, I turned left and hurried past the various concessions, now closed for the night. A glass elevator took me to the coronary care unit on the third floor, where I pushed my finger impatiently on the buzzer until I could identify myself and the nurse let me in.

I was surprised when I saw Mother, because she looked just the same: a thin, pale form beneath a light blanket. The same number of tubes and wires still tethered her to a bank of machines that whirred and sighed and bleeped in the same familiar, almost comforting, way.

Daddy and Ruth had arrived and were sitting in armless chairs on either side of the bed. Ruth glanced up when I entered, but Daddy didn't even seem to notice that I was there. My sister rose and pulled me aside. She spoke softly, her voice husky with emotion. "She's stable now, Hannah. But her heart is too weak."

I didn't realize I was crying until I felt tears slide down my cheeks. "What are we going to do?"

Ruth's fingers dug into my arm. "Daddy talked it over

with Mother. She's signed a paper that the next time her heart stops, they won't try to revive her."

Something inside me died. "Oh, no!"

"It's what I want, Hannah." My mother's voice was surprisingly strong. She raised an arm, then let it fall back onto the covers. "Living like this is no life."

I rushed to her side, knocking over the chair that Ruth had been sitting in. "Oh, Mom. Please. Don't!"

"It's my decision, darling."

"But you haven't even seen your great-granddaughter! You haven't met Chloe!"

Mother sighed, and turned her head toward my father. "She'll get to know her great-grandfather."

"*Please* don't talk like that! It sounds so final." I had faced death before, the possibility of my own. But that was easier somehow, because it would have been I who was doing the going. When I thought about a future without my mother, it tore at my heart.

Ruth stood behind me, a steadying hand on my back. "We love you so much, Mother."

Mother's mouth curved into a half smile and her violet eyes, shrunken within their sockets, moved from my tortured face to Ruth's. "Tell me more about Bali, Ruth." The subject was closed.

Ruth righted her chair and positioned herself next to the bed, while I alternately paced across the small room or stared out the window into the wet Baltimore night, consumed with self-pity. When Paul arrived after parking the car, Ruth was describing emerald hills and rice paddies, ancient Oriental temples with fat golden gods. My sister had a poet's way with words. Paul took up a position in the corner as if acknowledging that he wasn't an integral part of the family by blood but would be there if I needed him.

"I'm sorry you had to cut your trip short," Mother said when Ruth paused in her story to allow a nurse to check on the equipment Mom was attached to.

"I was coming home anyway, Mom." Ruth jerked her head in my direction. "Someone needs to keep Hannah on the straight and narrow."

If only she knew, I thought.

Paul spoke for the first time. "Hannah, have you told them?"

I gawped at him, like a stranded fish. How could it be that the events of the past four hours had flown so completely out of my head? Bali! What the hell did Bali have to do with anything? I had important news, and I'd nearly risked letting my mother go without telling her.

"Mom." I approached her bed. "Dad." I touched his hand where it rested on the covers. "They've arrested someone for the murder of Georgina's therapist."

Dad's jaw dropped, and my mother lifted her head slightly from her pillow.

"It was her father who did it, Dr. Voorhis."

"Dr. Voorhis?" My mother's pale face grew even paler. "Isn't he the children's pediatrician?"

I nodded and sat down.

"Why on earth?"

Dad stood behind me while I talked, his fingers drumming rhythmically on the metal frame of my chair, sending vibrations skittering up my back. I told the whole story, except for the part about Dr. Voorhis's attempt to silence me.

"They've taken him away," I added. "I think he'll have quite a headache in the morning."

Mom's eyes moved from my face to my father's. "Thank God."

"Have you told Georgina?" Ruth wanted to know.

"That's what we were doing when you called."

"Do you think Georgina finally realizes that those memories she had were strictly in her imagination?" Daddy sounded more hopeful that he had any right to be.

"I really don't know. Dr. Sturges had a powerful influence on her patients. All of them. It may be tough to overcome."

Ruth massaged her neck as if it were sore. "I thought you said that Georgina is seeing a new doctor."

"Scott says she is. We can always hope that the new guy doesn't see abuse lurking behind every tree."

"You *know* I didn't do anything to that child," Daddy said.

"We all know that, Daddy."

"Where's Georgina now?" Mom's voice was barely a whisper.

"I don't know, Mom. I'll see if I can find out." If Mother died while I was trying to locate Georgina, I would never forgive my sister.

"Do you want me to come?" Paul lurched to his feet. I shook my head. "I'm just going to make a phone call."

"There's a phone right here." Daddy pointed to the telephone on a bedside table.

I wanted a little privacy, but couldn't think of a graceful way to escape. I dialed my sister's number.

"Hello?" It was one of the twins.

"Sean?"

I had guessed right. "Hi, Aunt Hannah."

"Can I talk to your mommy?"

"She's not here."

That was a good sign. "How about your daddy?"

"Not here either. Want to talk to Mrs. Crombie?"

"Who's Mrs. Crombie?"

"She's the lady next door. Mommy started crying, so Daddy got Mrs. Crombie to come over. She made us popcorn."

"That's nice. Can I talk to Mrs. Crombie, Sean?" I held the phone away from my ear while Sean summoned the helpful neighbor with a shout so loud it made me wonder if she was watching my niece and nephews from her own home.

"You don't need to shout, Sean. I'm right here." Mrs. Crombie sounded upbeat and young, like one of the upwardly mobile professionals who lived on Georgina's street. She told me that Scott and Georgina had left for the hospital forty-five minutes ago, saying that she didn't know when to expect them home.

That was the best news I had heard all day. I wished the woman good-bye, then leaned back against the wall. I checked my watch. If they left the house forty-five minutes ago, they should be here now. Where the hell were they?

When I tuned back in, Ruth was talking about feng shui. All the beds in Bali were oriented with their heads toward some sacred mountain. Still no Georgina. Mother lay quietly, almost smiling while her machines beeped in a regular, reassuring rhythm. I talked myself into thinking that it was going to be all right. *Where there's life there's hope.*

My mouth was furry and dry, tasting of the garlic in the slice of pizza I'd had for lunch. "Want something to drink?"

Ruth nodded. "Tea would be nice." Dad just shook his head and pointed to a paper cup on the bedside table.

Paul came to life. "Let me help."

"That'd be great." I didn't want to be alone. Not for a single minute.

I was hungry, too, but I knew from past experience that at this hour, all the food concessions would be closed. Paul and I left the coronary care unit and went in search of the vending machines, which were tucked into an alcove farther along the hall. We bought a Coke and two teas.

When we returned I was delighted to find Scott and Georgina sitting in the waiting area just outside the door that led into the coronary care unit, holding hands. I noticed that Georgina had come away wearing her apron. A bright red corner of it peeked out where her coat fell open at her knees.

"Georgina?" Her face was red and puffy from crying, her eyelids swollen.

"Oh, Hannah!" She sprang to her feet and lunged in my direction, startling me so that I nearly dropped the Styrofoam cup I was holding. I spread my arms wide while Georgina wrapped herself around me. Paul lifted the cup from my hands, freeing me to hug Georgina properly.

"How's Mom?" Scott directed the question to Paul over my head.

"Stable for now."

Georgina released me and stepped back, her tear-stained face a mask of misery. "I'm so ashamed."

I felt like saying *You ought to be,* but was so glad that my sister seemed to have come around that I didn't dare. "She's asking for you," I said.

Georgina raised an eyebrow. "She is?"

"She wants to see you, Georgina."

Georgina turned to her husband. "I don't know what to do, Scott."

"It's up to you, honey. Remember what Dr. Loring said." He stared at his wife for a long time without blinking.

Georgina flopped onto a chair and patted the one next to her. "Can you sit down for a minute, Hannah?"

"Sure."

Paul dragged another chair over so we could all sit together. It took a while for Georgina to come to the point. She sat there peeling the frosted pink polish off her nails, not looking directly at me. "I've been thinking about what you said," she began. She chipped away at a nail with her index finger. "After you left, I telephoned Dr. Loring. He's helping me put things together."

I nodded, my hands wrapped around my cup. "And?"

"Suggestion can be a powerful thing."

"So I've heard."

"Dr. Loring indicated that I might have been unduly influenced by some of the other women in that therapy group."

Hallelujah! A crack in the facade. I hoped that if I waited long enough, it might split wide open and my real baby sister would arise from the ruins.

"Stephanie Golden said the same thing, Georgina. It wasn't until she withdrew from the group that she started thinking more clearly and began to question Dr. Sturges's diagnosis."

Georgina made the connection. "Hannah, you have to understand that all that stuff about the Cabbage Patch doll seemed so *real* to me. I could see her face just as plain as day. She had on a yellow flowered dress and little buttoned shoes." She shook her head. "But I checked into what you told me, and you're right. There's no way I could have had one."

I leaned against the back of the chair and exhaled. I felt dizzy, as if I'd been holding my breath for a week.

"I have to be honest," Georgina continued. "I'm still not one-hundred-percent sure that nothing ever happened, but after listening to you and to Dr. Loring, I'm willing to give Dad the benefit of the doubt."

After all we'd been though in the past seven weeks, I felt like tossing my teacup into the air and dancing a jig on the tabletop. Scott looked more thoughtful. "That therapy group was like a fire. Each member was a log. The more logs, the hotter the fire. But as the logs were pulled away . . ."

"When I pulled *myself* away," Georgina corrected, "it was if the fire grew cooler." She studied me silently, chewing on her lower lip. "But I still have a feeling that something happened in Sicily. If it wasn't Daddy . . . ?"

I grew suddenly cold, as if a cloud had passed over the sun. *Paolo? Charming, lighthearted Paolo?* I shivered. *No. No way.*

As if he had read my mind, Paul laid a comforting hand on my shoulder, then spoke directly to Georgina. "It's your mother who needs you now, Georgina. We may not have much time."

Scott grabbed his wife's upper arm and shook it. "Go!"

"But . . ."

Scott stood, took her hand, and pulled her to her feet. "Go, Georgina, or you may regret it for the rest of your life." He pulled a crumpled tissue out of his shirt pocket and waited for her to blow her nose and wipe her eyes. She turned a blotched face toward me.

"Ready?" I asked.

"Ready."

Outside our mother's room Georgina stood frozen, looking in. I knew she had to be taking in the machines and the sounds and smells of serious illness. Fresh tears brimmed in her eyes, and she must have seen what I did—Ruth and Dad flanking the bed; Paul perched on the arm of a chair talking to Emily on the telephone. And our mother.

Daddy spotted Georgina first. His face lit up, causing Ruth to pause in mid-sentence, turn her head, and follow his gaze toward the door. "Georgina!"

Georgina ignored him, brushing past Ruth without a word of greeting, and leaned over the bed. She grasped Mother's hand where it lay on top of the covers and pressed it to her cheek. "I'm so, so sorry."

Mother's eyes had been closed, but she opened them and smiled.

"How can you ever forgive me after all the terrible things I said?"

"We love you, Georgina." She reached up to touch her daughter's cheek, still glistening with tears. "We *both* love you."

I hoped that Georgina would apologize to Daddy then, but she didn't even look at him. She bowed her head and stared at the floor, then positioned herself on the side of the bed nearest Ruth.

I crossed the room and stood on the opposite side of the bed with my father, watching until Georgina's sobs subsided and Scott helped her settle into a chair he had dragged in from somewhere.

Mother's eyelids fluttered closed. I panicked, thinking she had died. I laid my hand on her chest and was comforted to find that it still rose and fell beneath the blanket, however slightly. She was asleep.

Daddy had taken Mother's hand and was rubbing it tenderly. Her skin was translucent and slipped easily, too easily over her bones. It was so thin, I worried it would tear. After a few moments, she awoke and beamed up at my father, a radiant smile reminiscent of happier times that quite took my breath away. "I'm ready, George." Her eyelids closed and I heard a shuddering sigh.

I didn't need the machines to tell me that Mother was gone, leaving her body, still warm, beneath my hand. Her spirit simply departed, fleeing its broken-down body and soaring, I knew with confidence, toward heaven. I gazed up, imagining I would see it, a flickering light like Tinker Bell, hovering near the ceiling—*flick-flick-flick*—gazing down upon her family with love. All the clapping in the world—*I believe! I believe!*—wouldn't bring Mother back now. Only her shell remained, pale and serene, the hint of a smile on its lips. What made Mother Mother had simply floated away.

One of the machines screamed; another bleated. Nurses rushed in from all points of the compass. One grabbed for the crash cart, but my father stayed her hand. "Not this time," he said. The nurse complied. "I'm sorry, sir." It was then that his face crumpled. Daddy's knees buckled and he slumped, racked with sobs, over my mother's body.

My tears wouldn't come. I imagined I saw Mom still, hovering near the window. Any minute her gossamer wings would batter against the pane and I would lift up the sash and release her spirit into the night.

Georgina had been curled in a chair, her cheek resting against her arm. Her hair had escaped from its clip and cascaded over her arm, the color of rust in the subdued light. When the alarms began to sound she ground a fist into her eye, focused on the scene around the bed, and said, "Daddy?"

Daddy sucked in his lips, struggling for control. Huge tears coursed down his cheeks and glistened in the shadow of a beard that had sprouted on his face over the past few days. Georgina's wail rent the night, more piercing than the machine that the nurse had just silenced. She fell across the bed. "It's my fault! It's all my fault!"

I bent over my sister. Her skin felt hot and damp, as if she had a fever. "Georgina, you know it's not your fault. Mother told you so herself."

Georgina's cheek was pressed against the blanket. I took her by both arms and pulled her away, but she laid a flat hand against my chest and shoved. "Leave me alone!"

The nurse drew the privacy curtains across the windows, leaving us to say our final farewells and give free rein to our grief. Ruth sat stiff as a mannequin, mascara-tinged tears marking crooked bluish paths along her cheeks. I turned to her as I had done as a child. "Oh, Ruth." We clung desperately to one another, and I began to weep. After a few minutes, Paul's embrace was large enough to encompass us both.

When I looked up again, Georgina was sobbing in Daddy's arms, her flushed cheek pressed against his chest. He smoothed a wayward strand of hair back behind her ear. Fragments of a familiar tune danced at the edges of my consciousness—*Hush little baby, don't you cry*—as if a TV were playing low somewhere in the next room. The song, in gravelly snatches, teased my ears until I realized that the familiar lullaby was coming from my father. Daddy was singing to Georgina, holding her securely in his arms and rocking, rocking, rocking.

About the Author

Marcia Talley's first novel, *Sing It to Her Bones*, won the 1998 Malice Domestic Grant, was a Featured Alternate of the Mystery Guild, and was nominated for an Agatha Award for Best First Novel. Her short stories have been featured in mystery magazines and collections. A former librarian and computer specialist, she lives in Annapolis, Maryland, with her husband, a professor at the U.S. Naval Academy. When she isn't traveling or sailing, she is busy writing the next Hannah Ives mystery.

9-2-11
Donation